The Roses
of
Ainsworth Manor

Nina Gates

BOHÈME ÉCLAT
PRESS

Published by Boheme Eclat Press LLC, Austin, Texas. First printing, December 2025, Copyright © 2025 by Nina Gates. All rights reserved. No portion of this book may be reproduced, stored, or transmitted in any form or by any means—electronic, mechanical, photocopying, recording, scanning, or otherwise, without written permission from the publisher or author.

ISBN: 979-8-9932132-4-8 ISBN: 979-8-9932132-5-5

Library of Congress Control Number: 2025926020

Author's Note: Language and Spelling

The Nell Ainsworth mysteries are set around the world and include characters from many countries and backgrounds. As an American writer, I primarily use American English spelling, with British and other regional terms, idioms, and occasional non-English words where they feel natural and clear in context. Any blend of usages is intentional, meant to welcome a wide range of readers, and reflects my voice and the needs of each story rather than strict adherence to a single regional or linguistic standard.

Contents

1

The Last Vigil

ROGER

His breathing is shallow and slow. He tries to stand, but his legs shake, and he sinks to the cold stone floor, his bones pressing against his ragged coat. The house is a silent witness. But silence means no one is coming—not now, maybe not ever. For the first time since he was abandoned, Roger closes his eyes and allows the emptiness to take him. He wonders, as his mind drifts freely between then and now, if this is how loyalty ends. Not with companionship, or praise for a job well done, but alone. A quiet surrender in an empty house.

When the clock chimes now, there's no strength to lift his head. All he can do is remember.

***

The estate once pulsed with life and purpose, and Roger had been at the heart of it. He patrolled the grounds alert for foxes in the hedgerows, errant squirrels, and delivery vans rumbling up the drive. His reward was the old man's affectionate hand ruffling his fur and the words that set him wagging: "You're a good boy, Roger." Roger's days moved in perfect rhythm with the house. He rose before dawn to the creak of floorboards and sounds of the staff beginning their work. In the big stone kitchen, his favorite destination, he found delicious smells and two waiting bowls. Cool fresh water filled one, and twice a day food appeared in the other. When he checked his bowl in the afternoons, often there were scraps for no reason at all—a bit of roast, leftover vegetables, and sometimes a biscuit. Cook had laughed at his surprise, gently patted his head, and said, "Who's the best boy? That's right, you are."

He went everywhere with the old man. Sometimes Roger napped in a patch of sunlight in the Great Hall while the man worked at his desk; sometimes he settled at his feet when visitors arrived. Midday walks were circuits through the gardens, chasing a tennis ball—or the gardener's hat if caught the wind. Evenings brought the finest reward; dozing by the fire, enveloped in warmth and familiar voices. In those days, he knew his place in the world.

One morning, he didn't see the man anymore.

The others left one by one. Sheets shrouded the furniture; lights switched off; doors closed. Winter settled in, and the house grew cold.

Roger waited.

Car sounds on the distant road stirred his hope. Some nights, he curled at the top of the stairs, certain that someone would come home soon. Keeping watch was a job too, and he meant to do it well. He walked empty hallways and sniffed at cracks beneath closed doors. Outdoors, he covered miles, tracing the edges of the property, nose to the frozen ground. He patrolled the gardens and growled at the wind when it rattled latches or swung a gate. In the boot room, he nudged a forgotten shoe into place on the mat.

Moonlight and sunlight marked time across the Great Hall. Some afternoons, after checking his empty bowl, Roger sat upright by the front door, ears at attention, listening hard for a familiar voice. He never barked unless he meant it. When footsteps echoed in his dreams, he snapped awake and stood watch at the landing. He grew thinner, and his coat dulled until one day he stopped checking his bowl when even the kitchen was too far.

Now his mind slides easily between past and present. Someone took him from the empty house once... a new home. He was a good boy then too, but there was shouting and pain he didn't understand. Someone needed him, and he protected as he was meant to. Their word "Bad!" still confuses him.

He is standing in front of the manor house once more... a car door slams. Faces looking back at him through rain-marked glass fade to nothing as the car drives away. Memories surface and dissolve until all that remains is the tick of the clock on the landing and the silence at the edge of life.

It has been a long time since Roger felt sure of anything, but he has learned one bitter lesson about the world: human rules cannot be trusted. Being a good dog isn't enough. Being devoted isn't enough. Nothing is enough when humans don't want you anymore.

***

He hears her before he smells her, and smells her before he sees her. Footsteps on the portico, the big door unlatches, then the scent of soap, flowers, and sweat. When she appears in the Hall, he hears a low growl, and realizes it's him. He doesn't mean to; it just happens, but his body trembles with the effort, and the growl escapes fearful and uncertain.

She sees him but doesn't run away. Her gaze rests on him briefly, then she moves on as if he isn't there. Without meeting his eyes, she walks past his hiding place under the sideboard and sets a bowl of water where morning sun warms the limestone tiles. Then she places a plate of cooked meat beside the water. Roger retreats further into the shadows.

She walks through his house throughout the day: moving boxes, folding white sheets, dusting, opening and closing doors. When the lights go out and he hears her climb the stairs, Roger crawls from beneath the sideboard, drinks the water, takes a few cautious bites of food, then retreats. In the early morning, he finishes the rest.

Over the next days, this becomes their careful dance: she sets food and water nearby and walks away; he creeps out at night to eat. With each meal, life returns, and Roger stays awake longer during daylight hours, watching her. Gradually, her scent fills the rooms until she's part of all that's familiar. If she doesn't come too close, he sometimes leaves the safety of the sideboard in the afternoons to lie in the patch of sunlight in the Hall. Today, he even falls asleep there.

She talks constantly while she works. Sometimes she says his name as if speaking to him, but it never sets his nerves on edge. Roger likes the sound of his name in her singsong voice. Her scent never mingles with another's; no second set of footsteps. Sometimes she stands at the window, watching the empty drive. He knows that stillness—the same waiting he has endured for so long. Roger wants to step closer, to let her know he understands what it means to wait for someone who never comes.

As his health is restored, he is drawn to follow her. He keeps his distance, learning her habits and sounds—boots on stone floors, soft thuds on carpets, the wet squelch when she works in the garden and tracks earth across the threshold.

She continues to ignore his presence, letting him decide how close feels safe. From doorways and corners, Roger watches as she moves furniture, arranges books and papers. Her movements carry no threat—no sudden gestures that might startle him into flight.

***

Roger pricks his ears, nose twitching. A car rumbles down the drive, gravel spitting under its tires. Not one he knows. He hides behind a bush at the edge of the forecourt. The big doors stand open, and inside, the woman moves about. Every instinct urges him to place himself between her and this unknown threat, but his body remembers too well what happened the last time he tried to protect someone.

A man steps out of the car, jacket pulled tight against the chill. Roger instinctively registers the man's smooth, efficient movements. Confidence. Unlike most humans, who rush forward oblivious to their surroundings, this one doesn't. He pauses just like Roger does; notices, then moves again. Roger's tail almost wags, then stills.

Roger lifts his nose to sniff the air. For him, every intake splits into a hundred notes: where humans sense only grass, Roger reads minerals, crushed blades where a deer walked at dawn, insects, earthworms, droppings from five different animals, last night's rain dripping from evergreen needles, a walnut shell two inches below the dirt, and deeper, a vole in its burrow. A thrush flutters in the shrub, and over it all—the distinct, layered scent of the stranger: soap, leather, metallic sharpness, and the restless scent of someone who has traveled far.

When the man's gaze finally finds Roger among the rose thorns, it carries no threat. Surprised, perhaps sympathetic, he makes no move toward the hiding place. He only nods, respectful, acknowledging the guardian watching him.

There is something different about this stranger—restraint. Roger finds himself curious, wondering what will happen when two wounded creatures finally meet the third.

2

The Interview

HENRY

H ENRY GUIDES HIS SENSIBLE car up the mile-long drive. The rolling Cornish countryside is dotted with hardy sheep in muddy woolen coats and the hesitant yellow of early daffodils pushing up from the cold earth. He passes great stands of oaks and chestnuts, their branches etched on a cloudless blue sky. Sunlight dapples through staggered rows of linden trees, arching overhead in a pale green haze. From here, he can just make out a small ornamental lake in the distance, still edged with ice. This is parkland shaped by centuries of painstaking cultivation.

Henry has only seen Ainsworth Manor in magazines and on TV. The East Wing and three thousand acres were granted to Roderick Ainsworth, the first Duke of Belward, by King George II, as a mark of royal favor. In 1815, the estate expanded to thirteen thousand acres in gratitude for the valor of Aleric Ainsworth, the third Duke, at Waterloo. John Nash, famed architect of Buckingham Palace, designed the new Center Hall and West Wing at the height of his renown. Nash blended, according to Netflix, eighty thousand square feet of Georgian taste with timeless Palladian balance, creating one of the finest houses in the world, and arguably the most beautiful in Britain.

Henry rounds the last curve and brakes without thinking. Honey-colored stone blazes in the late afternoon sun. Gold-accented balustrades crown the roofline, and tall gold-leafed window frames shimmer with fiery luster. The broad central block rises behind monumental columns. Classical colonnades sweep outward from the wings, cresting like waves. This—this is not a house, Henry thinks. This is a proclamation of British power, a living testament that the Ainsworths were empire-builders.

Henry reviews interview answers and etiquette rules: the correct greeting, the proper bow, the endless do's and don'ts, then pulls his car to a stop on the forecourt. He steps out and turns slowly, taking in the grandeur, suddenly conscious of how modest his third-hand Volvo looks amid splashing fountains and gated parterre gardens knotted in intricate geometry. He straightens his tie, runs a hand through his hair, and wonders what kind of woman chooses to live alone in such magnificent isolation.

He'd done considerable research for this interview: photos of the Duchess, posts on her official website and social pages. He'd read the Times and Guardian reviews of her books, and interviews in American Town & Country and British Vogue. He'd watched her on several morning shows and a charming clip from her appearance on Graham Norton. Surely there would be servants in uniform lined up at the door like a period drama, ready to size him up before he was allowed inside.

Instead, Victoria Eleanor Rose Spencer-Oxley Ainsworth, the Duchess of Belward herself, steps out of the house—boots caked with mud, hair tangled with twigs. From behind a leafless rosebush, she's watched by what might once have been a large German shepherd. If Henry hadn't known better, he might have mistaken her for grounds staff.

Striding across the forecourt, she extends a paint-stained hand.

"Nell Ainsworth," she says. "You're early. That's good. I hate lateness. Let's walk through the back gardens."

Without further ceremony, she swings herself into a topless Range Rover parked nearby. Henry hesitates, momentarily confused—she'd just said, "Let's walk through the gardens." The engine grumbles to life, and he climbs in beside her. She steers toward the East Wing, passes beneath an arched carriageway, through iron gates, and past the stable block into an empty carriage court. Henry begins to understand: in a place this size, simply reaching the back gardens without trekking through the house means a journey of nearly a quarter mile.

When they disembark, Nell leads the way down marble steps, edges rounded with age, and through another set of double gates toward what had once been formal parterre gardens. Roses now intertwine with nettles; statues lean at questionable angles, and geometric hedgerows sprawl into anarchic lines. Fountain basins choke with algae; gravel paths vanish beneath exuberant weeds. The scale is breathtaking: acres upon acres of meticulous design surrendering to nature's rebellion.

The dog has followed them and now trails about ten feet behind, stopping when they stop. He must have been handsome once, but now his ribs show beneath a patchy coat. Henry watches the strange interaction between woman and dog. Nell seems oblivious to the animal's devotion, or perhaps she simply trusts the dog will always follow. Either way, Henry can't help wondering—does she ever feed him?

"I contracted help to bring the front into shape, but we have not tackled the back yet," Nell says.

"How many staff do you keep?" Henry asks, stepping around a toppled urn.

"Define 'keep,'" Nell replies, striding past a rose arbor that looks ready to swallow the path whole.

From somewhere behind a massive rhododendron comes the sound of vigorous, off-key humming and the scrape of metal on stone. A wizened figure emerges, dragging a rusty wheelbarrow at a perilous angle. The man, seventyish, wearing Wellington boots and what appears to be yesterday's clothes, waves cheerily at Nell before promptly walking into a hedge.

"That's Fergus," Nell says matter-of-factly. "He's been here forty years. Knows every inch of the estate."

Henry watches Fergus extract himself from the shrubbery with the patience of someone who does that a lot. "And he's...?"

"Three sheets to the wind most days, yes." Nell's tone is dry but not unkind. "He could retire—full pension, cottage in the village." She watches the old man resume his meandering progress. "But this place is all he knows. Besides," she gestures at the wild beauty around them, "drunk or sober, Fergus understands roses better than any landscape architect I could hire."

The dog edges closer to Fergus, pausing a moment before moving near enough for an ear scratch. Fergus mumbles something that could be botanical Latin, mixed with Gaelic and nonsense. "Botanicalis befuddlium, flopsy-doggicus snackificus waggalorum, perplexidus muddius omnia splashium."

The dog listens intently, quite possibly nods, and leans into the old man's hand but glances warily back at Nell, ready to retreat if necessary.

Henry inclines his head, beginning to understand. The gardens might be in disarray, but they aren't abandoned. Not entirely.

Nell is already walking toward the house. "Come on. The real interview happens indoors. Fergus, don't fall in the fountain again!"

A distant, cheerful shout suggests Fergus hears her but is making no promises.

***

Inside, Nell leads Henry through a cavernous marble hall and up a staircase to the main floor, taking the steps two at a time while he just manages to keep pace. They enter Ainsworth's famous Great Hall. Henry pauses, transfixed by the vast painted ceiling edged in gold: luminous clouds, battling angels, chariots, naked cupids, maybe an alligator, all tumbling through impossibly blue skies. Nell, following his gaze, says, "It's Sir James Thornhill, in the style of Rubens, called *The Triumph of Celestial Forces*. I call it 'The Great Celestial Muddle.'"

A round table with an intricate marquetry top occupies the Hall's center near the colonnaded foyer. On it stands a Ming vase, probably priceless, at least four feet high. It's stuffed with even taller branches of budding blackthorn, cut, Henry suspects, from somewhere on the grounds and now forced into bloom by the house's warmth. Scattered across the table are a few stacks of books, a bronze sculpture of an English setter, and a dog leash curled in a silver bowl.

Dominating the center of a huge sterling salver is a single cream-colored envelope sealed with a circle of dark red wax—unopened.

Nell's office is the size of a ballroom, which it likely once was. Floorboards creak as Henry steps inside. This is not the expected dark English library-with-ticking-clock; instead, light pours through a row of tall windows facing the forecourt, curtained in billowing ballgowns of French blue silk, caught up in heavy ropes of braided gold bullion.

Opposite the windows stands a black marble fireplace as tall as Henry, its mantel wide enough to sleep on. In front of it, a single modern white leather Eames chair sits surrounded by more piles of books.

Nell's desk is a table—the largest slab of mahogany Henry's ever seen, at least fifteen feet long and nearly eight feet wide, its surface lost beneath teetering piles of books, neat stacks of yellow legal pads, and baskets full of dog-eared puzzle books. There's an elaborate sterling silver punch bowl crammed with hundreds of freshly sharpened pencils, an enormous lidded crystal jar filled to the brim with jelly beans, and another Ming porcelain vase overflowing with pink hothouse roses. Facing each other across the expanse are two modern white desk chairs, a startling contrast to the old-country formality.

Modern meets seventeenth-century, Henry thinks. The space is lush and eclectic. Either Nell has just moved in, or she doesn't care that people might expect more traditional decor. She drops into one of the office chairs and flips open a crossword.

Henry glances around. "I must admit, your office isn't what I imagined."

She looks up, cocking an eyebrow. "Would it help if I draped a velvet throw somewhere?"

He summons his training. "No—just unexpected."

She begins reading clues aloud, almost to herself. "Seven down—*asset in a crisis*, twelve letters, starts with 'D'."

Henry takes a seat on the opposite side of the table, feeling ridiculous sitting so far away in this cavernous room, and a little off balance, wondering if this whole setup is a test, or just an extension of her eccentricity. She asks him perfunctory questions—skills, references, favorite omelet fillings—but seems more interested in her puzzle than his careful answers.

He clears his throat. "Are you even listening?"

She doesn't bother to look up. "Of course not. I made up my mind in the first thirty seconds we met."

He blinks, unsure whether to be insulted or flattered.

The skinny German Shepherd sits unmoving in the doorway watching him with amber eyes.

Nell pencils in DECISIVENESS for seven down, then finally meets his eyes. "So, do you want the job or are you just here for the scenery?"

Henry glances down at the typed job description: *Personal Valet. Duties range from light estate maintenance to occasional crisis management.* He raises an eyebrow, pen poised. "One last question, Your Grace. How often do you entertain houseguests or... see friends here?"

Nell scoffs, not even looking up from her crossword. "Don't be ridiculous, Mr. Templeton. I don't have any friends. That's what I'm hiring you for."

Henry doesn't miss a beat. "Ah. Emotional support, emergency cocktails, and basic social camouflage?"

Nell looks at him, her surprising lavender-blue eyes direct and faintly amused. "Exactly. If anyone asks, you're the amicable one."

He jots it down. "Noted. *Must possess moderate charm, advanced breakfast skills, and willingness to be mistaken for the social circle.*"

Henry smiles. "And canine relations, I assume?"

Nell gestures toward the dog's muddy paws. "Roger doesn't belong to me. He was here when I moved in."

"How do you know his name is Roger?" Henry asks.

"His name is on his water bowl," replies Nell, as if Henry should have known that.

The interview had gone much worse than expected, Eleanor Ainsworth proving to be, by turns, incredibly beautiful, dazzlingly sharp, and utterly baffling. Maybe crazy. Henry tucks the job description into his coat and stands.

Ainsworth Manor's opulence and Nell's impossible directness collide in his mind. Although something—her quick wit, Roger's loyalty, the bizarreness of it all—tugs at him, he's made up his mind: this is not for him.

Whatever had happened in London—the scandal, the career implosion—maybe he is a little adrift, sure, but he isn't so desperate for penance that he'll haunt these halls, pretending to be a recluse's social circle.

He thanks Nell for the interview and crosses the gravel drive to his car, keys biting his palm. Already weighing next steps, Henry glances over his shoulder and stops.

There on the wide west lawn, Nell stands with a tennis ball, hurling it as far as she can, then running after it herself and throwing it again—over and over, undeterred. Roger watches each throw, shifting his gaze between her and the flight of the ball. He sits somber and attentive while Nell plays fetch for both of them. Henry isn't sure, but he thinks he might have seen the very tip of Roger's tail twitch, just once. The two of them alone, but entirely present for each other.

He hesitates, door half-open. What am I doing? *Get in the car, Henry.* This place is mad. She is mad. But so is running from his own life, isn't it? And maybe mad is exactly what he needs right now.

Henry shuts the car door. He takes a deep breath, straightens his coat, and walks toward the lawn.

Nell looks up, blonde hair wild, cheeks flushed. "Forget something?"

He nods. "Yes. The job. I'll take it."

3

Mail Is Never a Good Thing

NELL

THE LETTER HAS BEEN sitting on the hall table for a week, and Nell has perfected seventeen different routes through her own house to avoid looking at it directly. This morning's path involves the servants' stair behind the Ballroom, a detour through the Conservatory, and what Mrs. Patterson would undoubtedly call "undignified scrambling" through the Morning Room window.

She settles at her desk with today's crossword, determinedly not thinking about cream-colored envelopes with red wax seals. The puzzle is particularly satisfying this morning, a cryptic from The Guardian that requires actual thought rather than just filling in blanks.

"Eleven across," she says aloud to Roger, who has positioned himself in his usual patch of sunlight that allows him to watch the front door, a servants' hall, the rear stairs leading to the ground floor, the main stairway to the second and third floors, the Butler's Office, and Yellow Drawing Room, part of the Gallery and directly into the Ballroom, all at once. "*Coward's way out when facing unpleasant correspondence. Seven letters.*"

Roger opens one amber eye and gives her a look that suggests he knows exactly what she's avoiding.

"Don't judge me," Nell tells him. "You hide under furniture when strangers arrive. I hide from mail. We all have our coping mechanisms."

The answer comes to her suddenly: EVASION. She pencils it in with perhaps more force than necessary.

Henry's footsteps sound in the Hall outside the Ballroom. She's learned to recognize his particular rhythm, easy-going and steady like everything else about him. He appears in the doorway holding two cups of coffee and wearing an expression of patient resignation that she finds both irritating and oddly comforting.

"Good morning, Your Grace. Lovely day for a crossword."

"Every day is lovely for a crossword, Mr. Templeton. Unlike some activities I could mention."

Henry sets one cup in front of her and glances toward the hall. "The letter is still there."

"Is it? I hadn't noticed." She focuses intently on twelve down. "*Procrastination leads to this. Eight letters, starts with 'P'.*"

"PROBLEMS," Henry supplies without hesitation.

Nell glares at him over her reading glasses. "I don't recall asking for help."

"My apologies. Though in my experience, unopened letters rarely improve with age."

"In my experience, letters never contain good news. Wedding invitations are just expensive announcements that someone expects you to buy them a toaster. Bills are demands for money you'd rather spend on books. And personal correspondence..." She trails off, penciling in PROBLEMS. "Personal correspondence is usually someone explaining why they're disappointed in you."

Henry settles into the chair across from her, coffee cradled in his hands. "Not always."

"Name one time a letter brought genuinely good news."

"Acceptance to university. Job offers. Agents saying yes to manuscripts."

"Agents say yes by phone now. They only write letters to reject you." Nell flips to the next page. "Besides, this one is from France. I don't know anyone in France. All the more reason to let it sit until it spontaneously combusts."

"All the more reason to open it. And I seriously doubt you know no one in the entire country of France. Your great-uncle had a house in France, as I recall."

"Uncle Charles had that cottage in Provence, yes. But he's been dead three years, and I had to sell it to pay for the new roof here." She points upward with her pencil, as if Henry might need help remembering where the roof is. "And how do you know so much about me in such a short time?"

Henry sips his coffee. "First, you're a celebrity, so it isn't hard to find information about you on the internet, including the notorious YouTube video of your interpretive dance to 'God Save the Queen.' Which I hope to change."

"That I'm a celebrity, or that the whole world has seen my moves?"

"You may continue to be a celebrity if you must, but I'm going to remove your personal information from the internet," Henry says. "Second, I may have done a bit of research before taking the position. An old habit from my previous life." He pauses. "Third, his 'cottage,' as you old-moneyed aristocrats call it, was a thirty-five-bedroom château listed on the French national register of historic monuments. The estate records show your uncle died three years ago, but the succession was caught up in legal wrangling until recently. That's a long time for a place like this to sit empty, especially with only a skeleton staff."

"Previous work? What kind of previous work involves researching an employer's relatives and French property sales?"

"The kind that teaches one to ask questions before walking into unknown situations. Especially when said situations involve isolated Cornwall mansions with..." Henry glances toward where Roger is sleeping, "...complicated histories."

"Complicated histories indeed," Nell says. "The staff left when the maintenance fund Uncle Charles established dried up during probate. He'd planned for everything except a prolonged legal battle. Fergus stayed on for two years until illness put him in the hospital. He found Roger a temporary home with a neighbor, but something happened...I heard Roger was protecting a child, but the woman only saw aggression. She panicked, brought him back here, dropped him off and never told Fergus." She glances at Roger, who opens his eyes at his name.

She speaks softly, as if Roger might understand. "He'd been alone at the empty house for weeks when I arrived, nearly starved to death. The poor dog has been abandoned so many times, he doesn't trust anyone. Well, except old Fergus, who raised him as a puppy. Even with me..."

She regards Roger fondly, "He still won't let me touch him. I can't blame him for that."

"Nell, how does the duchess thing work? I thought only male heirs could inherit a title, but when I was researching you—for the job—I saw you are a duchess in your own right."

Nell digs through a tote bag on the floor and hands him a copy of a document. Henry sets his coffee on the desk, *Special Remainder in Letters Patent.*

After reading it, he looks up. "That's impressive. What does it mean?"

"It means it's incredibly complicated. It attached a Special Remainder to the dukedom that allowed Aleric to pass the title to daughters, should there be no male heir. Even so, my claim doesn't come through Aleric's direct line. He's more like a very distant uncle. My ancestor was Aleric's sister, Lavinia. Several generations after her, someone from her line married back into the Ainsworth family—actually into the same line as my uncle Charles. That's how I got the name and the blood. Normally I'd never inherit."

"Even with the Remainder?" Henry asks, puzzled.

"Right. But with the direct male lines extinct, pressure to save the title, and in consideration of Aleric's Remainder for heroism, the government accepted what they believe was the intention of the crown and recognized me as the only Ainsworth left who carries the legacy." She shakes her head with a wry smile. "It took years, and an act of Parliament, but now...it's mine. Though it was never supposed to be."

Henry nods and refills their coffee cups. They sit in comfortable silence while Nell works through the puzzle. Hearing no further mention of his name, Roger sighs and flops over onto his side, taking a break from Nell-watching while Henry is there. Outside, Cornwall's unpredictable weather is doing its usual performance—sunshine one moment, threatening clouds the next.

"Fourteen down is stumping me," Nell admits eventually. "*Hidden truth surfaces when barrier removed.* Ten letters."

Henry considers this. "REVELATION?"

She counts the spaces. "Perfect fit. Annoyingly perfect, actually."

"Nell." His voice has gone softer, more serious. "What if it's nothing terrible? What if it's just...correspondence?"

"Then why does it smell like tobacco and lavender? Normal letters smell like nothing. Or glue, if you're unlucky."

"Tobacco and lavender?"

"Old-fashioned scents. Either someone with peculiar taste in stationery, or..." She waves her hand vaguely. "I don't know. Something ghostly and dramatic."

Henry leans back in his chair, and she recognizes the expression that means his mind is working through possibilities. It's the same look he got when he reorganized her filing system and planned a hiring strategy for new staff. Everything about Henry suggests systems, order, and competence—all the things Nell has spent thirty-four years actively avoiding.

"What if I open it?" he offers.

The suggestion hits her like a small electric shock. She looks up from her crossword, startled by how tempting the offer sounds.

"You would do that?"

"If it would help."

"But it's addressed to me."

"Yes, but you're clearly not going to open it yourself. And if it contains something unpleasant, at least you won't have to read it in your own voice."

This logic is so perfectly Henry-like that Nell almost smiles. "You make it sound like hiring someone to eat vegetables for you."

"Similar principle. Unpleasant but necessary tasks are often easier when delegated."

Nell sets down her pencil and really looks at him. Henry Templeton, with his excellent manners and his steady hands, and his complete absence of judgment about her various neuroses. When was the last time someone offered to simply...help? Without wanting anything in return, without making it about their own inconvenience?

"You don't think I'm being ridiculous?"

"I think," Henry says carefully, "that everyone has things they'd rather not face alone."

Something in his tone suggests personal experience. Nell wonders, not for the first time, what exactly happened to Henry in London that drove him to answer job advertisements for remote estate management positions.

"The crossword clue was right," she says finally. "REVELATION. *Hidden truth surfaces when barrier removed.*"

"Is that a yes?"

Nell looks toward the hall, then at Roger, who is still lying on his side, but has opened both eyes and appears to be following the conversation with unusual interest. Finally, she nods.

"Yes. But if it's a ransom note, I'm blaming you for opening it."

Henry stands with that fluid grace of his and pauses at the doorway. "Any other disclaimers I should know about?"

"If it's from the Inland Revenue, I'm moving to Scotland. If it's from my Aunt Gilda, I'm moving to Mars."

"Noted."

She listens to his footsteps retreat. There is a crinkle of heavy cotton paper, then a soft snap as he lifts the wax seal. Roger raises his head, suddenly alert.

"Nell." Henry's voice has changed completely. "You need to hear this."

Her stomach drops. "Bad news. I told you."

"Worse than bad news."

Henry returns to Nell's office holding the opened letter like it might explode. His face has gone slightly pale, and Nell realizes she's never seen him look genuinely alarmed before. Even during their recent chaotic interviews with incompetent butlers, Henry maintained perfect composure.

"Read it to me," she says quietly. "In your voice, like you promised."

Henry clears his throat and begins:

Your Grace,

I write regarding information uncovered during my research into Ainsworth Manor and its former owners. What I have learned now places the reputation of the Dukes of Ainsworth—and, by extension, your own inheritance—in grave jeopardy.

The evidence in my possession shows that members of the household took part in high crimes, including, but not limited to, treason. If necessary, I will submit it to the appropriate authorities, the press, and every genealogical society in Britain.

There is, moreover, *another* matter *long buried, concerning the death of Lady Rose Ainsworth. Officially described as accidental, the records I hold suggest her demise may have been of a far more troubling nature.*

Nell's crossword puzzle slips from her lap.

I have no wish to see the Ainsworth name destroyed. There is a path by which the family's reputation might remain intact. Within the grounds of your estate lies something of extraordinary value, once belonging to Napoleon Bonaparte—a relic directly tied to these same events. I know its location. If you assist me in recovering it, every trace of this old scandal will remain private.

Expect to hear from me again soon. I urge you to treat this matter with the seriousness and confidentiality it warrants.

A Friend of the Truth

Nell sits in silence. Even Roger stops his near constant panting. Henry looks up from the letter, his expression grave. Nell's mind races. Rose Ainsworth. The ancestor she'd always been told died tragically young in an accident. Is he saying she was murdered? Over something Napoleon had hidden?

"Well," she says finally. "That's definitely worse than a tax bill."

"I assume Rose Ainsworth lived here at some point," Henry said.

Nell nods. "She was the daughter of Aleric and Catherine Ainsworth. Aleric was the 3rd Duke of Belward."

"The war hero? The British officer who helped Wellington defeat Napoleon at Waterloo?" Henry asked.

"That's right," Nell replied. "Rose died tragically young, in an accident in 1847—or at least, that's what everyone believed. But this letter suggests it was no accident."

"Nell, this is—"

"Blackmail. Yes, I gathered that." She retrieves her crossword from the floor. "Napoleon. That would explain the French postmark."

"You're taking this very calmly."

"I'm taking this the way I take all unpleasant surprises. By pretending it's a plot from one of my novels until I can process it properly." Nell looks at the crossword clue she'd been working on. *"Ancient secret surfaces when foundations disturbed.* Eleven letters."

Henry stares at her. "Are you seriously doing crosswords right now?"

"It helps me think. Besides, the answer is ARCHAEOLOGY, which seems à propos under the circumstances."

She pencils it in, then sets the puzzle aside and meets Henry's eyes directly.

"All right. Someone believes Rose Ainsworth was murdered over treasure hidden on the estate. They have evidence. They'll destroy my family's reputation if I don't find it." Nell takes a sip of her coffee, pleased that her hand remains steady. "Question is: do we believe them?"

"The Napoleon connection isn't entirely mad," Henry says. "This coast was crawling with French smugglers during the wars."

Nell nods. "Half the great houses have stories about mysterious packages and midnight landings."

Henry nods slowly. "So we're talking about a real historical mystery."

"With a real modern blackmailer who knows more than we do." Nell stands up, suddenly energized. "Well then. I suppose we'd better find out who killed Rose Ainsworth."

"We?"

"You opened the letter, Henry. You're involved now whether you like it or not."

She heads toward the door, then pauses and looks back at him. "Besides, you did say unpleasant tasks are easier when delegated. I'm delegating this one to both of us."

Henry follows her into the Hall. "Where do you want to start?" he asks.

Nell glances toward the portrait gallery, where generations of Ainsworth ancestors gaze down with varying expressions of dignity and disapproval. Somewhere among them is Rose, the tragic girl who supposedly fell from the cliffs.

"All we have to do," Nell says, "is dredge up every secret the Ainsworth family has ever hidden, find treasure Napoleon buried two hundred years ago, and catch a blackmailer."

Henry nods thoughtfully. "Oh, good. Just a regular Tuesday. I was worried it might be something difficult."

Roger stands and gives himself a good shake, as if agreeing with the plan.

"See?" Nell tells Henry. "Even Roger thinks it's a good idea. And he's usually quite sensible about these things."

Henry looks between Nell and the dog, both of whom appear remarkably unperturbed.

"Right," he says at last. "Then I suppose we're treasure hunting."

"We're mystery solving," Nell corrects. "The treasure is just a bonus."

4

The Winterhalter Portrait

HENRY

ENRY SITS CROSS-LEGGED IN front of the fire, on a blue damask sofa in Nell's Ballroom turned office, laptop balanced on his knees. Mrs. Patterson, whose knack for unearthing the house's forgotten treasures borders on the supernatural, had whisked the sofa out of one of the East Wing's unused sitting rooms of her own accord, and parked it squarely in front of Nell's fireplace. Henry expected Nell to object, but she didn't even blink. She explained that she's curious what a stuffy, fringed silk damask sofa and a mid-century modern Eames chair might say to each other. Then she'd laughed and said the chairs remind her of the two of them, leaving Henry to wonder exactly which one he's supposed to be.

Cornwall's morning fog blankets the gardens, the sky low and heavy with the threat of rain. Most mornings he prefers working in the Ballroom, with its row of floor-to-ceiling windows; it's far brighter than his office in the library. He's still coming to terms with what's required to run a historic estate of this size. Officially, he's Valet, Manager, Handyman, and part-time Assistant; unofficially, he does whatever Nell doesn't feel like doing that day. His ex-fiancée used to say he was too adaptable for his own good, forever filling gaps other people leave behind. He can hear her exasperated voice reminding him, "Spackle isn't a career plan." But here he is, patching leaks at Ainsworth Manor, literal and otherwise, one foggy morning after another.

Today, his focus is blackmail. He knows from experience that while blackmail is about money; the danger to Nell is that it's also about control—and once she gives it, she'll never get it back. No one who's blackmailed ever thinks they'll pay twice, but it rarely ends cleanly.

He taps his laptop awake and opens the folder he's labeled *Ainsworth Family History*. Inside are documents, scanned letters, and photographs. Some are his own; others digitized years earlier when the family began converting their archives. This is the task Nell dreads most: sorting through records, faded images, and brittle pages. But it's the patient, meticulous work Henry trained for at MI5, and excels at. He's used to solitary hours, the steady click of keys, and the satisfaction of unraveling a mystery one thread at a time.

Rose Ainsworth:

-Born in 1822, died in 1847, age 25, after a reported fall at the Black Tor cliffs.

-Last known sighting was at a garden picnic that June, described as "distracted, in fine spirits."

-Death certificate signed by Harold Whitby, local magistrate.

He takes a drink of his coffee, pulls up the scanned certificate to look for inconsistencies, and notes the hurried scrawl. *Cause of death: accidental. No witnesses.* The magistrate's signature was dated two days postmortem. How closely did anyone look at the details? Henry logs into the Cornwall digital archives and cross-references magistrate Whitby, a wealthy landowner. His name pops up re-peatedly in local scandals: questionable deaths, lost property claims, rumors of bribery. Henry's instincts, honed by years in Intelligence, flare—there's a pattern here. Henry flags it for closer review.

Next, Henry opens a faded photograph on the screen—a sepia group posed stiffly in the south rose garden. Rose stands at the center, young and striking—a ghostly version of Nell; the same eyes, angelic face, even the tumble of pale blonde hair is uncanny. To Rose's left stands a tall, handsome man in his mid-thirties, angular features. In the margin, a careful hand has written: *Thomas, June 1847, The new sundial.* Photography was rare then. Could this be the only photo of her? He squints. "And who was Thomas?" He says aloud, then looks around for Roger.

Roger is lying in the center of the Great Hall. There's no reply, just the persistent, woody crack of what sounds like a good-sized tree branch splintering in his powerful jaws. Henry returns to typing, then glances over his shoulder again, and sees bark, damp earth and leaf fragments scattered across the stone floor. Roger is in the center, gnawing away—each crunch paired with a muffled grunt of effort.

Mrs. Patterson can be heard next. "Roger? You know very well how I feel about forestry products indoors."

Roger stands, drops the branch with a thud, and ambles to where Mrs. Patterson—expert in canine negotiation—has already positioned a treat on the floor. She bends with a sigh, scoops up the mangled remains of Roger's project, handing them off to a grinning young footman. Order restored, Mrs. Patterson straightens. "Nero chewed a stick while Rome burned," she remarks, then sweeps off toward the Gallery, briskly wiping her hands on her apron, Roger trotting along behind.

Henry looks up at the portrait above the fireplace of a young man in an English battle uniform mounted on a rearing horse. His sword is drawn in perpetuity, forever poised for heroics. The gilded plaque beneath reads: *His Grace, the Duke of Belward, June 18, 1815,*

Waterloo. An idea forms, and he types *Rose Ainsworth oil portrait* into his internet search bar.

There are three etchings and two oil paintings of Rose listed in the results. The etchings are held in the Prints and Drawings collection at the Tate in London. One of the oil paintings is an 1843 work by Sir William Charles Ross, and hangs in the National Portrait Gallery, donated in 1847, *A Gift of His Grace, the Duke of Belward*. Henry clicks on the image and saves it. There's no image of the other oil; just a notation: *1846, Franz Xaver Winterhalter. Privately owned, Ainsworth Manor, Cornwall*. Henry hasn't seen that painting anywhere in the house. He makes a mental note to ask Mrs. Patterson about it, closes the laptop, and goes in search of Nell.

The formal dining room is between the main reception room and the library, and has always been one of the busiest rooms of the house. Throughout its 300-year history, it has hosted kings and queens, prime ministers and presidents, scientists, philosophers, rock and roll legends, and movie stars. During the First World War, Ainsworth served as a hospital, and this was a bright, convenient room for surgery. During the Second World War, Ainsworth was a seat of Allied intelligence operations. The carved mahogany table built to seat twenty-four was no doubt privy to countless daring military operations. It's said that Winston Churchill once sat at the head of this table, writing war plans in the very spot where Nell sits now. Most mornings these days it's set for only two, since Roger prefers to take his meals on the floor in the kitchen.

A monumental portrait of Catherine Ainsworth, wife of the third Duke, looms over Nell's head, immortalizing her on the moor with her loyal deerhound, braced against the wild Cornish wind. The painting commands the room in its hand-carved, foot-wide gold-leaf frame. Henry is struck by how small and almost childlike Nell looks beneath it, and he wonders if the house will have a portrait of her someday. He tries to imagine a formal oil painting of Nell and Roger leaning into a gale on the moor: one absorbed in a crossword, the other chewing a stick.

Henry sets his laptop on the table and fills his plate with a small mountain of eggs and sausage. The sideboard under the painting is set this morning with a silver coffee urn, a chilled carafe of fresh-squeezed orange juice, chafing dishes of eggs and breakfast meats, and a platter of muffins, bagels, and croissants next to a toaster. Henry can't help but be impressed. Meals are lavish, precisely timed and served by uniformed staff: mornings they're in khaki slacks and royal blue polos bearing the Ainsworth monogram. By noon, it's navy livery jackets with red cording and sharply pressed royal blue trousers. After six, maids switch to black dresses with immaculate collars and cuffs, and footmen to black jackets with white waistcoats and bow ties.

Silver is polished, cutlery is perfectly aligned, and the kitchen runs on a rhythm to match Mrs. Patterson's Edwardian standards of ceremony and punctuality. Her ledgers are rumored to be color-coded, tracking everything from seasonal linen rotations to the exact day each chandelier was last cleaned. Staff briefings are as efficient as military roll calls. No wonder the butler he hired lasted exactly seven hours.

"Look at this," Henry says.

Turning his screen toward Nell, he opens a letter from Rose to her cousin Emmeline. Nell abandons her toast and scoots closer to look over his arm. Henry highlights a passage for her, feeling that familiar thrill of discovery.

Dearest Emmy,

I fear trouble brews at Ainsworth. If all comes to ruin because of the terrible truth I must expose, promise me you'll still think well of me.

"Rose wrote this a week before she died," Henry says.

"What did Rose plan to expose?" Nell asks.

She looks over at Henry. "You look like you're preparing to break Cold War codes, not write estate reports."

Henry manages a half-smile. "Cold War codes were simpler. At least one knew who the enemy was."

"If we dig up all these secrets, are we going to make things worse?"

Henry shakes his head. "If we're careful, maybe we'll get to the truth without burning the place down."

She leans in, studying Rose's looping script. "Ever actually crack real codes?"

He hesitates. "That was more or less the job."

"You were a spy?"

He laughs. "Not the glamorous kind—more paperwork than vodka martinis."

Nell studies him. "But you've done this before. Unraveling crimes, asking dangerous questions."

Henry meets her eyes. "Yes."

Rain taps at the windows. Henry thinks of the high hopes and loyal intentions that once convinced him to trust the wrong people, and how he lost everything because of it. He understands Roger's caution; they both did what they believed was right, only to be betrayed for it.

Mrs. Patterson enters a moment later, eyebrows raised. "A proper estate manager uses paper, Mr. Templeton."

Nell grins, looking down and scribbling in the margin of her newspaper.

Henry angles his laptop so Nell and Mrs. Patterson can see the old photograph of Rose by the sundial, then swipes to her oil portrait at the National Gallery. "Have either of you seen a Winterhalter portrait of Rose in the house?"

Nell leans in, her hand resting lightly on Henry's forearm. Henry doesn't look at her, but the light touch of her fingers on his sleeve sends his thoughts briefly off-course.

"I've seen that portrait of her at the National Gallery several times. It's beautiful. I've never seen a Winterhalter of her, though. It's supposedly at Ainsworth?" Nell asks.

Henry looks up and nods.

"That's odd. A Winterhalter would be in one of the main rooms here. He was very famous; he painted the royal family."

Mrs. Patterson sniffs. "Which, if anyone were to ask me, sir, I'd say if she's here, she's minding her own business. Now, if you want to find missing umbrellas, that I can do for you."

Henry smiles, then taps the screen. "Have either of you heard of a Thomas in the Ainsworth family?"

Mrs. Patterson shakes her head. "Ainsworths are as thick as midges after the rain. Could be a relative, but might just as well be the mail carrier."

Mrs. Patterson produces a tarnished brass key, the tag barely legible: East Wing. "You might need this. It was in a locked drawer in the butler's desk. Young Daniel, our newest footman, pried it open for me this morning. There was an old ledger and some receipts, which it's my duty, sir, to put them on your desk." She pauses, glancing sidelong at Henry. "Which, as usual, sir, there's dust everywhere. But I suppose I'll just be the one to see to it."

Henry smiles faintly. "Of course. Thank you, Mrs. Patterson. And—sorry about the dust."

Mrs. Patterson remains unmoved. "Not your sorrow that cleans it, sir. But I'll see to it, same as always."

Nell leans back in her chair. "The original East Wing has twenty bedrooms, a handful of drawing rooms, some historic suites where famous visitors have stayed, service quarters and storage. It's the oldest part of the house, but the least occupied now, so that's probably the place to begin searching. The new West Wing was begun in 1816. It contains about thirty bedrooms, including the main family suites, along with studies, sitting rooms, and a second library. Spread across three floors, it has been home to generations of Ainsworths."

Henry pockets the key. After breakfast, he, Nell, and Roger will go in search of locked doors and lost paintings.

5

Finders Keepers

NELL

THE THREE OF THEM cross the Great Hall and climb the magnificent main staircase. On the first landing, a tall case clock keeps steady time, modernized years ago to run without winding. It's here that the staircase splits. Nell and Roger curve right; Henry goes left.

The stairs rise again to a broad landing on the second floor, where a large portrait of Ainsworth family women fills the wall. The ceilings here are lower, fourteen feet compared with eighteen to twenty-two feet on the main floor. To the left of the landing is the East Wing, and to the right is the West. Nell and Henry turn left into a wide corridor lined with rooms on both sides: ten to the left, ten to the right, plus storage and a drawing room. Each bedroom has its own adjoining spaces: sitting rooms, baths, dressing rooms. A few have small attached maid's quarters.

They move in a slow zigzag from one side of the corridor to the other, opening doors and walking through each suite. Sometimes they work alone, sometimes together, combing for a trace of Rose's portrait or another clue from the past. Each room is spotless and ready for guests: the chandeliers sparkle; there are new English floral chintz fabrics on the beds and windows; and the furniture is polished with Mrs. Patterson's special blend of waxes until it gleams.

Henry seems to enjoy Nell's guided tour, and they are both impressed anew with Mrs. Patterson's housekeeping, but the search brings them no closer to answers.

Nell reaches the end of the corridor first. There's a stairway leading up, and a door to the servants' stairs. She pushes the door open to show Henry. She's used these stairs before—they run behind the Library, Conservatory, and Morning Room, then descend to the ground floor. They climb too, up to the third floor and again to a half-floor of servants' rooms tucked under the eaves. Henry studies the staircase, seeing how the design allows the staff access to every level of the house without being seen. Nell closes the door and leads Henry and Roger up the next flight.

The third floor is different; less formal, more practical. They pass bright schoolrooms with desks and bookshelves, the nursery, and playrooms. Farther along are bedrooms for young visiting relatives, and suites for their governesses and nannies.

There are several storage rooms on this floor; the one at the center of the hall has a walnut door with a small oval brass plaque marked Luggage. Roger dutifully sniffs at the crack. Nell stands beside Henry as he tries the knob; when it doesn't turn, he slides the brass key into the lock and works it side to side until it yields. Before they can turn on a light, the door swings closed behind them with a soft click, plunging them into blackness.

Nell turns at the same moment Henry does, and they collide; she lets out a gasp, muffled by the shoulder she bumps. Henry steadies her with a hand at her waist. "It's just me," he says, reaching past her to feel along the wall. A moment later, the light flicks on.

"How did you know the switch would be there?" she asks, a little breathless, though she isn't sure whether it's from the jolt of fright or Henry's nearness. He smells nice, Nell thinks—warm and masculine, like cedar and spice and clean wool—and she has a sudden wild and overwhelming impulse to kiss him.

He looks into her eyes for a long moment, reading her mind. Then, that slow Henry smile…"Chapter Three of The Victorian Vixen: Destiny and Desire. Elizabeth and Frank are in a dark closet together. He finds the switch in the same place," he says.

Nell blinks. Surprised.

"Actually, I just guessed," Henry chuckles. "Although I'd like to point out that in the novel, Elizabeth kisses him. And, well… other things."

She blushes. "You're reading my books?"

"Of course." Henry winks. "And I'm learning a lot."

Nell rolls her eyes and turns away.

Dust hangs in the cone of light from a single bulb, stirred by their footfalls and slow to settle. Roger sneezes once, sits, sighs, and looks from Henry to Nell.

"These are Louis Vuitton," Henry says, peering at the mountain of old trunks stacked along the wall, canvas dulled like faded wallpaper.

"Some are," Nell answers. "The checkerboard ones, and the ones with the LVs. The painted chevrons are Goyard, and the one with the oval stamp by the lock is Moynat. That pale one at the end could be Au Départ."

"All French," Henry observes, and stoops to touch a grey trunk near the bottom. "This gray trunk doesn't have a pattern."

"That's Vuitton too," Nell says, "but older still. It's called Trianon canvas. It was coated in oil so rain would run off."

"Canvas, not leather?"

"An innovation," Nell says. "It was lighter weight, and it didn't soak through as easily. The older leather-topped trunks were curved so rain would run off, but they still leaked, plus they couldn't be stacked. These flat-topped trunks were built with poplar frames, lined with linen, and finished with brass corners so they would be stronger, much lighter, and could be stacked. People baby their bags today, but two hundred fifty years ago, they rode strapped down outside carriages in every sort of weather. They were made for endurance."

Henry runs his thumb along the edge of a blackened brass latch. "So the patterns are just decoration?"

Nell straightens. "Not at first. Vuitton used plain grey until the 1870s, then stripes—red and white, then beige and brown. 'Rayée,' he called it. When forgeries flooded Paris, he wanted to protect his brand. Next came Damier. The checkerboard." She pauses at a trunk, reading out, "*Marque L. Vuitton déposée—registered trademark*. His son Georges invented that after counterfeiters copied even the stripes."

"Interesting," Henry says, and looks closer. "And after that, the LV monogram?"

"Yes. It was supposed to be too elaborate to counterfeit." She gives a small shrug. "But it's still among the most copied in the world."

"I can't say that I enjoy traveling. It's just about getting there, and getting on with it," Henry says, almost apologetic.

Nell looks up at him and smiles while she re-pins an errant blonde wisp. "The point isn't to arrive, Henry. The point is to be perfectly, gloriously unarrived."

"Explain." Henry says.

"The beauty of travel is the in-betweenness," Nell says. "The delicious sense that time stands still when you're neither here nor there."

"Most people just take photographs," Henry observes.

Nell smiles. "Most people do."

There's a teasing edge to his voice. "I can imagine you traveling the way you write."

"Of course," Nell replies. "Traveling well is an art."

"Travel as a blank page?"

"Travel as a creative act," Nell says. "It's a highly personal way to experience the world, express yourself—maybe even transform yourself."

Henry nods, understanding. "If this were a chapter, would it be worth keeping?"

"Exactly," Nell says.

Furniture shapes huddle beneath their shrouds, pale forms in the weak electric light. She lifts the corner of one and finds a mahogany desk beneath, its surface dulled but sound. She makes a note to mention it to Mrs. Patterson. There's a suite on this floor without a proper desk, and this one would do very well.

Against the far wall, a massive gilded frame rests upside down. Henry and Nell stand side by side, tilting their heads to read the inverted brass plaque.

"*Xaver Winterhalter, 1846, Lady Rose Ainsworth*. How about that? The frame is here..." Henry says.

"But the painting's gone." Nell finishes his thought.

Henry carefully tilts the frame forward, and Nell steadies it while he checks the back. "There are nails—some missing, some bent. If a restorer had taken the painting out, they would've removed every nail carefully. They wouldn't risk tearing the canvas."

They exchange a look. The missing portrait was removed in haste, not professionally.

Nell scans the shadows. She sees a rectangle of narrow oak boards, joined at each corner—wooden bars fitted neatly together. It is propped against a nearby bureau, still assembled, corners squared. She touches the smooth oak. "Stretcher bars," she says.

"Stretcher bars?" Henry repeats, puzzled.

She gestures. "They support the canvas inside the frame, keep it tight like a drum. See here?" She points to a small heap of copper nails. "These would be hammered into the edges of the painting after it is wrapped around the bars. Whoever took the painting out of the frame, also pulled all the nails and removed the canvas from its support." She hands the wooden bars to Henry to check to see if the support fits inside the frame.

"Marries with the frame perfectly," Henry says. "The canvas was wrapped around these bars. But why not take the frame as well? It's beautiful."

"It's ten feet tall and six wide," Nell says. If someone took it and meant to hide it, the painting would be awfully large to store easily in the frame. Plus, it would weigh over a hundred pounds."

Henry laughs. "You sound like an American."

"I lived in California for a few years," Nell grins. "Habit. Americans don't really do metric. What next?" she asks.

"Lunch," Henry says. "Then we go looking for a rolled-up canvas."

6

The French Tutor

NELL

DESCENDING THE MAIN STAIRCASE with Henry and Roger, Nell hears the deep, resonant peal of the doorbell. Part summons, part announcement. The mechanism, a relic of earlier engineering, connects a pull-cord outside the front door to a system of wires and levers that activates a real bell in the foyer and downstairs in the staff rooms. They cross the Great Hall and reach the foyer just as Mrs. Patterson does. She swings the heavy door open in one motion as thunder crashes. Rain pours down in sheets, sweeping across the portico. A woman stands on the threshold, skittish and soaked, clutching a limp envelope with both hands as if it's all that keeps her upright. "I'm here to see Henry Templeton," she says.

Mrs. Patterson looks at Henry, who gives a brief nod. Pulling the door wider, Mrs. Patterson says, "You may as well come in, miss. No sense standing in the rain. Mind the floors; the stone gets slick."

The woman hesitates, eyes flitting between Nell and Henry, then steps over the threshold and thrusts the envelope toward Henry.

"Are you Mr. Templeton? I hope you can help me—please, someone may be watching."

Nell leans against the door to the gallery, arms crossed. From the look Henry gives her, she knows he's already cataloging the details: the woman's shoes; her coat, gripped at the collar; the tremor in her hand. Roger disappears beneath the sideboard, as he does when storms—literal or otherwise—roll through.

"How can we help you, Miss—?" Nell says.

"Eliza. Eliza Brookes. It's Mrs."

Her eyes search the faces in the hall—Mrs. Patterson, then Henry, then Nell. "I know I shouldn't be here, but it's... it's about Rose Ainsworth." Her voice drops. "My family was involved. A long time ago."

Henry exchanges a look with Nell, then says, "You'd better come through." His voice is even. "Let's talk in the library."

Mrs. Patterson takes the dripping coat and passes it to a waiting footman. "I'll see to tea," she says, then vanishes down the hall.

Henry leads them through the gallery, past the reception room, and into the library, where he's created his office.

Nell pauses at the entrance; she loves this room, a cathedral made of books. It's the sort of grave, masculine library that belongs in every proper country house. Walnut shelves climb skyward twenty feet on all sides, drawing the eye up toward a domed ceiling painted a subdued midnight blue, flecked with gold-leaf stars and constellations. Long library tables with shaded lamps and an arrangement of deep reading chairs anchor one end; at the other is Henry's desk and an enormous globe.

Set at the eastern corner of the house, the library opens onto a wide stone terrace. Comfortable sofas and generous chairs cluster around modern firepits, contrasting with the old flagstones. On days when the weather holds, Nell sits out there to read in the sun's warmth, or the shade of a big umbrella.

The library windows are dressed in a new dark green silk taffeta she chose because she loved how it billows and drapes to the floor. The designer she hired gathered the fabric in ropes of blue and green with heavy tassels. The ledges beneath are broad, ideal for perching with a book and watching rain sketch its way across the old glass. She remembers how, as a child, these windows became secret hideouts during evening games of hide-and-seek; once the shutters closed and the curtains were drawn, no one could spot her tucked into the shadows.

On blustery days, she likes to sit in front of the fire here and write her books longhand on yellow notepads. Henry, meanwhile, is almost always at his imposing desk, working steadily on his ever-present laptop. The room is just the right kind of cozy for rainy days like this.

Henry gestures for Eliza to have a seat, then takes the chair beside Nell. He leans forward, hands clasped and elbows resting on his knees. Eliza drops the envelope in front of him, onto the oval coffee table.

"I'm Eliza Brookes." She blurts again. Eliza is likely in her thirties, Nell thinks, though her short, dark bob, round cheeks, and quick nervous movements make her seem much younger. Pink flushes her skin; her nose and lashes give her an impression of stubborn innocence more than anything else. Henry meets her eyes. His voice is calm and direct. "Yes. How do you do? Why are you here, Mrs. Brookes?"

Eliza's eyes dart around the room, from the fire to the bookshelves, then back to Henry. "Someone's watching me. I need help."

"Why come to me?" Henry asks levelly.

"People in the village say you're some kind of investigator. That you work for the Duchess," Eliza says, her glance darting toward Nell, "is...is that true?"

"I'm Her Grace's valet and estate manager," Henry replies, not offering more. He watches her response.

Eliza turns to Nell, voice uncertain. "You should have this. It's about Rose." She slides the envelope further across the table, hands withdrawing as if the object carries a charge.

Henry takes the envelope, unclasps it, and tips the contents into his palm: a gold button, a torn piece of map, and a small book.

He turns the book over in his hands, then cracks it open. "It's a diary," he says, thumbing through the filled pages.

Nell lifts the button between finger and thumb. An eagle spreads its imperial wings. "Napoleon's French military?" she asks.

Henry nods once.

He unrolls the scrap of map, tracing the faded lines with a thumb, brow creased. "What is this? It looks old." He shows it to Eliza.

Eliza shakes her head, uncertain. "I'm not sure... It looks like a garden plan, but I couldn't say for certain. I'm not familiar with the estate besides what I've heard."

He passes it to Nell. She studies the layout and the faded watercolor illustrations. "Ainsworth," she says. "It's a map of the gardens."

Both she and Henry turn to Eliza.

Henry's tone stays gentle but firm. "Start at the beginning."

Eliza shifts, picking at the edge of her sleeve. "My family worked here for generations. An ancestor of mine, Sarah, was Rose Ainsworth's lady's maid. That diary," she nods to the book in Henry's hand, "it belonged to her."

"Whose diary?" Nell asks, needing the connection named.

"Sarah's," Eliza says. "She wrote about seeing Rose and Thomas arguing in the rose garden before Rose died."

Nell rolls the button in her palm. "Who was Thomas?"

"Thomas Duval," Eliza says. "He was Rose's French tutor. It's all in there."

Nell and Henry exchange a glance.

"Sarah wrote that Rose and Thomas were in love," Eliza continues.

Nell raises an eyebrow. "A French tutor. Hardly a romance the family would have encouraged in those years."

Eliza manages a wan smile. "It was kept secret. Rose was engaged to someone else."

"To whom?" Nell asks.

"I don't know," Eliza admits. "After Rose died, Sarah was told to stay silent."

Henry leans in. "Silent about what, exactly?"

Eliza's eyes lower. "I wish I knew. Maybe things Sarah saw. Or learned. She doesn't always say."

Nell sets the button down and meets Eliza's eyes. "Why bring this to us now?"

"I've received threats," Eliza says. "Notes at my door, someone following me from work, messages telling me not to talk about Rose. I'm afraid to keep these things at home, but I can't bring myself to destroy them either."

"When did the threats start?" Henry asks.

"Just after my mother died," Eliza says. "She kept this all locked away until last month. I didn't know any of it existed until I sorted through her things."

"Did you go to the police?" Henry asks.

Eliza shakes her head. "No. The notes warned me not to. I got rid of them."

Henry glances at the items on the table. "Does anyone know you're here?"

"No," Eliza says. "And I have to leave now, before someone notices."

She stands. Nell and Henry do as well. "Thank you for seeing me," Eliza says.

From under a table, Roger rises, eyes locked on the terrace doors, the fur along his spine bristling. Nell sees a blur passing outside, a suggestion of movement just beyond the glass. Eliza's eyes go wide. "I have to go."

She bolts from the library, winding her way through the house. Her hand snatches her coat from the rack by the front door. The door slams; the sound echoes down the limestone hall. An engine grinds to life outside, gravel spitting under the tires, and Eliza's car is gone.

Nell retraces her steps to the library. She opens the terrace door and peers out into the rain-soaked dark. Whatever she thought she'd seen isn't there now. Henry comes up beside her, but she doesn't mention it. The wind, she tells herself. Just the wind.

7

Insecurity

HENRY

LATER THAT NIGHT, HENRY moves through the dim house, Roger trailing at his chosen distance. It's routine for both of them: the nightly circuit, the ritual of reassurance. Each upstairs window he secures reminds him how many more lie vulnerable at ground level. There are dozens of entrances. For every door he locks, he knows there are others he isn't aware of. There are lengths of corridor he's never fully mapped: service passageways, back stairs, countless branching paths where someone could move throughout the house utterly undetected. Roger is perpetually alert, his ears swiveling at sounds only he can hear. In a place this sprawling, Henry knows Nell can't ever be entirely safe.

He recalls how, despite all the security at Buckingham Palace, an intruder once scaled a fourteen-foot wall lined with spikes and barbed wire, shimmied up a drainpipe, and found his way into the Queen's bedroom. Ainsworth has nowhere near Buckingham Palace's layers of security. He glances back at Roger, weighing the choice. Should Nell have another dog? One less wary, less scarred by whatever came before? If danger reached her, what would Roger do?

Even now, any hint of trouble sends him shrinking into the margins, present, but never quite ready to stand guard.

Henry passes the door to Nell's suite, not far from his own along the second-floor West Wing. The door stands ajar, light spilling out. She's still awake, so he knocks.

"Enter," Nell calls.

He steps in. She's on the blush velvet sofa by the fire, bottle of wine open, the envelope from Eliza emptied onto the low table. "Hi. Come in," she says. "Just who I wanted."

He pauses by a chair. "Mind if I join?"

"Please do." She hands him a glass.

He nods, taking a seat. "What's all this?"

Nell settles back into the cushions. "Sarah's diary. Rose's lady's maid."

He swirls the wine, watching the movement. "Anything useful?"

"Thomas warned Rose about something hidden on the grounds. Said it must never be found," Nell says.

"Interesting. What else?"

"Someone in the house might have been feeding battle plans to Napoleon," Nell says, her smile wry as she flips through the diary. "Here it says there were rumors in the village after Rose died that Thomas killed her and vanished into thin air the same night." She turns another page. "Sarah wrote about all sorts of warnings. Look..." Nell turns the book toward Henry and taps the pencil-dark scrawl with her finger. *The gardens hold more than roses. Do not dig too deep.* "Makes you wonder how many secrets these historic houses conceal."

"Nell, have you ever felt safe in this house?" Henry asks her frankly.

"Well," Nell says, "Honestly, I don't give it much thought. Although when Eliza was here today, I was a little concerned that I saw a shadow moving on the terrace outside the library."

Henry's gut tenses. "Why on earth didn't you tell me sooner?"

Roger lifts his head, ears angled, reading the irritation in Henry's voice, but he stays pressed to the wall, not coming closer.

"What can you do? Uncle Charles never believed in those kinds of things—cameras and alarms. He said it would ruin the house's spirit. He said, he was safe enough because he trusted his neighbors."

Henry's exasperation spills out, sharper with her than he's ever been, and he regrets it immediately. "I'm sure your neighbors are perfectly nice people, Nell. But there are millions of pounds of artwork in this house—Raphael, Rembrandt, Reynolds, Gainsborough. There's a Leonardo da Vinci drawing, for heaven's sake, in my bedroom. I've started the security plans for Ainsworth already, but after this, I'm not waiting. I'll do it myself if I have to."

She only nods.

The truth is, his plan was always to install a proper system. He's only been here a few weeks, but he started pulling together specs and making calls almost immediately. He's even lined up a couple of friends from MI5 to do a walk-through and point out blind spots. Now, though, the timeline speeds up, whether the family spirits like it or not.

Nell breaks into his thoughts. "Henry, about the art. Sarah says in her diary that Aleric had both portraits of Rose taken down after she died."

"Well," Henry says, "we know the one by William Charles Ross was donated to the National Portrait Gallery in 1847. The Winterhalter must have been put into storage. I'd like to know where it is."

"I'd love to know why," Nell says. "Sarah only wrote that Aleric couldn't bear to see them. Is that because of grief, or because on the night she died she confronted him about spying?"

"Maybe we'll find answers in the gardens. Let's start in the rose gardens tomorrow," Henry says, rising, meaning to call it a night. He pauses when Nell looks up at him. There's a soft, hesitant note in her voice he doesn't often hear.

"Do you want to hang out here a little while?"

He doesn't have to think about it. Yes, he realizes he does. He sits down beside her on the sofa, letting the tension slip away as Nell picks up her crossword and folds her legs beneath her.

As she puzzles out a clue, Henry leans forward, snagging the pencil and tackling the next one, side by side in the wash of firelight. No more talk of threats for now, just a comfortable, companionable sound of pages turning and the soft hiss of the burning logs. Across the room, Roger keeps his silent post, chin on the carpet, watching them with steadfast eyes.

"Nell, I hope this isn't too personal, but I want to understand all the players and the stakes in this game," Henry says quietly. "Are you planning to get married? I mean, what happens to Ainsworth Manor if you don't?"

Nell sips her wine, thoughtful. "The dukedom itself would die with me; the title would be extinct. The estate would pass to whomever I choose, or failing that, become a heritage trust, or revert in some fashion to the Crown."

He watches her face. "And you're all right with that?"

She leans back, regarding the ceiling. "Well, I'd rather not be the one to break a three-hundred-year chain, if that's what you mean. But I'll only marry for love. If it happens."

Henry can't help smiling. "The novelist wants romance?"

Nell looks over. "I want a love story. There's a difference."

Henry rolls the pencil between his fingers. "I grew up in orphanages and foster homes. Any family I've ever had, I've chosen myself. It's an advantage in its way. I'm free to move toward what matters to me."

Nell edges closer, a subtle brush of shoulder. "I like the sound of that."

8

Dogged Instincts

ROGER

ROGER SITS IN THE kitchen, ears angled toward one of his favorite sounds: bacon sizzling in a pan. He doesn't move. Chef's rule is non-negotiable: no sudden moves before Chef says "good morning."

A special bowl waits on the stone floor near the range, meant just for Roger. Chef doesn't look his way, but Roger knows the routine. Every morning, the bowl is filled with something new: Tuesday brings leftover roast; Wednesday means scrambled eggs. Sundays are unpredictable, but edible, so Roger abides.

Chef hums a song that sounds like "Baa Baa Black Sheep" but references marzipan. Roger likes humans who sing about food. He sniffs the air: bacon, biscuits, then Nell's fresh flowers and Henry's waxy leather shoes.

Henry and Nell enter a moment later to talk to Chef. Roger considers slipping out, just in case, but Chef merely waves a hand without turning. "Shoo, let His Majesty eat first." His Majesty is Roger, though Fergus calls him "dog." Chef lobs a crust behind his back without looking. Roger catches it mid-air, ignores the applause—a total professional.

He edges to a spot beneath the long oak table where a spoon is lying on the flagstones. He gives it a hope-filled lick, just in case. Nothing. But diligence is its own reward.

***

Later that morning, Roger is full—a rare and worthy achievement. He lumbers upstairs from the kitchen, winding through a warren of back hallways, up an incline and around another corner, then pushes the service door to the library open with his nose. One quick loop around the perimeter and he settles in the vestibule between the library and the dining room, where Nell and Henry are having a low-voiced disagreement by the sideboard. Nell pours steaming water into her cup. Henry sets a scrap of paper on the table that makes Roger sneeze.

Henry says the word "garden," a word Roger knows well, and calls the scrap of paper a "map." He will follow the humans today. If they stray, he will herd them. They do not know it, but he is the watcher now. And watching is the only purpose he has left.

Henry lays the piece of garden map on top of the estate plans, then stands suddenly. Roger does too. Henry says, "We should check it out before the rain starts again."

The three of them take the servants' stairs to the ground floor. Henry and Nell grab their coats from the Boot Room. Roger is already wearing his coat. Practical, he thinks.

Roger trots ahead of the humans and noses open the iron gates to the nearest rose garden. The air is damp and thick with the scent of earthworms and rain-soaked grass. Mist weather. It pins smells low to the ground and gathers them in dense pools in the weeds and leaf-litter. Nothing drifts in mist weather. The breeze has no reach.

But near the ground, every scent is sharp, fixed, impossible to miss unless you're human—no offense.

Roger sweeps the grass with a deep nose, moving in loose arcs across the path. Night-fox, strong by the hedge. Squirrel, skittish, under the old horse statue. He keeps clear. Horses are dramatic and unpredictable at both ends. He gives this one a look that means, "You stay there."

Footprints are pressed into the mud. Not Nell. Not Henry. Not Fergus. Roger draws in the unfamiliar scent, sampling it from every angle, circling back to verify, slow and thorough. He files it away in the part of his mind reserved for things that don't belong.

Henry opens another gate and steps gingerly onto the path. Nell follows, boots squelching with every step. Roger dashes ahead, turns to check their progress, then trots to the base of the sundial. The foreign footprint smells go round and round it, so Roger goes round and round it too.

He circles the sundial once more, partly to check his work, partly for show. It's important to look competent in front of the pack. A final sniff, and an extra lap just for effect. Then he halts at a patch ripe with the scents of old wood, moss, and trouble. Roger digs, paws sinking into the soft ground, savoring the itch of the earth under his nails. He's a good digger—it's one of his specialties, Roger thinks, and he can make quite an impressive hole when he really gets going.

Nell sighs, "Roger, no." Then, "Oh!" as his claws hit wood. Roger pauses, front legs elbow-deep in the hole, rear end pointed way up skyward. He looks at her, tilting his head: Yes, this is what I meant.

He backs out of the hole and gives himself a good shake, mud and bits of grass flying wide.

Henry raises an eyebrow, wiping dirt from his cheek and sleeves, then kneels beside the muddy hole. The box is old—older than

Roger, older than Fergus for that matter. Nell pulls it free, while Roger plants himself between the rose bushes and the open gate, tongue hanging out. Humans have fairly useless noses, Roger thinks. And why such small ears? It's no wonder they tire so easily from detective work. They might enjoy a nap in his Great Hall sun patch.

Henry sets the box on the path and stands to look at it. Roger looks at it too. Then Henry looks at Roger; so Roger looks at Henry. They stay that way for a long moment until Nell looks at both of them, shakes her head, and bends to brush off the loose dirt.

The box is sealed tight somehow, and Nell has to pry the lid open with the point of her trowel. Inside are sealed tin tubes. Nell opens one and reveals a waxed cloth bag containing papers—yellowed, thin, scrawled with marks. Roger resists sneezing. The other tube holds another waxed bag. Inside that is a ribbon; he eyes it warily. Ribbons mean collars, collars mean control, and control is for other dogs.

Henry frowns. Nell asks questions. Roger pants. Then his ears flick. The cigarette stub by the sundial—it's recent, nothing like the box's long-buried scent. He stands and pokes at the stub, pushing it closer to Nell's boot to get her attention. She almost notices, then turns to study the box again. Suddenly Roger catches a scent beyond the hedge—it barely reaches him in the damp. His fur goes up, and he gives Nell a look that says, "There's more here than what's in any box, and you're best to keep your boots ready." Nell smiles at him in the way humans do when they miss the point.

Roger jogs the perimeter of the rose garden as Nell and Henry gather up the box and head toward the house, talking in low, puzzled voices. Their words fade into background music against the symphony of leaf drip, bug buzz, rabbit droppings, and a bluebird jeering from the mossy head of the horse.

A twig snaps behind the hedge. Roger's fur bristles, and he lets out a low warning growl. There's a flash of movement—the edge of a boot, a hand pulling away, a glimpse of a coat that does not smell of anyone in the house. He barks, sprints to Nell and Henry, issues another bark—urgent, not decorative. By the time Nell and Henry turn, the garden is empty. Roger's hackles stay raised. He herds them inside the house, keeping his body between Nell and the wind, glancing over his shoulder again and again at the rose garden.

Later, as dusk descends and Henry and Nell reassure themselves that every danger belongs to the distant past, Roger lies by the downstairs door, still as stone, ears fixed on the place where the intruder slipped away. He alone knows the garden is not nearly as safe as it looks.

9

A Hero and a Traitor

HENRY

V IEWED FROM THE FRONT, Ainsworth Manor presents a facade level with the drive and lawns, but on the sides and
rear of the house, the ground slopes gently downward, exposing
a lower storey beneath the main floor. From the garden, a row of
windows, barely visible behind the ivy, reveals the service level where
the work of the house is done. This lower floor forms the functional
core of the estate: the kitchen, larder, pantry, housekeeper's office,
gunroom, and boot room occupy the eastern side, and are located
directly below the library, dining room, morning room, conservatory, silver room and butler's pantry.

The western wing of the house includes Nell's Ballroom, the
Music Room, the Orangerie, another working pantry, men's and
ladies' lounges, several sitting rooms, and a bedroom suite on the
main floor. Behind the ballroom, a hidden staircase rises, connecting
the service floor with those above.

Outside, symmetry reigns. Inside, the corridors and wings tell
a more complicated story. Built up over generations, each addition
is meant to keep the two halves close enough to function, but not
close enough to mingle. Beneath the rooms of the main floor, the

machinery of the house operates smoothly and out of sight. For the family, the grand spaces and polished drawing rooms are the ground floor. For the staff, that world is simply "upstairs."

Henry marvels at how the architecture of the house itself enforces the social order, and how willingly everyone maintains it. Especially the staff, who prefer not to mix with the family and their guests. The hidden corridors and back stairs allow them to work efficiently and without interruption.

Only one room in the house bridges the two worlds: the Boot Room.

The Boot Room sits on the east side of the house, on the ground floor, and opens directly onto the walled courtyard leading to the stables. It is the only family space below stairs; sportsmen and riders come in from the yard, shedding coats, boots, and dogs before mounting the stone steps to the main hall. The route leads through a paneled lobby and joins the principal hall just below the grand staircase. Henry reflects that the Boot Room is both a boundary and a ceasefire—order relaxes here in small but meaningful ways.

The room itself, with a connecting door to the gun room, is dim and cavernous, its walls paneled in waxed mahogany. Near the door, a large blue and white porcelain urn is stuffed with umbrellas, and another with walking sticks and a few golf clubs. There's a stone fireplace with glowing embers. Above it are framed oil paintings of dogs and horses, varnish cracked with age. The mantle holds polished silver trophies, one filled with well-worn tennis balls, another with dimpled golf balls, and a third with leather polo balls scarred from many a match.

Half a dozen wooden bootjacks line up in front of a bench polished smooth by nearly three hundred years of muddy behinds. A generous oak table dominates the center of the room—a broad, practical surface, its grain satin-soft from years of scouring. There's a bridle in need of mending at one end, and a cheerful tangle of dog leads mingled with coils of garden twine in a carved crystal bowl. Underneath the table is a large plaid dog bed stitched with the name Roger—currently holding its owner.

A neat row of wellingtons and riding boots stretches along one wall, upside down on wooden boot stands, allowing them to keep their shape and dry properly. Brass plaques with the names of family members are screwed into the paneling above sturdy coat pegs. Henry smiles when he sees he has a plaque now as well. Mrs. Patterson's doing, he'd wager.

Henry shrugs off his waxed Barbour jacket, helps Nell out of hers, then works his boots free and sets them aside. Nell wipes her hands on a nearby towel and passes it to him after he lifts the box onto the table. With a hand broom and dustpan, she brushes away the remaining dirt, revealing the tarred and lacquered wooden strongbox sheathed in copper, its seams neatly soldered. When they ease the lid up, Henry sees that the inner edge had been bedded into a groove of dark wax. Inside, the contents lie wrapped in oiled silk nestled within sealed tin tubes.

Henry holds the medal up to the light. It is a white cross, edged in gold, with a crowned portrait in the center and laurel leaves. "Look at this," Henry says. "It's the Grand Cross of the Legion of Honour, Napoleon's highest decoration. Only the elite received this—his greatest officers and statesmen."

"So whoever owned it was someone of consequence," Nell remarks.

"Oh, yes," Henry says, "only the best got these. You wore this scarlet sash across your chest and that silver star on the breast. Proof you'd done something extraordinary, and likely lived to tell the tale."

"And what about these?"

Henry sets the medal aside and sorts through crinkling parchment: maps scrawled with routes and coalition regiments, signed by Wellington himself, and more: a letter in French, the seal broken. At the box's corner, a heavy brass button embossed with Napoleon's eagle. It matches the one Eliza gave them.

"These are battle plans," Henry says. "For Wellington's push into France: reports, orders of march, the kind of thing a French commander could use to turn the tide of the Allied advance. These should never have left headquarters. If they did..." He looks at Nell. "You know what it suggests..."

"That Aleric Ainsworth—the country's decorated champion, one of Wellington's trusted military officers—was a spy?" Nell says.

Nell stands with her back to the fireplace, warming her hands behind her. "Ainsworth Manor was a royal reward, Henry, for Aleric's heroics at Waterloo. Both stories can't be true."

Henry turns the brass button in his fingers, considering. "Napoleon's eagle, Henry IV's cross... What does the letter say? It's in French."

Nell scans it, translating.

My dear friend, Our efforts have finally borne fruit and I am grateful for the essential information. I hope neither you nor I will be compromised as circumstances become so uncertain...

She looks up. "It goes on about leaving for Paris, settling affairs."

"If these belonged to Aleric, he wasn't some gallant defender; he was trading in secrets." Nell says. "Tell me, Henry, why else would a British officer have Napoleon's highest honor and Wellington's invasion plans buried in his garden?"

Henry thinks aloud. "Maybe this is what the blackmailer meant by evidence of high crimes. Maybe there's more like this."

Nell crosses her arms. "If this is true, Henry, it changes everything. About the family. About me. Aleric was granted the bulk of

Ainsworth Manor after Waterloo—both the land and the special remainder on the dukedom. If he were found to be a traitor, that would all be stripped away. The title for certain, and possibly the estate itself, would revert to the Crown. In one stroke, three hundred years of Ainsworth history and legacy could vanish."

Henry nods slowly. "This is serious."

"Even so," Nell says, "this isn't the treasure the blackmailer wants. There must be jewels or coins somewhere."

Henry lifts the Legion cross, weighing it. "I don't know. We're not finished," he says. "Rose's letter to her cousin—she spoke of exposing *a terrible truth*. Was she protecting her father, or planning to expose him? Someone went to great lengths to bury these things. I'm not sure they'd thank us for digging them up."

Nell starts up the stairs from the boot room to the main floor. Henry follows, the box balanced under one arm. Halfway up, his phone vibrates.

He shifts the box against the wall and checks the screen. The message is terse, but enough to stop him cold.

Merrick, MI5: The mistake's been accounted for. The officer admitted it. We'd like to discuss your return.

Nell continues talking as she climbs the stairwell. When she notices the silence behind her, she turns.

"Henry?"

He doesn't answer right away. Then clicks the screen dark, fits the phone into his pocket, and adjusts the box under his arm.

"Nothing," he says.

She studies him for a second, then turns back toward the light above, unaware that everything behind her has just changed.

***

In the library, Henry takes the contents out of the box: the medal, the letter, the battle plans—arranging them in a neat row on his desk. He slides the box beneath it and crosses to the sideboard. From the decanter, he pours a measured shot of bourbon, adds a few cubes from the silver ice bucket, and watches the glass fog over.

He takes a slow sip, then crosses to the hearth and stands with his back to the fire. MI5 had recruited him straight from university—a scholarship kid, mathematics, philosophy, and law, with no family ties to complicate things. He'd barely finished his final exams when MI5 brought him to London for assessment—aptitude tests, interviews disguised in small talk. Then came the induction: three days in a windowless room, surrounded by people who looked perfectly ordinary. Ordinary enough to blend into any crowd.

The first lesson hadn't been about weapons or tradecraft. It was learning to hold two conflicting ideas at once. For example, the obvious answer is often wrong, and people will always prefer a story that confirms what they already believe. Training went fast: classroom briefings one week, field rotations the next. They called it Investigative Skills Training: formal analysis mixed with surveillance practice in city streets, pattern recognition, and the discipline of writing concise reports where one misplaced word could derail an operation.

At Thames House, the pace was relentless. Behavioral analysis, mock interviews, and case exercises that tested how you handled imperfect information. You learned what to say and what to withhold; you learned to act or to wait. They'd told him the best intelligence work isn't clever; it's precise.

He'd adapted out of necessity. That was the unspoken rule: adapt or disappear. You didn't complain, and you didn't seek information above your clearance. By his first posting, he could sit across from someone, listen to every word, and already be three moves ahead. It was satisfying work—until the part where it wasn't.

He turns, picks up the poker, and knocks the logs apart. Sparks leap, flash, then die. The fire settles, the bourbon warms in his hand, and he watches the flames shift and fold.

In those early years, he had believed that if he mastered every procedure, every nuance of a briefing—he could stay ahead of the chaos. But chaos has its own rules. He pulls out his phone and reads the message from his former boss again. For all the discipline and detachment MI5 had instilled, none of it prepared him for what it felt like to be abruptly discarded—or called back.

A soft knock breaks his focus. He turns. Nell stands in the doorway, changed into a soft pink sweater, frayed jeans cropped just above her ankles, backless Gucci loafers. She has a crossword book tucked under her arm.

"Mind if I sit by the fire?" she asks.

He clears his throat. "No, please do."

She crosses the room, kicks off her loafers, and settles into one of the chairs near the hearth. She flips the crossword open, humming as she reads.

Henry returns to his desk, but he's not really working. Every so often, he glances up—tracks the movement of her pencil, the way she sits with one leg folded beneath her, how she brushes her hair off her face and twists a strand around her fingers without noticing.

He looks at her longer than he means to and corrects himself automatically, reaches for his pen, taps it once against the desk, and brings his eyes back to the page. Attraction is just another kind of distraction. His interest in Nell, if that's what this is, is an impossible situation. The distance between them is measured in habit, his life in London, and in the reality of working together. Nothing about her fits his world. And yet he has felt more at peace, and more at home here than he's ever felt anywhere.

She looks over, and he knows in an instant: if he goes back to London, she'll slip beyond reach—out of his orbit, gone for good.

After a moment, she says, "Six letters. *Something you try to ignore until you can't.* Any ideas?"

He's spent his life reading people, managing outcomes, denying what he wants. But there's no denying this, and the line holding him back is thin. She can't possibly know what would happen if he crossed it. He does. And that's the problem.

"Desire," he says, the firelight flaring against the gold edge of the medal on his desk.

10

Another Letter

NELL

NELL FINDS HENRY IN the Great Hall, in black shorts and a gray tee, hunched on a gilt Louis XVI armchair in deep green velvet, knotting his running shoes. He gets to his feet the moment he spots her, offers a brisk "Morning," then sits down again to finish tying the other shoe.

"Hi." Nell folds her arms. What is it about a gentlemanly man that makes him so much more attractive than other men? "Are you running today?"

Henry stands to stretch against one of the soaring marble columns, looking her way, amused. "Am I that obvious?"

She laughs. "It was a shot in the dark. I don't know what gave you away. Can I come?"

"You want to go running with me?"

"I do know how to run, Henry. And since you're the only man currently standing half-naked in my hall—" She arches an eyebrow, casting a quick look up and down. "You're the easy choice."

Henry says. "And I'm cheap too."

Nell laughs. He gestures toward the grand staircase. "Go for it."

Nell bounds upstairs to change and comes down later in neon pink running shorts and a matching tee shirt.

As she descends, Henry shields his eyes. "I should've brought sunglasses for this."

Nell grins. "Is that for my blinding outfit or my beauty?"

He pauses, his expression sincere. "Both."

Their eyes meet for a moment before Nell breaks the spell, rolling her eyes and giving her ponytail a flip.

They turn left out of the front door and jog the length of the house toward the west wall, cutting through a stone archway, where double iron gates stand open. From this portico, it's one long straight path for almost a mile through groomed fields. Roger runs ahead, far down the path now, swerving off occasionally to follow the scent of a deer or fox—at least, that's Nell's guess.

Their trainers crunch on the gravel. Nell matches her stride to Henry's, falling in step beside him. Roger trots along on the grass, moving with an easy, ground-covering gait. I bet he knows this route well, Nell thinks. It may have been one of his old patrol circuits. He doesn't venture out by himself anymore, but he runs it almost every morning with Henry. For a quarter mile, Nell says nothing, focusing on the rhythmic sound of their shoes. Then, without preamble: "Henry, there's something I have to tell you."

He glances over. "Now what?"

"I got another letter this morning," Nell says.

"What did it say?"

Nell just looks at him.

"You didn't open it. Right. Hall table?"

"It's underneath something from the Horticultural Society. And a card from my dentist." She exhales. "I thought with everything going on, I shouldn't let it molder for a week."

Nell had half expected Henry to be annoyed. If he is, he doesn't show it.

"Character growth?" he offers.

She snorts. "Don't get carried away."

***

They finish their run breathless and flushed, slowing to a walk as the house comes into view.

Nell nudges his arm. "All right, MI5. Why the daily self-inflicted cardio?"

He considers for a moment. "There was a case," he says at last. "Domestic cell, very quiet, very competent. My team was running a live surveillance handover on a bridge in London—one team trailing out, one team picking up. I was in the van, screens and audio, making calls on who was who in a crowd of about three hundred commuters."

He watches his breath cloud in front of him. "We had one chance to identify the courier. Wrong person, and we'd scare the whole network underground. Miss him, and something very large and very loud was going to happen on a Monday morning."

"What happened?" she asks.

"We got him," Henry says. "By three seconds. My spotter saw a bag change, I saw the hand signal, called it, and the grab team moved. They opened the rucksack later. It wasn't a sandwich." He swallows. "People walked over that bridge the next day like it was nothing more than part of their commute, which is exactly how it should be. But from our side..." He trails off, searching for the right words. "From our side, you know exactly how close it was to not being fine."

They walk a few steps in silence. Roger finds a stick, decides against it, drops it again.

"A week later," Henry continues, "one of the junior officers on my team froze on a much smaller job. No bomb, just a tail that got messy. He was a good officer. It rattled him anyway. I realised then that you don't get to switch the pressure off just because the moment's passed. You have to be ready for the next one, when it's mundane and when it's not."

Nell looks over at him. "So you run."

"So I run," he agrees. "Back then it was to make sure I could trust my body to keep up with my head. These days..." He glances toward the house, toward her. "These days it's how I remind myself I did that job well. That I didn't break under it. And that I don't have to be on that bridge every morning to stay the kind of person who can move when it matters."

Nell glances over, softer now. "And here I thought it was just to show off your calves."

"That's a secondary benefit."

Roger lopes up the path ahead of them, tongue lolling.

She reaches out, briefly brushing her fingers against his hand. "For what it's worth, I'm glad you were on that bridge. And I'm glad you're here now instead."

He exhales, something in his shoulders easing. "So am I. If the worst thing I do before breakfast is run in pointless circles around a Cornish estate with a disreputable German shepherd, things are improving."

Henry collapses onto the broad front steps, stretching out his legs and watching Roger flop into a patch of shade, panting. Nell ducks inside, returns a moment later with two bottles of water and a bowl for Roger, then goes in again and reappears holding a pale blue envelope. She drops beside Henry on the step; balancing the letter on her knee while twisting her ponytail into a chignon. The envelope wobbles, and Henry reaches over to steady it before it falls, his hand grazing her thigh.

Nell watches as he inspects the envelope, turning it over in his hands. He slides his thumb under the flap and draws out a single folded page. "It's in French," Henry says. "I can read it to you, but you'll have to translate."

Nell turns toward him, leaning back just enough to clasp her hands around one knee.

Henry clears his throat and begins. His French halting, each word uniquely mangled. Nell can't help smiling—a blend of affection and admiration at his willingness to brave her correspondence.

She peeks over his arm. "Let's see, this is curious."

Dear friend,

At the foot of the old oak, the one who loyally served the Emperor entrusted what L'Orient never carried into the depths.

A friend of the lost cause.

"Where's the old oak?" he asks.

"There are thousands of oaks on the property," she says. "But this one sounds distinctive."

"The Emperor is Napoleon, no doubt," he says. "But what about L'Orient? Could that be the ship Admiral Nelson sank at the Battle of the Nile?"

Nell tilts her head. "I've never heard of it."

"L'Orient was the French flagship—huge, more than a hundred guns," Henry explains. "The British destroyed it at Aboukir Bay in 1798 at the Battle of the Nile. Blew up spectacularly. Legend says Napoleon's treasure went down too."

Nell studies the letter, brow furrowed. "But why would Napoleon have all his treasure on a single ship?"

Henry leans back on his hands, considering. "L'Orient led Napoleon's fleet in the Egypt campaign. He seized Malta on the way, took a fortune in gold and silver from the Knights of St. John—Maltese treasure. It was supposed to fund his whole expedition."

Nell is fascinated. "And it was still on his ship." She stands and brushes gravel off her shorts, and holds out a hand to Henry.

"A good portion, yes." Henry takes her hand and stands, straightening. "The crew never really had a chance to unload it—maybe they thought the ship was safe, anchored as it was. But Nelson surprised them. A cannonball found the magazine and—" he makes a silent gesture for explosion. "Most of the treasure went down and was never seen again. That's the story, anyway. If this letter's to be believed, some never made it aboard. Someone smuggled out a share and brought it to England."

Nell considers picking up Roger's bowl, but decides he might like to have one in front of the house too, along with his others. "So, most of Napoleon's treasure was lost at sea, but some part of it is hidden here at Ainsworth. I'm still not sure I get it though."

Henry explains, "Napoleon left Egypt, abandoned his army, went back to France, seized power in a coup and crowned himself, essentially, dictator for life."

"That's convenient," Nell laughs and trails Henry through the house to the library.

Henry continues, "This coast was thick with smugglers and spies during those years. After Napoleon's defeat in 1814, then his escape, then Waterloo—all chaos. Maybe the loot stayed buried."

"So the letter's talk of a *lost cause* ties in with Napoleon's defeat. And the treasure might still be here." Nell muses.

Henry says. "The blackmailer is convinced Napoleon's treasure was brought here and buried. He implies that someone at Ainsworth Manor did it."

He guides her to a large oil painting near the desk, a wild, stormy maritime painting of British and French ships locked in fierce battle, cannon fire lighting up the black water. "There—that's the Battle of the Nile." He points to a ship, its mainmast wreathed in flames. "That's L'Orient, just before the explosion."

Nell leans closer to the brass plaque on the mahogany frame. *The Battle of the Nile by Philip James de Loutherbourg.* "Oh, Henry. She presses her palm to her chest. How tragic. I never thought a painting could feel so terrifying."

"This is what we're tangled up in," Henry says.

Nell turns toward him. "So this is the second letter from the blackmailer we were waiting for."

"No," he shakes his head. "I don't think so. This one's from someone else."

"What? How can you tell? Both letters were mailed from Paris."

"It's just a hunch," he shrugs. "Experience, I guess. The handwriting is different. Stylometry," Henry says. "It's a branch of literary forensics. It uses various clues to distinguish authorship. Each of these letters has a completely different style. I'd even guess the first one is from a man, and this one is from a woman."

"So unless these two people are working together, we might have an edge," Nell says, enthusiasm in her voice.

"If we can figure out where this oak is, we may be able to beat the blackmailer at his own game," Henry agrees. "He said the next letter is coming soon."

"Henry, we have to find that tree—and fast."

Henry nods, thinking aloud. "They both want us to find the treasure. The blackmailer wants it for himself. But this second writer—what's their motive? This new letter makes me more uneasy. It's... cagier. More of a wildcard."

"And we're running out of time," Nell says.

11

Reality Cheque

NELL

NELL SKETCHES THE OUTLINE of her next novel at her desk in the Ballroom, absently tapping a pencil against her legal pad. She smiles. The habit is Henry's. She pauses, leans back, and wonders, not for the first time, how she came to be marooned on a remote Cornish estate, tangled in someone else's secrets and facing blackmail for a past that was never hers. Trouble doesn't stalk her so much as she has a knack for wandering straight into its arms.

There was the time in Thailand when she accidentally joined a smuggling investigation after staying at a guesthouse that turned out to be laundering rare orchids. And when she worked at a vineyard in Tuscany, and had a near miss with an irate wild boar who didn't appreciate her shortcut through the vines. On the other hand, that Italian chef had made it quite worthwhile. Then again, there was the time she agreed to dog-sit for an Icelandic novelist and spent a week in Reykjavík trying to rescue a sheepdog from a geothermal field.

Her aunt Gilda—brilliant and beautiful, with pure white hair swept into a classic back-combed newscaster style she's surely worn since birth—insists that Nell's entire life is a plot twist. Once a diplomat, now the proud owner of a Virginia horse farm and an enviable townhouse in Georgetown, Gilda has never married. She claims it's far more fun to entertain a turnstile of glamorous boyfriends: ambassadors, polo players, the occasional retired spy—all eager to help her out of (or into) the next social escapade.

Just last year, she phoned Nell from a Paris gala to report she'd accidentally RSVP'd to the wrong embassy and been seated beside a prince—whom she went on to date for three weeks before declaring him utterly lovely, but drearily sincere. Gilda raised Nell after her parents, both field scientists, vanished on an expedition in the Malaysian jungle. Nell likes to think she's nothing like her aunt, but as she sits in her ballroom-turned-office, spinning turmoil into novels, she wonders if they're more alike than she thought.

Henry arrives balancing a tray with two plates, two cups, and the chrome Alfi thermal coffeepot that signals proper coffee, not the instant Nell endured before he and Mrs. Patterson arrived. There's also a basket of her favorite chocolate croissants from the village bakery.

He sets the tray on her table but doesn't move away, just stands there, looking at her.

She looks up. "Uh-oh. When you bring pain au chocolat, it's never good news."

"Nell, we need to talk numbers," he says quietly, laying a printed page in front of her. "It's not about pride or tradition. It's just math. The house, the people—it all costs far more than you think."

She lifts the page, eyeing the neat columns on his spreadsheet. "I try not to think about it."

Henry smiles. "Then let me do the thinking. Just for this conversation." He taps the page. "Staff alone: a butler, head housekeeper, kitchen staff, at least four housemaids, footmen, a chauffeur for the cars, a head gardener, junior gardeners, a groundskeeper and at least two, better three people for general maintenance... You'll need thirty people at a minimum to run this place properly. That's not counting temp workers."

"And I suppose none of them accept payment in gratitude or home-baked scones," Nell mutters.

"Alas, people do grow fond of money." He continues, "Salaries will land somewhere near £1,000,000 a year. Add £80,000 for heating and repairs. Upkeep and emergencies? God help us if the water pipes leak again. We're looking at a million a year, before you count a penny for your roses."

She pushes back from the table and walks to the window, silent.

Nell turns, her eyes narrowing slightly. "How did Uncle Charles do it?"

Henry sighs, rubbing the back of his neck. "Truth? He didn't. He was bleeding money too. Spent fourteen million on renovations and upgrades those last five years—still couldn't keep up with the ongoing costs, let alone the surprises. The estate is beautiful, but it's a financial drain."

He pauses. "We have to find another solution—something sustainable, that doesn't mean selling off parts of the property."

Nell always thinks best when she's moving. She leads the way through the Great Hall; Henry takes two jackets from the brass rack, passes one to her, and follows her outside. She heads down the steps and turns right. It's a beautiful early spring morning; the grass finally greening after all the rain. It's chilly, but Nell is bundled in camel wool trousers and a thick cashmere turtleneck. Her hair is twisted into a knot at the nape of her neck, pinned with a pencil in a loose chignon. She wears low boots with flat heels and, as usual, no jewelry.

"What do you propose?" she asks, slowing so he can catch up.

He pauses to pull a weed, then falls into step. "We need to look to the future," he says. "Running this estate takes more than income and inheritance. We have to find a sustainable financial solution.

Maybe opening part of the property to limited public access, hosting events here, and starting a trust to help fund upkeep without selling off the land."

She stops, studying his face as he slips on his deerskin gloves and eyes the condition of the lawn. "It won't be easy," he admits. "But Uncle Charles tried to do it all privately, spent a fortune. It still wasn't enough."

Nell nods and pulls on her own gloves, then quickens her pace toward the east portico, propelled by the crisp morning air and the nervous energy of decisions to come. The portico is an arched, iron-gated opening between the gravel carriageway at the front of the house and the stable yard beyond.

"Opening the house to visitors—even just the gardens, and maybe a handful of rooms—could pay for most of what we need," Henry says.

Nell's jaw sets, and she crosses the stable yard toward the rear carriage gate. "I don't want strangers poking through my family's mess. It's not a museum, Henry."

"I know," he says gently, his boots crunching on the gravel. "But if we do nothing, there won't be a family house left to protect. And it doesn't have to be forever. Give it a year. Let the public in one day a week. We keep the second and third floors private. If it doesn't help, we'll revisit. If it does, we keep the doors open and pay everyone on time."

Nell knows that opening private estates like Ainsworth for limited public access has become a viable way to cover substantial upkeep costs. Her neighbors are already doing it. It would give the estate financial stability without permanent loss of privacy and could generate steady income to support the estate's preservation.

She pushes open the big iron carriage gate. "If we do this," she says, "I want the guides well-trained. And you'll need to put some things away."

Henry grins. "You have my word. We'll keep the Minton under lock and key."

She gives a reluctant laugh. "All right then, Mr. Templeton. Set up your interviews. If the house is going to be on show, it should at least be in expert hands."

Henry closes the gate after Roger, and they both follow Nell through the gardens, Henry looking triumphant and relieved. "Thank you. You won't regret it."

She turns to look into Henry's eyes and thinks about how much she needs his intelligence and level head. If it weren't for her complicated past, and this working arrangement, he might have been someone she could have fallen in love with.

Henry tilts his head and smiles at her. "So, Your Grace—or should I curtsey and call you 'Princess' instead?"

Nell laughed. "Oh, please don't. Although I'd quite like to see you attempt a curtsy. It isn't as easy as it looks, especially after a couple of martinis."

A brisk walk brings them to the old Potting Building at the far southern end of the gardens. She shrugs off her jacket and hangs it on a hook just inside the door. She holds out her hand, and Henry hands her his coat as well.

"The 'Duchess' part is straightforward. Standard issue for tedious British aristocrats with an excess of hyphens and oil paintings. But 'Princess' is thanks to my mother, who was officially Princess Margareta of Lichtenheim."

"Lichtenheim?" Henry says, pulling up a stool. "That sounds made up."

"It might as well be," Nell says, standing in front of him, arms crossed. "It's a tiny kingdom between Austria and 'someplace else,' officially vanished before anyone in my generation learned to spell it. But on the Continent, titles die hard. Relatives, eccentric society pages, and American fashion magazines keep the whole 'princess' thing alive. Legally, I'm Ninth Duchess of Belward. To my mother's family and a handful of charming European hoteliers, though, I'm Princess Eleanor of Nowhere in Particular."

The Potting Building is one of Nell's favorite spots on the estate, nestled at the edge of the walled garden and built from the same honeyed Cornish stone as the house. Inside, sunlight pours through arched windows that still hold the original leaded glass panes. The floor's black and white tiles are worn smooth, and the paneled walls are pretty, in a fresh Ladurée green. The best part: every cupboard and door has been adorned with trompe l'oeil paintings—baskets of fruit, scattered garden tools, even a painted linen apron next to Nell's real one. Somewhere, she's sure, Bunny Mellon is nodding in approval.

A green worktable stretches the length of the room, crowned by a thick marble top riddled with years of scratches, chips, and water stains. At center stands a deep stone sink with a copper faucet. Overhead, the ceiling beams are the same soft green as the walls, and above the sink, a real marble shelf holds trompe l'oeil clay pots. The potting building is a cheerful and clever wink at gardens both real and imagined, that never fails to make her smile.

On sunny days, Nell writes here with the doors thrown open to the breeze, surrounded by the cheerful illusion of neatly stacked garden books and orderly tools, both painted and real. The room is an artist's daydream and a writer's sanctuary.

Henry grins. "So you're telling me you're a real-life princess?"

"I'm telling you I can sometimes get a free dessert in Vienna if I remember to look suitably mysterious. The main perk is confusing people at society dinners. Although I did inherit the crown jewels."

"Really?" Henry's eyes widen.

Nell grins. "Well, actually, yes. But in college, when I offered to loan my 'royal' pearls to a friend for a dance, she flat-out refused to wear them when she learned they were all that remained of the Lichtenheim royal treasury. She said if the crown jewels of a vanished kingdom went missing on her watch, she'd have to flee the country, and purple taffeta isn't ideal for life on the run."

Henry watches Nell from his stool as she moves around the potting room, opening cabinets, then drawers and shelves above the desk.

"Mind if I ask what you're hunting?" he says.

"I wondered if there's mention of a distinct oak in the old garden logs or maps, but the years we need are missing."

She moves aside a stack of terracotta pots, even kneels to look beneath the desk, but there's nothing on the floor but an old seed catalogue. Nell sits back on her heels, frowning.

"They're not here, Henry. Someone's taken them."

"Are you sure?" Henry says, standing to help look.

"Yes," Nell says, stepping aside to show him the interior of a cabinet filled with bound books. She points. "This section should hold the garden plans for every decade since 1800. Each volume covers twenty years. But the volumes from 1800 to 1860 are gone."

"Where are the originals?" Henry asks, curious.

"The UK National Archives," Nell says, then smiles, realizing how odd it must sound to have one's garden notes in a museum.

"Is this building normally locked?"

"No," Nell replies. "I'm the only one who ever comes out here. Real potting is done near the greenhouse."

Henry's tone is quiet. "So... who else is searching for that tree?"

Nell tilts her head and shrugs. "I don't know, but this is becoming quite a party."

12

Open House

HENRY

THE NEXT AFTERNOON, NELL marches a trail back and forth across the faded Turkish rug in the library, leaving a Hansel-and-Gretel path of jelly beans, which Roger seems happy to clean up.

"I'm telling you, Henry, I've come around to your way of thinking. You're right—people love old houses. You know how it is—everyone loves the romance of a country house, but when they get inside, nothing delights them more than judging someone else's curtains."

Henry looks up from his laptop and sits back in his chair, surprised. "By 'everyone,' are you speaking of the masses or just indulging your own curtain obsession?"

Nell wags her finger. "Everyone. Especially the poking, nosy sort—exactly who we need in order to solve this mystery."

He twirls his pen with what Nell calls "inconceivable MI5 dexterity," and says, "So your plan is to lure in local aristo-watchers with the promise of drawing-room drama and buried treasure—hoping some heritage enthusiast with a sideline in blackmail shows up sporting a Napoleon hat?"

"Well, just the village for now. I want to beta-test this tour thing." Nell says decisively.

"I admit," Henry concedes, "we might scare up some leads. I just want to be sure you're ready for people commenting on the upholstery, or posting your teapot to Instagram with the hashtag *shabbychicfail*?"

Nell gasps, hand to heart. "Sir, you wound me. I'll have you know shabby chic is a lifestyle here. Besides, this circus was your suggestion, remember?"

"And if you capture our mysterious blackmailer?" Henry asks.

"Then I'll charm him or her into confessing over Victoria sponge. Just like Jeanette in The Swooning Countess," Nell says brightly. "People always tell me things. I have one of those faces."

"Maybe it's because you always have jelly beans in your pockets."

She stops in front of his desk. "You handle the finances and keep track of everyone's alibis. Then, when someone slips up—"

Henry finishes, "—Roger pounces and saves the day."

They both look at Roger.

"I'll make a list of our visitors as we get responses—and don't worry. I promise not to mention murder, the ghost, or stolen garden plans in my flyer."

"That's a relief." Henry scribbles a note on his legal pad, then pauses and looks up. "Wait. What? We have a ghost?"

Nell nods solemnly. "In the stable block."

***

Henry notes that the library, which used to be his office, has transformed under Nell into "Tour Central," a hub filled with flyers, brochures, and half-empty coffee cups until Mrs. Patterson sweeps

through and collects them, muttering about "anarchy" and "civilization deteriorating by degrees."

He stops behind Nell's chair, looking over her shoulder as she
wrestles with her latest creation, a poster that's a masterpiece of uneven fonts, irregular spacing, and a photograph of Roger scowling.

"You've really captured Roger's spirit of civic enthusiasm."

"That's his headshot face," Nell says. "I was aiming for noble."

Henry reads aloud:

AINSWORTH MANOR: OPEN FOR INTRIGUE!
DEBUT HISTORIC HOUSE TOUR!
MYSTERY GUARANTEED!
ROSES, RELICS, REFRESHMENTS.

"Perfect, right?" Nell says, "It practically screams titillating
chaos."

Henry reaches for his coffee. "That it does."

She chews on the end of her marker as she finishes the poster.
"Do you think it's dishonest if I put 'refreshments' but it's just
emergencies-only gingersnaps?"

Henry doesn't respond, just hands her a to-do list on a clipboard—Nell doodles a rose in the corner because, priorities.

They wrangle over logistics—how to secure the gardens, which
rooms are off-limits, and whether Fergus should be present (no).
Henry makes a few notes, careful not to notice Nell's nervous energy. He hears what sits beneath Nell's humor: the strain of letting
strangers tramp through her private life. Still, the plan goes forward.

He reminds her about security. "Don't trust anyone who talks
about Napoleon as if he's still writing them letters." It wins a laugh,
which was the point. He watches her shoulders relax for a moment,
anyway. Then she wonders aloud about her welcome speech and
whether to mention the blackmail letter. Henry doesn't answer; he's
not sure whether she's serious, but he's wise enough not to ask.

Nell's phone buzzes constantly over the next two days. She stares at the screen. "Do you answer on the first ring? Is that desperate?"

"If you answer before it rings, that's desperate," Henry says.

Roger swipes a flyer and ducks under the table, chewing thoughtfully. Henry retrieves it, sighing. "Do you think he's trying to tell us something?"

"Probably that our marketing needs work," Nell says.

To Henry's surprise, Nell's "Debut Historic House Tour" fills almost immediately—twenty-five visitors signed up in the first two days, most of them local. He scans the list she hands him: an antiques dealer, Eliza Brookes and her husband Edgar, Dr. Marcus Penhaligon, an Oxford military historian, Magnus Clay, a rose enthusiast, and Mr. Payne, a horticulturist who has already phoned twice about the sundial.

They draw up a plan for discreet observation. Nell will charm the guests; Henry will look for clues. Roger will, well, Roger will do what Roger does best. Hide under the sideboard. There is a brief debate about whether he ought to wear a Welcome Dog bandana. Roger yawns and leaves the room.

***

Tour day arrives, and Nell gathers the guests in the Great Hall.

"Good morning, everyone! Welcome to Ainsworth Manor—family home, local landmark, and ongoing liability."

There's a polite ripple of laughter.

"We're so pleased you're here and hope to get to know each of you today, so please be sure to introduce yourselves."

She pauses, adjusts her notes, and smiles at the crowd. "We'll start here in the hall, which has seen more generations of Ainsworth drama than I can summarize without refreshments."

Another laugh drifts through the hall. Henry shifts a little, moving nearer to one column for a clearer view. From there, he can see everything: Nell at the top of the shallow steps on the landing, the guests fanning out across the geometric pattern of the marble floor. Sunlight filters in mottled gold through high mullioned windows, a painter's composition in order and symmetry.

She glances over; he gives her an encouraging nod. Henry folds his arms and waits, part-sentinel, part-detective. Something is about to go right, or about to go wrong, and he still can't tell which.

"The East Wing was originally the main house. It was built by the first Duke in the early 1700s. The central block and west wing were added later, a gift from the Crown to Aleric Ainsworth in recognition of his heroism at Waterloo in 1815. Most of the changes you'll see date from later generations, some visionary, some... less so."

A few appreciative smiles pass through the group. Henry notes the polite shuffling of notebooks; collectors, historians, and the merely curious.

"Charles Ainsworth, 8th Duke of Belward, my uncle Charlie, took his responsibilities seriously. He inherited the estate after the title passed out of the 3rd Duke's line, following the death of Aleric's son Clarence, who left no heir. Under Charles, Ainsworth underwent its most ambitious restoration since the nineteenth century: structural reinforcement, stonework cleaning, the restoration of priceless art, and the revival of its gardens. The roof repairs, which are a vast and costly undertaking, began under his supervision."

Henry studies Nell, fascinated. Most people, even Nell herself perhaps, see her as a little unruly. He used to think she colored outside the lines simply because she never stopped to ask why they were there. But as he watches her weaving through the crowded room, he sees she isn't careless at all. Nell understands society's rules perfectly; but she knows which ones are sensible and which exist solely to ensure people stay in predictable lanes, where they can be managed. Nell sees the world as it actually is, not how people tell her it is.

She values manners. In her hands, courtesy is a kind of social currency, which might be worrisome in someone less kind. Permission to Nell is irrelevant. She knows with absolute confidence that she belongs anywhere she wants to be. She's disarming, sometimes exasperating, but impossible to look away from.

Nell makes life feel as though everything is possible.

In the library, Nell pauses beside a glass case, gesturing at the medal within. "This was presented to Aleric Ainsworth in recognition of bravery at Waterloo. Wellington himself signed the citation."

Dr. Marcus Penhaligon, notepad open, drifts closer. "A fascinating artifact, Your Grace," he says. "Bravery cited in dispatches is a rare honor." He looks at Henry. "Out of curiosity, have you ever read the original citation?"

Penhaligon stands out in the group, Henry thinks. He's slim and immaculately neat, with close-cropped greying hair, rimless glasses, and a precise, almost fussy manner of speaking. His Oxford vowels are soft, but his questions are pointed and delivered with a gentility bordering on slyness.

Henry shakes his head. "Ainsworth has a copy, but the original is on display at the Wellington Museum in London. We're lucky to have the medal here. You're from Oxford?" Henry asks.

"Yes," he says. "I teach military history, Wellington's campaigns in particular. I'm especially interested in his staff; the headquarters officers who handled intelligence, signals, and liaison with the allied contingents; and in the rumors that still trail Waterloo. History has a way of polishing its heroes. Even by English standards, the battle was a muddled affair: orders went astray, intelligence reports were conflicting, and a few reputations were, shall we say, rehabilitated afterward to maintain morale."

Nell smiles, "You're implying Aleric's record was exaggerated?"

"A question worth examining," Penhaligon replies. "There were breakdowns in communication, moments of near disaster, perhaps even lapses in discretion that might look different when viewed through the prism of victory." He hesitates just long enough to make her uneasy. "If not outright instances of espionage." He moves away, leaving Henry with a sense that Dr. Penhaligon's interest in Aleric Ainsworth is more than academic.

As the group moves toward the Conservatory, Henry introduces himself to Lady Penvale and her mother-in-law, the Dowager Countess of Penvale, who claims she's "known the Ainsworths since they had horses."

He also meets Mr. Simms, the secondary-school art master. Lagging the group, he stands in front of a painting of Aleric Ainsworth and his son Clarence near the Conservatory doors, his head angled as if closely studying the brushwork. He asks no questions, only makes sounds under his breath. When Henry greets him, Simms looks up, startled. He gives a quick smile that doesn't quite reach his eyes, and rejoins the group.

At the rear of the group walk Eliza Brookes and her husband. He towers over her, his jacket pulling slightly at the seams. He surveys the crowd with heavy-lidded eyes that probably miss very little, Henry thinks. When Henry moves to pass, he shifts a half-step, casually blocking the corridor.

"Are you Mr. Templeton?" He asks, but it isn't a question.

"Yes," Henry replies evenly. "How do you do?" He glances toward Eliza as he speaks, wondering whether she's mentioned their previous conversation.

Eliza extends her hand, perhaps a touch too quickly. "How do you do, Mr. Templeton? I'm Eliza Brookes. This is my husband, Edgar Whitby."

Her voice is pleasant, but she doesn't smile. While her husband watches, she keeps perfectly still, her hand withdrawing the moment Henry releases it. Whitby. The name is familiar. The magistrate who signed Rose Ainsworth's death certificate in 1847 had been a Whitby. Coincidence, perhaps, but Henry's never believed much in those. Eliza's husband doesn't move for a moment, then nods and steps aside, gesturing for Henry to continue.

Eduard Leclair introduces himself as they pass back through the gallery. He is more formally dressed than the other guests in a dark suit and tie; his silver hair is brushed carefully back and caught in a low ponytail, reminiscent of a seventeenth-century courtier.

"An extraordinary collection, Mr. Templeton," he says, his English touched with a Parisian accent, the vowels drawn out like silk. "The mahogany desk, Louis XVI style, no? Or perhaps reclaimed Regency?"

"I'm afraid I don't know much about furniture, Mr. Leclair, but I can certainly find out for you," Henry replies. "I do know the French pieces are largely original to the house."

"Ah." Leclair inclines his head, smiling as though at some private amusement. "Furniture can be confusing. The distinction between period and style...it is a language of its own, yes? Still, they are beautiful things." He pauses. "If Miss Ainsworth should ever wish to part with a few items, I have clients who would pay very respectably for work of this caliber. I also do restoration work."

Henry finds it interesting that someone so obviously formal would specifically drop Nell's title.

He produces a slim ivory card, his fingers careful and unhurried. "For future convenience," he says pleasantly. "Circumstances, as we know, do... evolve."

Before Henry can answer, Leclair gives a courteous bow and drifts away toward the next doorway, pausing to admire a portrait as if nothing of consequence had passed between them.

**

One of the new tour guides has taken over from Nell and is leading the remaining group from the gardens, wrapping up the tour. Some visitors have already climbed into their cars and are making their way out of the parking area behind the stable yard.

Henry is just about to close the gate to the south rose garden when he spots a figure crouched beside the sundial. Mr Payne, in a brown coat rather too short in the sleeves, is bent beside the sundial, prodding at the soil with a small hand trowel.

"Hello, Mr. Payne?" Henry says. "I hadn't realized the garden tour included gardening."

"Ah, Mr. Templeton." Payne straightens, still smiling. "You found me at last. I phoned twice about this sundial; you may remember. Quite an unusual specimen—bronze plate, early nineteenth century. I wanted to see if the original base was still visible beneath the moss."

"You thought of checking during the tour?"

"Best light of the day," Payne says easily, brushing soil from his palms. "And one never knows when these old pieces will be disturbed—or replaced." He glances toward the other guests along the path. "Better to study them while one can. I'll admit, I've been in the gardens several times since His Grace died."

"You have?" Henry says, surprised.

"I was sure no one would mind, since there was no one here. Of course, I haven't been back since the Duchess of Belward moved in," Payne replies.

"Of course," Henry says. "What did you do when you were here before Her Grace moved in?"

"Oh, this and that," Payne says lightly. "I enjoy exploring. Sometimes take cuttings if I see something interesting. You know, at one time, these grand houses were open to visitors."

"Perhaps when Jane Austen was alive," Henry says evenly. "Now I think it's trespassing and theft."

Payne nods once. "Then I'm glad to see the house is in capable hands with the Duchess now." He tucks the trowel into his coat pocket as though it were standard equipment and walks away toward the departing visitors. He pauses at the gate to look back at the sundial, then gives Henry a wave.

Henry closes the gates to the rose garden, then pauses, taking in the view before returning to the house. From here, the southern grounds unfold in elegant tiers—clipped parterres nearest the terrace, followed by the rose gardens, tennis court, pool, and gently sloping lawns. Beyond these lie the working garden buildings, and farther still, thousands of acres of parkland roll into the misty distance—a cultivated wilderness designed to seem effortless but demanding constant care.

He straightens a cuff pointlessly; it's already neat. The scale of the estate always astounds him. Every hedge, every statue, every scrap of gravel depends on someone's care, someone like him, at least in name if not always in practice. Ainsworth Manor looks serene in the fading light, but Henry knows from experience how easily order frays: a gate left unlatched, one door not locked, a single window left open. Drawing a slow breath, he feels the beauty and the burden of this place. He could no more guard every inch than stop dusk creeping across the lawns. Still, habit makes him scan the grounds once more before heading inside.

The message from Merrick still lingers on his phone. Henry tells himself he'll answer tonight, after he's thought it through. He knows he won't. Half a dozen drafts live in his head—every version reasonable, none sent.

The phone feels heavier than it should. The words are so simple: Yes, I'll return. Or, no, simpler still.

He closes his hand around the device, as if to keep it from replying for him.

***

The day unraveled quickly after the tour: Mrs Patterson's questions about invoices, a missing key, and the surprise downpour that sent everyone running for cover. By the time the last visitor had gone, the house had taken on that peculiar end-of-day quiet, the sound of things waiting to be tidied for the evening.

Henry finds Nell in her office at last, writing at her desk, half-hidden behind her ever-present bouquet of roses and a massive crystal jar filled to the brim with jelly beans. For someone so small, everything about Nell is larger than life—her decorating, her ideas, her charm. He glances at Roger, sprawled across the floor; even her dog is epic in scale.

"That might be the largest quantity of jelly beans I've ever seen assembled in one place," he says, leaning on the doorframe.

Nell smiles without looking up. "Occupational hazard. Sugar improves creativity."

"So that's the secret to your impressive number of novels." He crosses to the chair opposite her. "I came to see how you thought the tour went. Thought we might compare notes before anything gets rewritten in folklore."

"I'd call it a success," she says. "Nobody fell into the ha-ha, and Mr. Simms didn't steal any doorknobs as far as I know." She studies him. "You seem far away, though. Everything all right?"

Henry meets her eyes briefly, then looks toward the windows where rain is dripping on the glass. "Of course," he says lightly. "Long day, that's all."

She nods, but seems unconvinced, and reaches for another jelly bean from the small mound near her laptop. "Then take one of these. They fix everything."

He smiles, takes the offered sweet, and pockets it without tasting it. Later, when he reaches for his phone, he finds the jelly bean is stuck to the back—untouched, a little sticky, and still there beside Merrick's unanswered message.

13

French Connection

NELL

NELL SELECTS A WHITE tennis skirt with crisp pleats and a matching polo, pops the collar, and threads a pink ribbon through her ponytail. Her phone buzzes on the windowsill.

Henry: Wait for you out back

She pulls a sweater over her head at the last minute and skips downstairs. From the Boot Room, she grabs a fresh can of tennis balls, and spots Henry outside, deep in conversation with Lewis, the new gardener. Lewis stands barefoot in the gravel, a clump of lavender in one hand. Both men look up as she steps outside, their conversation halting. Henry's gaze drops to Nell's bare legs, just once, before he smiles and slides on his sunglasses.

Nell waves. "Hi, Lewis. Was that downward dog I saw you doing while digging up bindweed?"

Lewis's reply is pure Zen: "The body follows the mind, Your Grace. Every weed is an opportunity for inner peace."

"Henry, Lewis is writing a gardening book—*Help Your Rhododendrons Find Their Dharma,*" Nell tells him.

"We were discussing realigning the rose beds by chakra," Henry says.

Nell taps her racket on her knee as she and Henry stroll toward the courts.

"What do you think of Lewis? He's my first official hire."

Henry eyes her sideways. "What were your hiring criteria?"

She grins. "He's certainly easy on the eyes."

Henry shakes his head. "He prunes according to the moon calendar."

Nell laughs. "Maybe so, but he's the only one around here who isn't scared of Mrs. Patterson."

They drop their gear onto a bench, and the conversation shifts to the house tour. Nell serves first, and they volley back and forth.

"Did you know Eliza's husband's last name isn't Brookes?" she says. "It's Whitby."

"Yes, I had the pleasure of meeting Mr. Whitby." Henry's racquet connects with a crisp thwack. "Same last name as the magistrate who signed Rose's death certificate."

"Do you think there's a connection?" Nell asks, returning his serve.

"Don't know. Worth looking into." Henry pauses before adding, "Eliza didn't look happy to be with him yesterday. I can't imagine why; he has a lovely personality."

Nell laughs, tossing the ball up for her next serve. "I wonder what he does for a living. He has enormous muscles—something physical, clearly."

Henry returns it easily. "What did you make of Mr. Payne?"

"He had a trowel in his pocket," Nell says, laughing again.

"Yes," Henry replies, "and he was using it to investigate the moss at the base of the sundial."

Nell serves again, the ball slicing neatly across the court.

Henry sends the ball back, not nearly as hard as he could. "What about Mr. Penhaligon, the military history expert?"

Nell runs for the return, breathless. "He certainly stands out for having both the knowledge and a motive for blackmail."

"Oh?" Henry raises a brow. "Disgruntled historian."

"He might be more interested in the historical significance of Napoleon's treasure than the money." She hits the ball—it spins wide and goes out. Henry collects it and lobs it gently back.

"With his contacts and research, it isn't hard to imagine him having access to documents that might embarrass the family."

They play in rhythm for another twenty minutes before calling it a draw, both a little winded.

"I met Miss Danforth, the village librarian," Nell says. "Jenny said Uncle Charles let her borrow books from the Ainsworth library."

"I didn't meet her," Henry says, walking back toward the house. "But did you know your uncle has all of your books in the library?"

"Really?" Nell says. "I wondered how you'd built such an in--depth knowledge of my backlist."

"I'm a huge fan," Henry says.

"Funny. You don't seem like the romance type," Nell says.

"He had them all bound in leather."

"That's sweet."

"Speaking of sweet," Henry adds, deadpan. "I may never look at whipped cream the same way again after chapter fourteen of *The Restless Rogue*."

Nell nearly drops her tennis racquet. "Oh god. That was... that scene was supposed to be comedic, not, you know... sensual."

"If you ever need a research assistant..." Henry replies, "I'd like to offer my services."

She laughs and flips a tennis ball at him.

Roger follows them at his usual safe distance on the path from the courts, preferring the shaded side. The tennis ball arcs wide past Henry and rolls toward him. Nell turns, still smiling, to see if Roger shows any interest in chasing it. He watches the ball skip a tuft of grass, bounce, then stop. He approaches it cautiously—nose working, tail still, gives it a small nudge, and watches it roll a few inches away before leaving it there.

"Not interested," Henry says softly to Nell.

Nell shakes her head and glances back again. "He will be. One day."

Roger doesn't look at the ball again, but when the wind catches it and sends it rolling behind him on the path, Nell notices he flinches then keeps walking.

"Who's Lady Penvale?" Henry asks.

"Oh, I meant to talk to her, but got pulled away," Nell says. "Deirdre. Deirdre Marsh, Countess of Penvale; she's married to Randolph Marsh, Earl of Penvale. They're neighbors to the west at Clairview Park. The Marshes have been there for eons—seat of the Earls of Penvale since the 1700s. Deirdre came with her mother-in-law, the Dowager Countess."

"She said she's known the Ainsworths since they had horses," Henry says. "What does that mean?"

Nell smiles. "It means she's old money in the very oldest sense. She remembers when the Ainsworths were practically royalty out here and never forgets anyone. Or anything."

The three of them—Henry, Nell, and Roger—are sitting on the terrace outside the library, having coffee and a bowl of water when Mrs. Patterson appears in the doorway, smoothing her starched white apron. "Excuse me, Your Grace—Mr. Templeton—have you a moment?"

Nell looks up from re-tying her shoe. "Of course, Mrs. Patterson. Is something wrong?"

"Not wrong, exactly," says the housekeeper, stepping outside as though summoned to testify. "The desk you wanted from third-floor storage has been brought down and set in the second-floor blue bedroom in the East Wing—as requested. Fine piece once it had a proper polish." She clears her throat. "While I was there, I took it upon myself to review the inventories. As you're aware, every room has its own record, and the blue bedroom is no exception."

Henry raises an eyebrow. "Inventories, plural?"

"Of course, sir," she replies crisply. "A house this size cannot be run from memory. Each room holds its own complete list—furniture, ornaments, even draperies if they're worth the ink. It's the only practical defense against the sheer number of feet tromping through—family, guests, staff, visitors, contractors. I imagine even you can see the difficulty." She purses her lips, visibly pleased with her airtight logic.

"The upstairs maids and the housekeepers—well, obviously not the late housekeepers—conduct a full count yearly and an informal one every month."

Nell is relieved, on balance, that the late housekeepers are no longer conducting inventories in person. Though in a historic house this size, she wouldn't rule out an occasional spectral audit. She can almost picture them gathering in the linen closets, counting pillowcases by moonlight.

Then, with a modest sniff: "I wasn't His Grace's housekeeper, mind you—that was Mrs. Linton. Capable woman, kept decent records—though not, I daresay, as thorough as my own. Still, credit where it's due."

Nell smiles. "Thank you, Mrs. Patterson. What did you find?"

Mrs. Patterson reaches into her apron pocket and unfolds a slip of paper with an efficient snap. "The blue bedroom once held a fruitwood writing desk, originally Mr. Philippe Moreau's. Brought from Paris in 1810. Record shows Mr. Moreau returned to France in June 1815—without it."

She adjusts her glasses. "Not that I'm looking for things to fill my time, Your Grace," she says, clearly implying the opposite, "but I wanted to know why the desk was missing. There ought to have been a desk, so I took time out of my day, as one does, to find out."

Mrs. Patterson fixes her glasses on her nose, consults her clipboard, and looks up. "If I may."

"Please do," Nell says, already bracing herself.

"Mind you," Mrs. Patterson says, "I'm not one to pull the rug out from under the kettle."

"Of course not, Mrs. Patterson."

Satisfied, Mrs. Patterson begins:

Blue Bedroom Inventory, Ainsworth Manor: One Biennais writing desk, continental fruitwood. Inlaid with black walnut and mother-of-pearl; compartments in the secretaire top; brass lion-head pulls; acanthus leaf carving at the feet. Crescent-shaped *ink stain inside the right-hand drawer. Lozenge stamp—capital N with laurel leaves, above a small Napoleonic bee—far rear, right side rail.*

She glances up, unsmiling.

Provenance: Monsieur Philippe Moreau, brought from Paris in 1810. Desk remained after his departure, June 1815.

Henry, still baffled, tries for logic. "What date is that inventory, Mrs. Patterson?"

Mrs. Patterson gives him an almost pitying look. "Inventory rolls over, month to month, year to year, sir. Unless something is marked out or added. Obviously."

Henry searches for footing. "So this is the current inventory of the blue bedroom? From 1810 until... today?"

Mrs. Patterson demurs. "No, sir. This is the current inventory from 1730 to today. Ten pages, sir. We don't go changing things every five minutes here, like most places."

Henry sighs. "Has the blue bedroom been blue since 1730?"

She consults her pages efficiently. "Yes, sir. Except the twenty years between 1950 and 1970, when someone tried Harvest Gold." She pauses, then adds, "It did not last."

Nell bites her lip to keep from laughing. "Thank you, Mrs. Patterson."

Nell says. "I wonder why Mr. Moreau would leave his desk here. Biennais was an excellent furniture maker."

"Upon engagement, Ma'am. That means he was probably employed here. But if he was in the blue bedroom on the family floor, he wasn't any kind of servant." Mrs. Patterson says.

Henry asks, "Mrs. Patterson, I don't suppose there are records from as far back as 1815 that mention who Philippe Moreau was, are there?"

Mrs. Patterson looks mildly affronted, lips set in a tight line. "Why, of course there are, Mr. Templeton. Everyone who's ever set foot in this house is recorded somewhere—staff rolls, contractor logs, visitor books. There are also the housekeeper's journals and the butler's journals. A property like Ainsworth runs on handwriting and accurate ledgers, sir; without them, the whole thing would collapse into anarchy."

She folds her hands as if to underline the point.

Nell has noticed that for Mrs. Patterson there is no middle ground between perfection and anarchy—her favorite word, and, Nell suspects, her private measure of civilization.

"If Monsieur Moreau was a tutor of some sort," Mrs. Patterson says, "he'd appear on the household staff list for those years. I can have them brought down from the attic records room. I expect they'll be in good order—my predecessors may not have had my precision, but they certainly knew the value of neat columns."

"So we could know exactly when he came and when he left," Nell says, already thinking ahead. "Mrs. Patterson, please also bring the records on Thomas Duval. He was a French tutor around 1847."

Mrs. Patterson exhales—the measured sigh of one who has a dozen other duties waiting below stairs—then straightens her clipboard and gives a brisk nod. "Very good, ma'am. I shall see what can be unearthed."

She turns smartly toward the library, the rattle of her keys a declaration of service rendered for the greater good of world order.

Mrs. Patterson closes the door behind her, leaving Nell and Henry alone again on the terrace.

**

Nell parks her old green Range Rover on the street in the village, just in front of her favorite bakery. She removes her scarf and gloves as she steps inside, tucking them into the pocket of her brown suede jacket and holding out her hand when she sees her old friend.

"Lord Jonathan! So good to see you. How have you been?"

The Holland & Holland representative—immaculately dressed in tweed and a dark tie—is already on his feet, his accent soft, precise, unmistakably Mayfair.

"Your Grace, always such a pleasure."

"Thank you for driving out," Nell says. "Next time I'll come in."

Jonathan replies with an easy smile. "Please call me Jonathan. We've been to college parties together."

Nell laughs. "Then you must call me Nell; you've seen me naked."

He grins, tipping his head. "A swim in the St. Andrews quad fountain doesn't really count."

"Try telling that to the photographers," she says, shaking her head. "It's good to see you again, Jonathan."

"You too. I didn't realize you were still down here."

"For my sins," she says lightly. "How's your family? All still at Drysden Hall?"

"Mostly. My father's retired to Scotland; my brother's running the estate now. I just shuttle between clients and gunrooms."

"Which explains all the green boxes." Nell notes Holland & Holland's trademark green stack. "You never travel light."

"Not when it comes to firearms." Jonathan's amusement shows. "Old habits die hard."

Nell tilts her head. "You've always stuck with dangerous habits."

"Not always." He winks, flashing the same perfect model smile he had at university. "But let me know if you ever change your mind."

"Deal," Nell laughs. "Now, what have you brought me?"

She flags down a passing server and orders a cappuccino and her favourite pastry—the pain au chocolat that's made this bakery famous from here to London in the single year it's been open.

"Do you want to go through these now, or try them on at home?" Jonathan asks.

"Oh, I'll take the clothes home," Nell says. "But I want to see the bag."

"Of course," Jonathan says. "I was hoping you'd say that. It's beautiful."

He lifts the lid from the top box and separates the layers of cream tissue, drawing out a leather briefcase-style bag.

"Nell, this is our very best full-grain, vegetable-tanned bridle leather. We've burnished it to a subtle waxed sheen in the walnut brown you requested. All the fittings are solid brass. As you know, we custom-forge these in small runs. They each have our H&H crown-and-scroll hallmark—discreetly, of course. The buckles and handle rivets are modeled after gun slip fittings—functional, yet the precision alone makes them ornamental."

"It's lovely, Jonathan. Thank you," Nell says.

"Reinforced handles, double-stitched seams. No plastic, no glue," he says.

Nell smiles. "It's perfect. Understated and practical. Just like Henry."

They chat for a while over their cappuccinos, then Jonathan carries Nell's boxes to her car and they make plans to meet for dinner the next time she's in Mayfair.

Nell decides to stop into Emily Miller's flower shop while she's in town to see if she'll help with arrangements for the next Ainsworth house tour. As Nell turns from the car, she sees Eliza's husband going into Eduard Leclair's antique shop, and decides to check with Leclair about restoring the sideboard in the Great Hall. As she pulls open the door, the men stop talking. Edgar Whitby tips his cap and walks past Nell without a word.

"Hello," Nell says. "I saw you were open and thought I'd stop in. I hope I didn't disturb a meeting."

Leclair is smooth and charming. "Not at all, Miss Ainsworth, enchanté. How can I help you today?"

"Nothing urgent," Nell replies. "I haven't visited since you bought the shop from Mr. Baines and wanted to see your offerings. Henry gave me your card. I need some restoration done and would love to see examples of your work."

Something about the place is naggingly familiar, but she cannot decide what it is. The furniture on display is exquisite; Mr. Leclair has excellent taste.

Then she sees it and nearly gasps—a fruitwood three-drawer writing desk with brass lion-head pulls.

The desk is French polished, inlaid with bands of black walnut and mother-of-pearl at the corners. There is a secretaire top with compartments, a single drawer, and even carved acanthus leaves at the feet.

That's my desk.

"Would you care for a glass of champagne, Miss Ainsworth?" Leclair offers.

"Yes," Nell says. "Wonderful. Thank you."

When he steps off the floor, Nell quickly opens the right-hand drawer on the desk, searching for the moon-shaped ink stain.

It's there. Of course it is, she thinks. I knew it would be.

At that instant, she hears Leclair behind her.

She slides the drawer closed and pivots, hoping she does not seem startled.

"Ah, Mr. Leclair, I'm interested in this George III chair." She turns her back on the desk and gestures to a nearby carved mahogany chair.

"A fine choice. That is one of the best examples of George III dining chairs I've seen," Leclair says, handing her a glass of champagne.

"We have a dining chair that is really quite beyond repair, and I think this will match perfectly," Nell says.

She marvels Leclair seems unconcerned about displaying Ainsworth's desk so openly—then realizes he has no reason to believe she has ever seen it before or that she even knows it is missing from the house.

Unbelievable, Nell thinks. Angry, but almost impressed at the man's audacity.

Nell sips her champagne and browses the shop for a few more minutes, then makes a point of looking at her watch. "Oh, heavens, look at the time. I'm running late as usual."

Leclair smiles. "I'll send you the tear sheet for the chair this afternoon."

"Thank you," Nell says, checking her watch again. "And now I really must go."

As she steps out of the shop, lost in thought, Nell nearly collides with Jenny Danforth, the village librarian.

"Oh! Sorry about that," Jenny says, cheeks coloring. "I wasn't watching where I was going."

"Hi, Jenny. I was hoping to catch you at the library," Nell replies, recovering.

Jenny gives a nervous little laugh. "Lucky you caught me now... I was just heading back. What can I do for you today, ma'am?"

Nell falls into step beside her. "I'm looking for records of Ainsworth landscaping between about 1810 and 1847. I know it's a long shot, but I'm hoping to find out if there was a distinctive large oak tree near the house back then."

Jenny hesitates, shifting her tote bag to the other shoulder. "Well, um... it's funny you mention that. Several people have asked about Ainsworth's old landscape plans lately."

Nell blinks. "Really?"

Jenny nods, avoiding Nell's eyes. "Yes, but, uh—of course, I try never to share who asks for what. That's something we take seriously. Privacy, you know. I wish I could help more."

Nell nods, sensing Jenny's discomfort. "I wouldn't want you to break a confidence."

Jenny exhales, relieved not to be pressed. She slows as they reach the steps of the library. Nell says goodbye and is about to turn when Jenny glances quickly up and down the street.

"Ma'am, Clairview Park has a larger library than the village. I don't believe I'd be violating any rules if I say that Lady Marsh has been kind enough to allow me to check out materials from their extensive local history files. If you're looking for specific information on Ainsworth's grounds—certain tree surveys or plans, for example—I'd definitely try Clairview. Materials move around, but you might find something... relevant."

Nell notices the slight emphasis and wonders if Jenny is nudging her. "Thank you, Jenny. I appreciate it."

Jenny offers an uneasy, polite smile. "Anytime, Your Grace."

As Nell drives home, she realizes what's familiar about Leclair's antique shop. It smells like lavender and tobacco.

14

Uniformity

HENRY

H ENRY STANDS WITH ROGER on the gravel in the forecourt. Nell's Range Rover trundles down the lane toward the village, the end of her scarf flipping and twirling where it has slipped free of her partially closed driver's-side door. Henry shakes his head as she disappears around the curve. He turns, watching as spray lifts from the tops of the water plumes in the fountains, driven off by the stiff westerly breeze.

Wind had come sharp from the west another time, too, not long ago. They had been out walking, and a gust had cut across the field just as Nell turned to say something to him. The scarf—her latest, a thin silk one patterned in watercolor stripes—caught the air and slipped from her neck before she noticed.

"Oh, bother," she'd laughed, and chased it.

He'd called for her to leave it, but she was already running down the slope. The scarf snagged once, then freed itself, carried toward the ha-ha. The drop-off—nine feet deep, cunningly hidden by grass—is a sunken barrier invented to keep sheep and cattle out of the gardens while preserving an unbroken view of the lawns. Ainsworth is famous for them. They are everywhere: invisible, sudden, and steep enough to surprise even old hands.

Nell flew after the scarf, quick and careless, hair breaking loose from its pins.

"Nell—wait!"

Too late. The grass underfoot was slick with rain from the night before. She skidded, her knees buckled, and momentum carried her to the edge of the ha-ha—for an instant she balanced there, the scarf fluttering below her like a flag.

He'd moved without thinking, reaching her in time to catch her arm and pull her back. The shock of her weight in his arms, the scent of cold wool and her hair, the startled silence before she laughed. Mud streaked her sleeve to the elbow. The scarf lay half down the embankment, motionless now.

She looked up at him, breathless. "I nearly had it."

He held her a moment longer than necessary. "You nearly didn't."

Henry looks over at Roger and wonders if he's remembering the same thing.

***

Henry picks up his coat and briefcase from the library, and by the time Nell reaches the village, he's already following the B-roads toward Truro.

He leaves his car in the long-term lot beside the station and boards the mid-morning Great Western service to Paddington. The journey takes just over four hours—a blur of hedgerows, slate roofs, and the transformation from green fields to city sprawl. He spends most of it reviewing digitized Ainsworth correspondence from the early nineteenth century, marking notes as the fields give way to brick terraces.

He meets Merrick at a private club off St. James's. Decanted wine sits on the table between them, with two stemmed glasses and a small crystal bowl filled with nuts.

"So that's it?" Henry asks. "One text out of the blue, and suddenly my name's cleared?"

Merrick nods once. "The Home Office Liaison signed off last week. Personnel Security verified your reinstatement—official clearance restored as of yesterday, assuming that is, you sign on the dotted line tomorrow, and take care of the usual paperwork."

Henry gives a short laugh. "Just like that."

"Not 'just like that,'" Merrick corrects. "It took months of back-channel work to get this done. The file's been sealed; the board is satisfied. You're no longer under internal review."

Henry leans back. "And does the department intend to apologize for destroying my career and my reputation, or do they only send wine and paperwork?"

Merrick laughs outright but doesn't sound apologetic. "Apologies aren't really our currency, you know that. But they are prepared to bring you back handsomely, with a promotion to Division Head and a pay grade most men would kill for."

Henry studies him. "I suppose I should be grateful."

"You should be pragmatic, Henry," Merrick says. "They wouldn't recall you if they didn't need you. And the fact that the Liaison even agreed to reopen your file, that should tell you how urgent this assignment is."

Henry's eyes narrow. "What assignment?"

Merrick slides a thin folder across the table. The seal on the cover reads: *Personnel Security Branch—Restricted.*

Henry looks around the room. Two MPs stand at the fireplace, discussing a pension reform bill that hasn't made the news. One pours a measure from a decanter and says, "If Treasury moves the date, the markets won't blink." The other nods; by morning, it will. At the next table, a banker from Canary Wharf signs a confidentiality addendum before passing an envelope to a defense procurement contractor. No one glances over. Just another day's worth of business—leaving no trace of the deal except what follows in the markets or a government briefing.

This room has seen politics, policy, and profit mingle for centuries. Lunches outline treaties, handshakes close mergers, ministers take notes they'll claim as their own in committee rooms later. A server sets down small plates and refreshes their glasses.

"The reinstatement was only step one," Merrick says. "Now comes the part I'm not supposed to tell you until you sign the papers."

Henry raises an eyebrow, not opening the file. "I'm listening."

"There's been another leak inside Whitehall. A small but targeted breach—briefings pulled from Personnel Security files, mostly dormant clearances. Yours among them."

"Mine?"

Merrick nods. "Someone inside the vetting system accessed restricted profiles tied to the old Baltic operation."

Henry stares at him. "That file was sealed."

"It was," Merrick says. "Which means whoever opened it knew exactly what to look for. They're calling it a counter-state threat. I call it unfinished business."

"Why isn't Six on this? This isn't our jurisdiction anymore."

"Because," Merrick says, "the breach happened on British soil. That makes it Five's jurisdiction—however much they'd like to forget whose operation it was."

Henry's mouth tightens. "And you want me to clean it up."

"I want you to do what you do best. Follow the threads no one else sees," Merrick replies. "You're field-experienced, with ties to both agencies and NATO-joint cases. Surely you can see this is a political hot-potato."

"It sounds like I'd be right back inside the same, as the Americans say, 'goat rodeo,' as before."

Merrick smiles. "You have clearance again, a promotion, re-sources, and carte blanche from the Liaison's office. It's your field, Henry, if you want it."

Merrick fills both glasses. "Of course, it won't be clean."

Henry looks at him for a long moment. "You think I'll bite because of money."

"I think you'll bite because whoever did this knows about '24—about the operation you took the fall for."

The words land between them like a dropped file.

Henry leans back, exhaling slowly. "And if I say no?"

Merrick shrugs. "Then enjoy your exile. But this isn't about a paycheck, and you know it. It's about cleaning the last smudges off your name."

He looks at the wine, blood-dark and still, says nothing, then stands. "Thank you. I mean, really—thank you, Arthur. I'll give it serious thought. For now, I have a train to catch."

"You'll stay the night at The Connaught," Merrick says. "It's on the department. The least we can do. Enjoy it; it's a unicorn. You can face the sharks tomorrow."

Henry raises an eyebrow. "You've already booked it?"

Merrick replies. "The Sutherland Suite—much nicer than Thames House accommodations, I assure you. They'll charge it to internal ops."

Henry nods and slips his phone from his jacket. "Give me a minute."

As Henry walks toward the hallway, he passes a pair of men in suits angled together over a phone—one tilts the screen to the other and says, "With this schedule, Cabinet will have the votes lined up by Thursday." The second man nods, taps the screen, and slides it into his pocket. A steward discreetly passes between tables, carrying crystal water glasses on a silver tray.

In the marble corridor, he stops and opens his phone. The silence is always astonishing in this place and only serves to intensify the somber elegance—similar to Ainsworth in that way. Attendants move soundlessly in and out of side doors; every surface is polished to a reflective glow. The flowers are abundant; the lighting is low; the art on the walls is worth more than most people's houses and hangs beside furniture that predates most countries' constitutions. One would never guess how much of the world has been steered from this deceptively civilized place for centuries.

Henry opens his messages and types: *Still in London. All fine. Back tomorrow.* He watches the cursor blink, then presses send before he can reconsider.

When he returns to the table, Merrick is swirling the last of his wine and appears amused. He reaches into his pocket and slides a folded card across the mahogany table.

"She's back," he says.

Henry picks up the card. Beneath the scrawled number is a familiar name—*Christine Lyle.* He tenses. "You're joking."

"Not in the least. She wrapped up her assignment in Vienna last week. She's wanted on the same task force we discussed." Merrick's tone is casual, but he seems to assess every expression on Henry's face.

Henry folds the card without reading it again. "You set this up."

"No," Merrick says evenly. "I only suggested it. She asked if you'd been reinstated."

Henry laughs once. "Of course she did."

Merrick stands. "Don't look so grim, old friend. It's only work. And besides," he says, picking up his briefcase, "the Connaught has a very fine bar. You might find the evening less lonely than you expect."

Henry says nothing and pockets the card. He stops for his coat, and they go out into the cool Mayfair air.

Henry checks into his suite, orders room service, and then heads down to the bar.

The Connaught Bar, with its palette of lavender, olive, and dusty pink, spans three rooms. The décor is inspired by 1920s Cubist art, softened by silver-leafed walls and pale oak paneling. There are no stools at the bar itself; it's only a sparkling stage for glasses, bottles, and bartenders. Instead, groups of comfortable curved armchairs are arranged inward to encourage intimate conversations around small, silver-studded black leather tables. Henry has always liked this bar and the balance it strikes between art and order. The sounds are muted but musical—shaking ice, clinking glass, low voices—and martinis mixed table-side from a trolley.

He takes a seat in one of the corner armchairs and orders a club soda with lime. Nell will be standing at the window in her office about now, staring out over the grounds as she always does before she goes up to her room to read. He still doesn't understand the ritual, the way she looks down the lane and waits. Roger sits three windows down and waits too.

Henry's phone lies facedown beside the glass. He resists the urge to text her again. He registers the familiar scent of Chanel No. 5 just a second before he hears his name.

"Henry."

He turns toward the voice and rises automatically when he sees her, but he's unprepared for the effect she still has on him. Standing a few feet away is the personified image of the memories he's tried to bury. Christine Lyle—a tall beauty with flaming red hair swept up from a long neck. She's wearing high-heeled sandals and a black wrap dress that sets off her curves and her porcelain skin. Henry sucks in a breath. The years haven't dimmed her beauty, only refined it into something more poised, and probably more dangerous.

For a moment, he just drinks her in, frozen where he stands. Then Christine smiles, slow and self-assured. "I heard you were back."

Henry moves toward her, and they clasp hands and kiss on both cheeks.

"Yes, but only tonight," he says, still taking her in.

"That's what you always said."

Her laugh carries easily across the room, drawing smiles and a few polite glances. Henry feels his chest tighten with some combination of what? Nostalgia? Longing? Warning?

Christine gestures to the empty seat opposite him. "May I?"

"Of course, yes, please." The bartender arrives. "Another round, sir?"

Henry doesn't have to answer. Christine does it for him. "Two vodka martinis. Shaken, glacially cold, with an extra olive. No bitters."

She meets Henry's eyes. "We have so much to catch up on."

"It's good to see you, Christine," Henry says.

"You didn't call."

"I wasn't sure I should."

"You should always call. I'll always pick up." She smiles. "I text too."

Their drinks arrive, and Christine lifts hers and takes a sip. Her green eyes have always reminded Henry of a spring field under frost.

"You look well," she says, and slides an olive off the skewer with perfect white teeth. "Rural life suits you, though you've always been better in a suit. You wear the most beautiful suits and ties." She smiles.

Henry stirs the olive in his glass. "I'm flattered that you remember."

"I'm paid to." Her voice is smoky.

Henry is momentarily confused. Christine always spoke beyond the surface of the conversation. Then, as now, he frequently found himself not sure what they were talking about.

"Merrick tells me you're back with us." She says, "I'm on the same project."

"That must make him happy."

"More than it makes you?" she says.

"I haven't decided yet," Henry says.

Christine chuckles. "About me, or the job?"

He raises his glass slightly and smiles. "Whichever one gets me in less trouble. You do tend to complicate simple decisions."

Christine excuses herself, leaving her clutch where it rests beside the martini glass. The bar has filled up, voices layered, the faint sound of a shaker carrying through the room.

He reaches for his phone, then stops. The display is blank. No reply. That's Nell. He almost laughs at the difference between Christine and Nell's approaches to communication.

How does anyone connect with Nell? Everyone seems to like her, but Henry isn't surprised when she says she has no friends. When he took over her correspondence, not that she's noticed, she had 69,743 unanswered emails. Most people live by their phones; she keeps the latest model but treats it like a decoration. Henry's a profiler by trade, yet Nell's the only person he's ever met who is impossible to reach, much less understand. Like the scarves—what is that all about?

Wherever she goes, she misplaces a scarf. He finds them on shelves in the library, on doorknobs, in hedges, stuffed between chair cushions, half-buried in his car boot. Fergus brought one in last week that had been tied around a garden hoe. Like that one, each seems to find its way back to her eventually, claimed as "not lost, just visiting." How do you reason with someone who assigns motive to inanimate objects? He's never asked what they cost; he suspects he'd be shocked at the answer.

Christine returns, perfume first, gracefully confident. She slides back onto the chair beside him and moves her clutch to the side.

"You were smiling," she says.

"Was I?"

"Thinking of Cornwall?" She asks, amused.

"Oh. No. Well." He says, startled. "I don't know. I guess I was."

"What is it like there?" Christine asks.

"Oh...It's...ah...fields. Weather. Sheep."

Christine orders another drink, her tone light, the curve of her mouth inviting. "Forget the countryside, Henry. You're home now."

He looks at Christine, the glass cold in his hand, the sounds of Mayfair gathering around them. He sees his reflection in the mirror beside them, her face turned slightly toward him, and realizes how easily he could step right back into this familiar life. London and the old Service close in together. Like a uniform he never stopped wearing.

"It's late," he says.

"Not for London." She lays a hand across his wrist, light as a question. "We could go upstairs. Talk properly."

He doesn't move. From where he sits, Cornwall is on another planet entirely.

Christine asks, "Do you still think about the past?"

"Only when it refuses to stay there."

She smiles. "Then you haven't changed at all."

For a moment they stay like that, two veterans of the same war, pretending it never ended.

Henry finishes his drink, sets the glass down with care, and stands. "I should be going. I've taken care of this. It's already on my room."

"You're sure?" She tilts her head.

"Not even remotely sure." He gives a small, tired smile. "It was very good to see you. Goodnight, Christine."

He turns and leaves the bar, heading back to his room alone.

***

Henry wakes early. He slept well. He collects his polished shoes from outside the door, works out in the hotel gym, then showers and shaves, moving automatically.

The first suit he has put on in months hangs on its wooden hanger, still sheathed in plastic from the cleaner's in Truro. He buttons the cuffs, smooths the silk tie, and studies himself in the mirror—the lines sharper again, the uniform restored. He feels like the other Henry. The one he knows well, like the suit. Like the life he left behind.

Downstairs, the lobby smells of wood polish and morning coffee. A porter nods as he passes.

Breakfast at The Connaught is served at Jean-Georges, the hotel's all-day restaurant located on the ground floor overlooking Mount Street and Carlos Place. The restaurant was designed by architect John Heah, with floor-to-ceiling windows and modern stained-glass panels by French artist Jean-Michel Othoniel. The pale oak woodwork, limestone flooring, and low, curved furnishings in muted greys and creams are contemporary but calm, contrasting with the Connaught's darker, more traditional interiors.

Henry sits at a table by the window. The menu features croissants, pastries from Nicolas Rouzaud's patisserie, eggs any style, smoked salmon, and fresh-pressed juices, served with coffee or tea on white china trimmed in silver. Perfect and predictable. He orders scrambled eggs with smoked salmon, toast, and coffee and reads The Times. Just like he used to.

He stirs his coffee, but instead of thinking about today's meetings, he recalls a recent morning at Ainsworth—as far from predictable as breakfast can get.

He'd come downstairs expecting the usual: Nell working a crossword, cold toast at her elbow. Instead, he found her lying full-length in the center of the enormous dining room table, arms crossed like a defiant Victorian corpse, hair splayed in a fan.

"Nell?" he hazarded, torn between amusement and alarm.

"Shhh," she whispered, eyes shut. "I'm Rose. Or I might be. We're holding a séance."

"You and...who?" He'd asked, looking around.

"Roger and I," Nell said, as if Roger's credentials in spiritual matters were undisputed.

Henry's brow furrowed. He glanced over his shoulder, hesitated, then bent down to look beneath the table, where Roger lay sprawled asleep, indifferent to both the living and the dead.

She'd propped herself up on one elbow and, with the peculiar logic he'd come to call "Nell-based," explained that someone must know what happened to Rose. If a ghost haunts Ainsworth, besides the one in the stables—obviously—the dining room is the place most likely to have heard all the family scandals. "If you want answers, you start at the scene of the crime, Henry. This is basic tablework."

Henry, who'd read a hundred procedural manuals, could only reply, "That isn't a method practiced by British law enforcement as far as I know. But they might want to consider it."

Later, passing Mrs. Patterson, he'd been met with a dry, "Let me know how many I should expect for breakfast tomorrow, Mr. Templeton."

Henry looks around at the well-dressed businesspeople this morning and tries to imagine them lying in the center of their dining room table for any reason at all, let alone pronouncing themselves a vessel for familial revelation. He feels, with a ridiculous and un-expected pang of longing, that he'd trade every egg-white omelette in the city to be back at Ainsworth—even if breakfast with Nell is occasionally taken on the table instead of around it.

The actual mystery, Henry thinks, the thing no séance can explain—isn't what happened to Rose that fateful night, but what happened to his once perfectly sensible and orderly existence, and how nonsense has become so essential to his happiness.

After breakfast and a pleasant nod from the doorman, Henry steps outside into a brisk, sunny morning and sets off for Mill-bank. He has the route already mapped in his mind: across Berkeley Square, down through St. James's, then over the river to Thames House.

Henry had once walked this route every morning from a small flat off Berkeley Square, a place he'd chosen for its private courtyard and easy access to the river. The lease is gone now, surrendered in the same flurry of decisions that followed his dismissal from MI5 and the collapse of his engagement. Furniture sold, books boxed, the ring returned to Tiffany's on Bond Street.

Cornwall had been meant to be a temporary job, a holding pattern until he decided what came next. Somewhere along the way, between hiring staff, searching for a blackmailer, and learning Nell's coffee order, it had started to feel like real life.

At Carlos Place he stops.

Traffic gathers at the corner, a black cab idling. Someone's wayward scarf flutters against a railing.

His hand lifts as if to straighten his tie, then drops. He checks his watch for no reason, straightens his cuffs. Looks once toward Berkeley Square. Then the other way, toward Bond Street, and instead of turning east, he turns west.

Ten minutes later, he arrives at 155 New Bond Street.

A sales associate approaches—young, composed. "Good morning, sir. Welcome to Hermès. May I help you find something special?"

"Yes," he says. "A scarf." Then, after a moment: "It's a gift."

"Of course." She opens a drawer lined with silks folded by color. There are saddles and bridles, constellations, and animals. She lifts one after another: rose, green, saffron. Then a blue pattern catches his eye, floral, with forget-me-nots.

"This one," he says. "Beautiful choice, sir," she replies.

He nods. "Forget-me-nots because she loses them. Scarves."

The woman smiles politely, unsure how to answer that.

Henry signs the receipt, takes the orange bag, steps back onto Bond Street, and turns toward home.

15

Horses and Sources

NELL

"EIGHT ACROSS. TEN-LETTER WORD for *unfriendly*," she says aloud.

Roger looks at her from his spot by the fire, chin on the ground, head between his paws.

Nell answers for him. "ANTISOCIAL."

Roger doesn't move.

"Yes," she says, "That's you."

She fills in the boxes. When she looks up, the dining room feels bigger than normal. She misses Henry. He would have had this puzzle finished before the toast cooled. He usually does.

Where is he, anyway? She starts the next line, pencil poised, and says to Roger, "Nine letters. *Portable communication device.*"

Roger sighs.

Penciling in "CELLPHONE," she remembers her phone, picks it up, and notices a text from Henry.

Back for tea. Terrace if it's nice.

Nell smiles at Roger. "Good thinking," and calls toward the hallway. "Mrs. Patterson?"

After a moment, Mrs. Patterson appears, wiping her hands. "Just came from the library, ma'am. Left another one of those boxes on Mr. Templeton's desk. It's becoming a museum in there."

"I'll tell him," Nell says, still smiling. "Tea at four on the terrace, please."

When Mrs. Patterson leaves, Nell considers her phone again. "Since I have you here," she says to it, "let's see if Lady Penvale is at home."

She rings Clairview Park to ask if she can use the library. The butler answers and asks her to hold. Then Lady Penvale herself comes on the line.

"Nell!" she says, "I was standing right here. Yes. Delighted." Before Nell can explain about her research on the Ainsworth landscaping, she's invited to come for the library and, if she's up for it, a short hack before lunch.

"Just ratcatcher, Nell. Can't wait to see you!"

Roger lifts his head when Nell stands. His ears twitch forward, then flatten.

***

Nell dresses for her ride more casually than usual. She pulls her hair into a ponytail and ties it with a brown silk ribbon. Since Deirdre had said "ratcatcher," Nell forgoes the white shirt and stock tie in favor of a pale pink dress shirt and a brown men's necktie patterned with tiny gold horseshoes, tied in a neat four-in-hand knot. She chooses beige breeches, an oatmeal cashmere waistcoat, and a brown tweed hacking jacket shot through with threads of pink and yellow. She'd had it made a bit longer, cut close with slanted pockets. It has a single long vent at the back, so it looks more graceful in the saddle.

She pauses over her boots. She thinks briefly about wearing her old, formal black dress boots that are broken in and comfortable, but decides on the brown field boots instead—less comfortable, but more neighborly. Technically, field boots ought to be more forgiving, since the laces at the ankle allow them to flex nicely, but these are new, bought to replace the pair she had somehow lost.

Roger sits in her doorway, pants, and looks worried, while she pulls on her boots, fastens her jacket and checks her line in the mirror. Equestrian fashion has its periodic revivals. Nell always enjoys whenever "riding chic" appears in the glossies. Women invariably rush to buy £800 boots that can't survive a puddle. Or have silly furbelows like high heels, zippers on the inside of the leg, or faux spur straps. If they had the least sense, she tells Roger as she bends to fasten her spurs, they'd go straight to a tack shop and buy the real thing for half the price, and twice the leather. Then they could actually ride in them too.

She tells Roger once more to be a good boy and that she'll be back, then grabs her gloves and brown velvet helmet from the boot room and stuffs them into a large cognac Longchamp tote. Henry gave her the tote on the optimistic theory that putting things in one place might mean she lost fewer of them.

She slips a folded hoof pick and a handful of peppermints into her pockets. Thinking for a moment, she adds her wallet to the bag, along with her old favourite scarf—Hermès Jumping in pink—a beige cable-knit cashmere pullover, and a Dr. Harris lip balm, because adventure is no excuse for chapped lips. In all likelihood, she'll now just lose the entire bag and everything in it, but she's decided to humor him. Henry is, after all, the organizational expert.

***

Clairview Park sits in the middle of a two-thousand-acre estate—a smaller, friendlier scale than Ainsworth, but still a house with a name that carries weight. The house itself is a pale honey-colored stone rectangle that sits on a shallow rise above a long, ornamental lake. Its facade is balanced and symmetrical. Inside it has Adam-style windows and delicate plasterwork, giving it a much lighter look than its Georgian bulk suggests.

The approach winds through parkland with wide lawns, clusters of ancient oak and cedar, and miles of carefully maintained fences. The drive curves past a walled garden and the stable complex, still filled with horses—and ends in a broad gravel sweep before the front steps. Beyond the house, the grounds trail off into distant woodland and a sudden drop into a valley visible from the south terrace. Despite all of that, Clairview feels lived-in rather than a showplace.

Deirdre Marsh, Countess of Penvale, has a knack for softening over-the-top drama. The house still hosts the occasional hunt breakfast or charity gala, but it's just as likely one will find her hacking through the lower fields or walking the dogs along the bridleway. Clairview is also open to visitors during part of the year, and Nell wants to be sure to talk to her about that.

Nell parks at the stable, and Deirdre meets her at the car with a warm hug.

"Perfect timing," Deirdre says, stepping toward the mounting block, gloves half-buttoned. "If we ride now, we might be back before the next shower. The forecast says it's meant to hold till noon—but they've said that before."

Nell shades her eyes. "I brought the wrong coat, for optimism."

Deirdre looks approvingly at her jacket. "You look amazing, Nell. Huntsman?"

"Bookster," Nell says. "I found an antique pattern from the 1920s at Ainsworth, and they made it up for me. I had them make three, since I lose things."

She had tried the modern double-vented jackets the kids are wearing for shows these days. They are a bit roomier on the ground, but in the saddle she always ended up sitting on the flaps one way or another, so she gave them to charity and went back to the tried-and-true.

The groom brings the horses up and halts nearby, holding the reins. Nell and Deirdre check their girths out of habit, and Nell picks up the feet of her gelding, Sam, a beautiful dark bay Warmblood, one at a time. Satisfied, she takes the reins, runs the stirrups down, and leads him to the mounting steps.

"We'll take the south fields," Deirdre says, "loop by the wood, and be back before elevenses. I'll make sure you have time for your scholarly business after luncheon."

"Thank you. I wanted to look at Clairview's local records." Nell says.

"And you will. After a ride, books always behave better."

Nell smiles. "That so?"

Deirdre laughs. "Absolutely. Fresh air frightens the dust right out of them."

***

The groom steadies Nell's horse, and she mounts easily, breathing in the wonderful smell of horse and leather. How she loves the creak of the saddle, a soft snort, and the faint clink of metal. Deirdre swings up beside her—the seat of someone who has been riding all her life. Hands light on the reins.

"Ready?" the countess asks, turning her mare toward the open drive with the subtlest pressure of her lower leg.

"Lead on," Nell says. "Before the weather changes its mind."

They move off side by side on a loose rein; the horses falling into a rhythmic walk as the gravel gives way to grass. A rook calls somewhere above.

"Nell, it's so good to see you," Deirdre says as her mare and Sam lower and lift their heads in time with the steady swing of their backs. "I met Henry at your house tour. He's so charming—and handsome. However did you find him?"

"He found me, thank heavens," Nell says, adjusting her reins as Sam gives a little shake of his head. "And he hasn't run for the hills yet. Between Henry's upgrades and Mrs. Patterson's scone diplomacy, I daresay Ainsworth has never been so well managed—or so well fed."

Deirdre laughs. "How did the tour go?"

"Reasonably well," Nell replies. "But truly, I don't know how you do it. People asked questions I didn't know the answers to, and they were so disappointed. I was tempted to make things up just to make them happy."

"All locals?" Deirdre asks, grinning.

"Yes," Nell says, "mostly."

Deirdre nods, leaning forward to rub her mare's neck. The horse sighs, ears flicking back, then forward again.

"Speaking of local, do you know anything about Mr. Leclair in the village?" Nell asks.

"If you mean Leclair of Leclair Antiques, little enough," Deirdre replies. "He seems knowledgeable. He's been on several house tours here. He's very interested in our furniture. Randolph said he's considering having him appraise some of the more valuable pieces at Clairview and do some restorations."

Deirdre tucks a stray strand of hair behind her ear and looks at the sky. "If we want to get a hand gallop in, we should probably set off now. Gives us time to cool them down before we get to the barn."

Nell grins, shifting in the saddle as Sam bobs his head impatiently. "He heard you. If Sam had his way, I'd just point him at the horizon and hold on."

Deirdre laughs. "That's the best part, isn't it?

"Agreed," Nell says, collecting her reins.

Deirdre leans forward, patting her mare's neck. "Daisy keeps looking for an excuse to throw in a celebratory buck. If I land in a hedge, just wave as you go by."

Nell winks. "Only if you promise to do the same."

Deirdre nudges her mare forward, and the two horses break into a lively canter, their hoofbeats and Deirdre's laughter carrying across the field.

***

After lunch, Deirdre walks across the house with Nell to the library. "I have a Historical Society board meeting at one o'clock, but feel free to stay as long as you like, Nell. There's a card catalog over by the big globe, and everything is organized by Dewey Decimal. If you can't find anything, just text Jenny Danforth—she knows this place inside out."

Jenny was right: the Clairview Park library is enormous, twenty-thousand volumes, Deirdre had said, with sections for local history and estate records. Nell fingers through the card catalog, starting under *Ainsworth Estate—Gardens*. She scans the subject headings for anything tied to *tree surveys, planting records,* or *landscape*. Nothing jumps out. Next, she tries *Estate Records* and *Maps—Ainsworth*. Finally, she finds a card labeled *Ainsworth: Tree Surveys & Plans, 1800–1850—Manuscript Collection, Bound, Drawer 3.*

She walks over to the long bank of wooden drawers and pulls on the handle for Drawer 3. The space inside is empty. Nell checks nearby drawers, just in case something was not filed correctly, but it's definitely missing. Frowning, she takes out her phone and texts Jenny:

Hi Jenny, I'm at Clairview Park. Lady Penvale says you're the expert. Drawer 3 missing Ainsworth estate tree survey.

Ten minutes later, Nell's phone buzzes.

Jenny: Hi, I checked out those documents from Clairview Park for someone. Have not been returned—overdue.

Nell: Can you tell me who has them?

Jenny: I'm sorry, I can't disclose. Confidential info.

Nell's mind connects the dots instantly. Someone else has linked Napoleon's treasure to the old oak at Ainsworth. Is that what Jenny is trying to tell her? Nell is collecting her things and returning materials to the shelves when she hears the soft click of the library door.

Deirdre crosses the room, cheeks still pink from this morning's ride, her hair in a blunt-cut, chin-length bob. She always looks healthy and self-assured, Nell thinks.

The internet is currently obsessed with the "old money" aesthetic. They would be so disappointed, Nell thinks, to know that a real old-money look rarely involves buying anything new—heaven forbid anything flashy. The key thing mainstream media and influencers miss is that the look is a lifestyle, and it depends entirely on not trying. But there's a world of difference between not trying because a woman thinks, why bother? and not trying because she knows without a doubt she's already perfect. Whatever "old money" aesthetic exists is built on the latter.

Real old-money women like Deirdre don't need to impress anyone; they already belong and always have. Their names guarantee access to the right schools, the right circles, a good job if they want one, and a favorable marriage if they don't.

Nell has known Deirdre—who could be a recruitment poster for the old-money look—since university. Her brunette hair has never been coloured, so it's thick and healthy. She buys Mane & Tail shampoo and conditioner at the tack shop, figuring if it works for her horse, it will work for her. Skincare comes from the chemist: Ivory soap, Pond's cold cream, and a basic moisturiser like Oil of Olay.

She is scrubbed fresh and wears not a spot of makeup, unless it's a tinted lip balm and a swipe of bronzer brushed where the sun hits naturally; she has no interest in what is popularly known as "sculpting."

She wears hand-me-down cashmere from N. Peal, Johnstons of Elgin, or Pringle. If she's feeling modern, it's Loro Piana. If she wears a watch—and Deirdre does—it's a Reverso or the smallest, most feminine Cartier Tank: no oversized men's pieces, nothing that would call attention to her. She sports a plain gold wedding band on her left hand and a battered signet ring on her right, the only daytime jewellery other than the pearls her great-grandmother gave her. No diamonds before six.

She wouldn't dream of using fillers or extensions to change her natural features. Her look isn't about showing off, looking young, or looking "hot." It's built on a foundation of certainty that she is enough, and she always will be.

"Did you find what you were looking for?" Deirdre asks.

Nell shakes her head. "No, I'm sorry to say I struck out. This is a real needle in a haystack. I'm looking for a distinctive old oak that stood somewhere on Ainsworth land sometime in the past two centuries."

Deirdre laughs with genuine sympathy. "Oh, I can see how that might be difficult, what with thirteen thousand acres and who knows how many stubborn old oaks."

Nell smiles. "Thank you anyway, and thank you again for the lovely ride this morning."

Deirdre grins. "Listen, I haven't seen the responses. Are you planning on coming to the Hunt Ball tonight? I know you're a member and you've got your colors, even if you don't always keep up with the hounds. Randolph and I are hosting, and we would love to see you, and Henry too, if you can drag him out. Promise you'll come."

Nell hesitates for a moment, then nods. "If there's dancing and champagne, how can I possibly refuse?"

16

Boots and Breadcrumbs

HENRY

H ENRY HEARS THE STEADY cadence of Nell's boots on the vestibule's wood floor long before she reaches the library. It's a sound he's come to know—a stride that doesn't hurry. Nell moves like someone who knows exactly who she is, what she wants, and fully expects time to wait on her. He's never seen her rush. Some women dash around like nervous squirrels, chasing minutes. Nell isn't like that.

She knocks on the open door. "Hi. May I come in? How was London? Roger missed you on his run this morning."

"Yes, please," Henry says, and looks up. When he sees her, he nearly drops the file he's holding, fumbles for composure, and looks down to rummage in his desk just to keep occupied. "It was good. Met up with some people I know." He's conflicted—he doesn't want to lie to her, but he's not ready to talk about the job offer yet. Maybe she won't press.

Nell lowers herself into the chair across from him, cheeks bright from her ride and a kind of contentment radiating from her. He wonders if it's the horse or if maybe, just maybe, it's him. "You know, you're making it very difficult to focus."

She raises an eyebrow. "Because I tracked mud on the carpet again?"

"Because you look entirely too good in those boots," Henry says before he can think better of it.

She fires back, "If I had known that was all it took to distract you, I would have left my spurs on."

"Don't tempt me. I'm only human," Henry says, and smiles.

Nell lays her helmet on his desk. "Careful, Henry. Comments like that might get you a reputation as a ladies' man."

"Or a boot collector," Henry says.

Nell laughs.

"If collecting boots brings women in riding clothes in here," Henry says, "I'll start immediately."

Nell crosses her legs, pulling off one glove, then the other. "I parked out front when I saw your car."

"What's your fee for a riding lesson?" he asks.

"I'd never have the patience. But Deirdre might teach you. She used to be a riding instructor. And she has very nice horses."

He nods, grateful for the normalcy. "Mrs. Patterson said you'd gone to Clairview. How was your ride?"

Nell brightens. "The ride was great. More luck in the saddle than I had in the Clairview library. I was hoping to find some details on Ainsworth's old landscaping, maybe a tree survey that mentions a particular oak."

"At Clairview?"

She shrugs. "Bigger collection than ours, full of plans, old surveys. Clairview's trying very hard to be Chatsworth: all those floor-to-ceiling shelves and rolling ladders, like someone looked at the Chatsworth library and thought, 'Yes, but what if we added even more books no one can reach without a safety harness?'"

"But why do they have books on Ainsworth at Clairview?" Henry asks again.

"Because they've got everything on the local area—estate maps, garden plans, surveys. If anyone in the 1800s so much as sneezed near an oak, someone surely logged it."

Henry notices Nell clearly loves talking about books. "I thought English country house libraries were just for reading dark Victorian novels."

Nell shakes her head, warming to the subject. "At Clairview, the library—the pretty book room—and the estate archives, where maps, rentals, surveys, plans, and correspondence are kept, are the same place. We do it differently at Ainsworth. As you know, our library holds only books, and we have a separate archive room on the third floor for records."

"So the person who managed the library was, in effect, the keeper of the history of the house and surrounding area," Henry says.

"In many places, yes," Nell replies. "Especially on big estates, where the family's land more or less was the local area."

"Who has the largest library?"

Nell is thoughtful. "It's complicated. Ainsworth has fifteen thousand volumes, but we have two libraries here. Clairview has twenty thousand. Blickling Hall in Norfolk claims the biggest National Trust country-house library—fifteen thousand books in one gallery. Chatsworth has more books overall—forty thousand, I think," she laughs, "but it cheats by hiding them in about six libraries. And then there's Blenheim; size-wise, the Long Library there is famous for being one of the longest rooms in a private house—about 180 feet."

"Wow," Henry says.

"The books I looked for at Clairview were checked out," Nell says.

He's thoughtful, chewing that over. "Who else wants a book about Ainsworth landscaping in the 1800s?"

Nell sighs. "Maybe the same person who stole our garden plans from the Potting Building." She looks tired for a moment. "I really don't know where to go from here."

Mrs. Patterson arrives precisely as the clock strikes four, pushing a fully loaded tea cart ahead of her like a parade float. She glances from Nell to Henry, eyebrows raised, and asks crisply, "Tea here, or shall we have it on the terrace, as Her Grace instructed earlier?"

Henry looks at Nell, sunlight pouring in from the terrace windows, the day unexpectedly warm for spring. Nell flashes a smile. "Let's go out—I did say it was too nice to stay inside."

They settle on the terrace, then, shielding their eyes, change seats again so they're looking away from the sun. Mrs. Patterson unloads the tea tray, the newspaper, and a tiered silver server onto the low table in front of the outdoor settee, and leaves them, taking the trolley with her.

Nell pours tea, her mood shifting suddenly. "Oh! I nearly forgot—I stopped at Leclair Antiques and you'll never guess what I saw—my desk. Or rather, Philippe's desk. Matches Mrs. Patterson's description to the letter: even the little crescent moon ink stain in the right-hand drawer."

Henry files this instantly. "This feels like something."

Nell sets her cup down. "It's not much, but the desk could be a clue."

Henry lays a napkin on his lap, selects two sandwiches from the tray, and leans back. "I believe you that the desk at Leclair's came from Ainsworth," he says. "Maybe someone pinched it while the house sat empty after your uncle died. But the desk may have nothing to do with the blackmailer, Nell—don't get your hopes up."

"Let's recap what we know so far," Nell says. "This is turning into one of my novels."

"If only," Henry says. "In your novels, someone usually has their shirt off by now."

She waves his teasing away and launches into her analysis:

"The blackmailer claims to have information that will embarrass the family if we don't hand over Napoleon's treasure. The second letter told us that part of Napoleon's treasure from L'Orient is buried near an old oak tree on the property."

Henry nods, catching up.

She powers on: "We know Aleric Ainsworth was a spy for the French, and that Rose and Thomas stashed a box with incriminating evidence in the garden."

Henry holds up a hand. "Whoa, not so fast. We don't know for sure that Aleric was a spy. And we don't know Thomas and Rose hid the box. All we have is Sarah's report of an argument."

Nell beams, undeterred. "Correct. I can tell you are good at this." She goes right on: "We know Philippe Moreau and Thomas Duval were French tutors here. Philippe from 1810 to June 1815, Thomas from 1845 to 1847—the year Rose died."

Henry gestures to the files laid out between them. "Those dates check with the employment records. Mrs. Patterson's inventory says Philippe brought a very fine desk with him, and left it here."

"Yes. The desk that's currently for sale in Eduard Leclair's antique shop," Nell adds, scowling.

Henry leans forward and sets his cup on the table. "I'd like to get a look at that desk. And talk to Mr. Leclair."

Nell sighs. "Getting it back won't be easy. If Leclair is bold enough to walk off with a valuable desk, he probably has forged receipts too."

"He's open until nine tomorrow night," Henry says, opening the morning post. "I'll stop in then, when it's quiet. Mind staying here, Nell? It might raise less suspicion if we don't double-team him."

She nods. "Agreed; I'll wait here."

Henry doesn't answer. He just looks at her.

"You look like someone about to confess to a minor crime," Nell says. "Did you reorganize my files again?"

"Worse," he says. "I went shopping."

That gets her attention. She leans forward. "For yourself?"

"For you." He goes into the library, comes back, and sets the orange bag in front of her. "You keep losing scarves."

"Henry," Nell says, "that bag is the color of financial ruin."

"Open it before you insult my fiscal responsibility," he says.

She peels back the tissue and lifts the silk free, forget-me-nots blooming blue and bright across her hands. Henry is struck by how unapologetically unnecessary it is, and how perfectly it suits her, a woman who orients herself by how things feel long before she asks whether they're practical.

"Oh," she says quietly. "It's... utterly irresponsible. And beautiful."

"Consider it a professional investment," he replies. "They're forget-me-nots."

She looks up, clearly hit harder than she'd like to admit. "You're getting alarmingly good at this being-nice thing. I refuse to be outdone. I have something for you too."

"You do?" Henry says.

Nell disappears into the house and returns a minute later with a large, dark-green box he recognizes immediately.

"Holland & Holland," she says.

He takes it, suddenly uncertain. "You didn't have to—"

"I know," she cuts in. "You were muttering about needing a 'proper grown-up brief-bag' last month. Do you remember?"

"I was muttering in the privacy of my own brain," he says.

"Your 'own brain' is not as private as you think." She nods at the box. "Open it."

Inside, the leather gleams: dark, structured, expensive, but under-the-radar. No designer logos, just his own initials stamped underneath the flap. She watches his face as he takes that in.

"If you insist on impersonating the competent adult in this arrangement, you'll need somewhere dignified to put your spreadsheets," Nell says.

Henry laughs, fingertips resting on the handle as if he isn't quite sure he's allowed to keep it. "You bought this for me."

"I ordered it before you ran off to London and started impulse-purchasing couture plants for my neck," she says. "I was going to wait for an occasion, but apparently today is 'mutual financial recklessness' day."

Henry looks up, meets her eyes. "Thank you." It's rare that Henry would ever choose something for himself simply because it's beautiful. How instinctive that is for Nell, who lives by color, comfort, and small luxuries that make the world more bearable.

She shrugs, suddenly awkward. "Consider it a professional investment. Less time dropping your laptop, more time rescuing your employer from ruin."

For a moment, they just sit there: Henry holding the bag, Nell with the scarf draped around her neck.

"Henry?" she says at last.

"Yes?"

"If Mrs. Patterson asks, the scarf was on clearance and the bag fell off a lorry. In Belgium."

He grins. "At your service. We'll present a united, unconvincing front."

She tightens the scarf. "See? Teamwork. Oh, and Henry, Deirdre invited us to the Hunt Ball at Clairview tonight. Want to go with me?"

Henry leans back, eyebrows raised. "Not that this is unusual, but you truly puzzle me. You never entertain; you have no friends—unless we're counting me and Roger, who'd rather eat the upholstery than socialize. Yet you attract ten event invitations a week and have two hundred thousand Instagram followers. Are you secretly running a cult?"

"It's worse than that," Nell laughs. "You're only my friend because I sign your checks, and Roger's not so much antisocial as terminally indifferent. But he came with the house, and I need you to run my life, so I'm stuck. It's easier with strangers, Henry. They only get what I post—flattering lighting, clever captions, absolutely no evidence of dog hair or anxiety."

Henry shakes his head, grinning. "You broadcast mysterious elegance to the world, then barricade yourself in an eight-thou-sand-square-metre mansion with a deranged German Shepherd. Honestly, it's a paradox worthy of its own Netflix special."

Nell makes a face. "Netflix has already contacted me about another special. And anyway, my public persona works out delightful-ly. I keep my personal mysteries, my audience stays enchanted, and you remain the last man standing."

She winks, and Henry and Roger follow her into the library. "And posting tea trays. Never underestimate the power of a good scone." She sweeps up her helmet from the desk. "I'm going up to change. Shall I ask Mrs. Patterson to give our dinner to the staff tonight?"

"Yes and yes," Henry says. "It'll throw her plans, but I expect they'll be happy. I saw her in the East Wing earlier—she was directing a platoon of maids and footmen like they were storming a fortress. Furniture everywhere. What do I need to wear, and when?"

"Black tie," Nell calls over her shoulder. "Eight sharp. I'll meet you in the Hall a few minutes before."

***

At a quarter to eight, Henry—dressed to the nines—steps into the Great Hall, waiting for Nell. Roger has established his usual dignified quarters beneath the sideboard—a general at rest, remote and stoical, surveying a wild constellation of bright yellow tennis balls. Nell's offerings, hopeful, all orbit untouched around him, marking Roger's front lines.

Nell descends the stairs in a billowing black silk taffeta ball skirt, paired with a short-sleeved black cashmere sweater and matching cardigan tossed casually over her shoulders. A wide sash spans her waist in burgundy and green plaid, which Henry assumes are the hunt club's colors. He's never seen her dressed up like this. Her hair is pulled into a sleek chignon, with not a stray wisp or pencil in sight. She's wearing jewelry for the first time he can remember—sparkling diamond butterflies at each ear.

Henry takes in the transformation. "Wow. You clean up well."

She smiles. "Thanks, you too," and finesses a fresh tennis ball from her skirt pocket.

"He is not accepting callers," Henry observes.

Nell rolls the ball across the stone floor. Roger, unmoved by this act of diplomacy, rests his head between his paws, eyebrows lifting and then lowering as he glances from Nell to Henry.

"He's not convinced by persistence—or bribery. You and he have that in common."

Nell arches a brow. "Do we?"

"You're both experts at keeping the world at bay."

She rolls her eyes, then, nearly vulnerable: "Roger's got cause. What's my excuse?"

"Not all fortresses are built by choice," Henry says.

Nell seems to weigh this. "Well, if I ever disappear beneath a piece of furniture, just roll jelly beans my way."

"I'll try that first," he says. "I've never seen you in actual jewels."

Nell brushes a finger over an earring. "Aunt Gilda gave me these. Graff diamonds." Her voice softens. "Spectacular. Probably the spoils of some prince or Italian count."

"Aunt Gilda must be quite something," Henry says, wondering if Aunt Gilda is as unreal and fairy-like as Nell.

"She's something, all right," Nell laughs.

17

In the Pink

HENRY

SWAYING FLAMES IN TALL iron torches cast a golden light over the clipped lawns and the winding gravel drive to Clairview Park. Cars pull up in a steady procession, headlights sweeping across the forecourt. Attendants in dark coats move swiftly to meet each car, opening doors and offering a steady hand as guests step out. A brief exchange—a greeting, a ticket stub—then the engine quiets as drivers ease the cars away to an outlying lot for parking. New arrivals adjust bow ties and smooth gowns, laughter bubbling up as friends spot one another and trade greetings. Pair by pair, guests move up the broad stone steps, drawn by the flood of music and warm light spilling through open doors.

Henry and Nell make their way into the ballroom, pausing to take in the glitter of chandeliers and the bright swell of conversation. Henry's eyes scan the crowd, always alert, even here. He leans in, lowering his voice. "You love animals. I'm surprised you take part in hunt events, Nell."

She waves hello to a woman in a long tartan skirt. "Oh gosh, no! I'd never hunt an animal. Foxhunting's been illegal here for ages, thank heavens. All the meets now are drag hunts or hunt rides; but those are really just an excuse to gallop across muddy fields and jump hedges."

"So the foxes are safe, dinner's served, and all anyone hunts tonight is gossip?" Henry says.

Nell grins and hands him a glass from a passing tray. "Exactly. If anyone chases through the shrubbery, it'll be for a runaway spaniel or a lost earring. The only thing truly traditional now is the hangover."

Deirdre and Randolph approach. "Foxes are strictly honorary," Deirdra says, picking up the conversation. "The closest we'll get tonight is a cocktail named The Clever Vixen and a charity auction for fox-shaped boot jacks."

Deirdre and Randolph make a striking pair, with her in a long gold lamé column from Ralph Lauren's fall collection and Randolph in his hunt coat with a burgundy velvet collar. They greet Nell and Henry warmly—cheek kisses, laughter, and a quick exchange about Nell and Deirdre's morning ride. Randolph teases Nell about her sash, while Deirdre points out to Henry the hunt staff clustered in scarlet coats and gleaming black riding boots with brown tops near the entrance.

"Only the huntsman, master, and whippers-in earn the right to wear pinks; everyone else is in black or navy."

Henry asks, "Pinks?"

Randolph smiles. "They're called pinks because of an old London tailor named Mr. Pink, who supplied red hunt coats to the aristocracy. The tradition stuck, so a scarlet coat is still a 'pink.' It's likely folklore, though. Scholars actually dispute the tailor story. It might just be an old nickname for the shade of red, or a reference to the sharp, 'in the pink' appearance the coat gives."

"Around here," Deirdre laughs, "the Mr. Pink legend is the one people like best."

Nell smiles and turns just in time to spot Eduard Leclair slipping through the crowd. She catches Henry's eye, and he quietly angles Deirdre's and Randolph's attention toward Leclair.

Nell says quietly, "Mr. Leclair's antique shop has a desk for sale identical to one that disappeared from Ainsworth recently."

Deirdre's eyes widen. "I didn't know you'd lost a desk."

"I didn't either," Nell replies, "until Mrs. Patterson reviewed her inventory records. It vanished after my uncle died."

"Maybe when the house was vacant," Deirdre suggests.

Randolph takes a sip of champagne. "Art and antiques, especially at this level, are a banker's headache. They are prime targets for theft and money-laundering schemes. Anything with high value and little oversight moves fast, and sometimes with little paperwork. In banking, we are required to scrutinize transactions like these for provenance and legitimacy, especially pedigrees, if you will. The trouble is, there are no consistent global anti-money laundering regulations for the antiques market compared to other financial sectors, so it's an attractive haven for criminals seeking to legitimize illicit proceeds."

"Money laundering. I didn't even consider that." Nell says, "I was only thinking that we lost a desk."

Randolph glances over her head at the dancers whirling past, then tips his chin nearer. "Most people don't," he says. "If you're missing a high-value desk, someone may already have copied it." He shifts his weight, absently tracing the pattern of condensation on his champagne glass. "All a dealer has to do is adjust the paperwork, move the fake, and sell the legitimate item. He gets twice the profit."

"How does the money laundering work?" Nell asks, fascinated.

Randolph says, "Antiquities of all kinds can be moved across borders with fake invoices and then sold, integrating them into the legitimate economy. Small items with high value, like gold, jewels, and coins, are especially easy to transport discreetly."

Like buried treasure, Henry thinks, but doesn't say.

Henry adds, "Dealers can provide false or scant documentation about provenance. It gets hard to trace if the item was looted, stolen, or bought with dirty money."

"And easier to sell in the legitimate market." Nell glances from Randolph to Henry, making sure she understands. "Making dirty money clean."

Randolph nods with a half-smile. "A few years ago, there was an infamous case involving an antiquities dealer who sold looted artifacts to museums and private collectors at inflated prices, using fraudulent paperwork and layering transactions through multiple entities and auctions. It enabled him to clean millions in criminal proceeds."

Henry nods,

"I'm so sorry, Nell," Deirdre whispers. "What will you do?"

"Henry is going to investigate tomorrow evening. We'll see what turns up." Nell looks up at him as if he can work miracles.

Henry wants to warn her not to pin too many hopes on this, though he isn't sure whether he means hopes about him or about solving the mystery. A tightness gathers in his chest as he realizes how much he doesn't want to disappoint her.

Deirdre's brow furrows as she lowers her voice. "Actually, Nell, when Mary and I toured Ainsworth the other day..." She looks at Henry. "You met my mother-in-law. We noticed something odd in the ballroom. The portrait of Rose Ainsworth was gone. Aleric's portrait had been hung in its place. Was that your decision?"

"No," Nell shakes her head. "Deirdre, the painting you and Lady Penvale remember—was it a Winterhalter? There's a Winterhalter of

Rose Ainsworth listed online as being part of the house's collection, but I've never seen it."

Deirdre nods. "That's the one. Your uncle told Mary he had come across it in a storage room several years back and had it restored before hanging it in the Ballroom."

Nell takes a sip of her champagne, looking thoughtful. "I don't remember seeing Rose's portrait at all when I was a child. But I'm sorry to say, I hadn't set foot in Ainsworth for years before my uncle died. The portrait above the ballroom fireplace now, of Aleric, that used to be over the library mantel, right?"

Deirdre confirms. "Yes, that's what Mary remembered. The painting of Rose must have disappeared after your uncle passed."

Randolph considers for a moment. "A Winterhalter of Rose Ainsworth would be a tough piece to move discreetly. A portrait of a known sitter, especially by an old master, stands out in the art world. Any reputable dealer or collector would recognize it immediately, and it would raise a lot of red flags at auction or in a private sale."

Henry nods at Randolph. "Agreed. Stolen art is not my specialty, but I know that highly distinctive, well-documented portraits by major artists are much harder to launder or fence than more anonymous or common works. Their provenance, subject, and artist make them easily recognizable, and any appearance on the market would be noticed by institutions, historians, and legal authorities."

Randolph waves to a friend across the crowd, then leans closer to Nell with a reassuring smile. "Nell, don't hesitate to call me. Either of you—if I can be of any assistance." Deirdre squeezes Nell's hand before she and Randolph drift off to greet other guests. "See you in a bit," she says over her shoulder.

As the music swells, Henry flashes Nell a smile. "Can you risk a dance with me, or is the Ainsworth security detail prohibited from basic ballroom maneuvers?"

Nell raises an eyebrow. "I'll risk it, but you'd better not step on my toes, Agent Templeton. These are new shoes."

"Lose the other ones?"

"It seems so," Nell says, letting him lead her onto the floor.

Henry soaks in the music and the bright spin of the night. "I may need a refresher. Do I lead, or is this the part where we argue about it in step?"

"Lead on, sir," Nell smiles.

Henry spins her and then pulls her in dramatically with a smile. She lets out a surprised laugh and lands lightly against his chest. They circle the floor in a foxtrot, then a waltz. Henry wonders he has never felt so in tune with someone so incredibly different from him. Nell is like a hothouse flower: rare, exotic, temperamental, and unpredictable. Henry is as steady, and he thinks, probably as boring as they come.

His fiancée had been cut from exactly the same cloth as he is. Reasonable, practical, and level-headed. Pretty too. She was a successful professional. She loved him. There was no reason whatsoever that they shouldn't have gotten married. But despite how right everything was on paper, he felt nothing like this when they danced. No electricity, no wildness. Just two reasonable people tracing patterns across the floor, waiting for a spark that never came.

Nell's laughter rings in his ears as they turn, and the world is music and motion. At the edge of the floor, a woman whispers to her companion, "Look at those two. Don't they move beautifully together?" Her friend answers, "They do. Perhaps they've been dancing together for years."

Henry, ever observant, notes the doors, the faces in the crowd, the escape routes; habits he can't unlearn. Yet as Nell's hand finds his, he's untethered. There's MI5 and London, ambition and duty, hovering just beyond the light and music. But Henry recognizes what he's begun to want: belonging, not just purpose. Here and now, with Nell—strange, radiant, enigmatic Nell—he feels both seen and needed, and fearfully alive.

He spins her, and the chandeliers shimmer overhead. "You know, this could get complicated."

Nell looks up at him. "Us? Or this adventure?"

"Both," he says, leading her expertly through another turn.

She smiles. "Henry, things in my life have always been complicated. That has never stopped me."

As the waltz slows, Henry feels a tap on his shoulder. He turns to see a man who could model country menswear. Tall, good-looking and Cornish through and through, confident with an easy charm. He smiles broadly at Nell. "May I cut in, for old times' sake?"

Henry hesitates, but Nell laughs. "I'd love that, Jeremy. It's good to see you." As Jeremy whisks her away, Henry feels an unexpected pang. Is it protectiveness, or perhaps envy? He tries not to watch too closely as they dance.

When Nell returns, Jeremy spins her with one last wink before disappearing.

Henry can't help but ask, "Old friend?"

"Jeremy Beckwith," Nell says. Her tone is casual, but her eyes are troubled. "We were at school together. He wanted to talk for a moment. He works with Dr. Penhaligon at Oxford. Do you remember him from the house tour?"

"Penhaligon? Yes, I do," Henry says, stepping aside to let a couple pass. "The Oxford military history professor."

"Correct. Jeremy said Penhaligon's been digging into Aleric's army records for the past year and found something called an 'S-class' code for Waterloo. Do you know what that means?"

Henry's focus sharpens. "Usually means suspected intelligence work."

Nell nods. "That's what Penhaligon told Jeremy." She lowers her voice. "That Aleric's code marked him as a spy, but it was hushed up because of what he did at Waterloo. He's supposedly planning a book. Jeremy implied Penhaligon's got financial troubles and needs the money."

"That gives him both motive and means," Henry says, looking at the crowd. The social whirl of the evening continues, but his mind is already filing away every detail.

***

According to Nell, the Hunt Ball ended the year on a banner note. Dancing had given way to dinner, and then the charity auction. Nell raised her paddle for a saddle, laughing off comments about not owning a horse. Afterward, there was more dancing, then relaxed circles of old friends chatting, scattered throughout the elegant reception rooms on the main floor.

The pianist plays something low and clever as the staff move through the rooms, collecting stray champagne glasses and dessert plates. A woman near the piano tallies the auction results on her phone.

"Ready?" Nell asks.

"As I'll ever be."

Henry and Nell pass the blue drawing room, aglow with the remnants of music and laughter. Small knots of club members are breaking up; their voices low. Some lean together on sofas, or gather near half-empty glasses, faces rosy and eyelids heavy; others stand and exchange handshakes and tired kisses on the cheek. A clutch of young men say their last, half-teasing farewells to friends, and a few couples pause in the entryway, searching for misplaced wraps or gloves or draping arms around each other in silent support.

They find Deirdre near the front doors, Randolph's hunt coat hugging her shoulders.

"Thank you," Nell says, smiling. "A smashing success, Deirdre. Please give our love to Randolph. We lost track of him before we could say goodnight."

Deirdre gives a laugh. "He slipped out to the stables with the committee to see his new horse. I'll tell him you remembered him. He'll be sorry to have missed you." She kisses Nell's cheek, then Henry's, inviting them to come ride soon. Henry inclines his head, offering his thanks. There's warmth in Deirdre's brief touch to his arm. With a parting smile, she wishes them a safe drive home and steps back so they can pass through the open doors.

The breeze is cool on Henry's face, and the sky shows the first hint of dawn as they descend the steps, carefully sidestepping two chatting women in evening gowns, barefoot now, with a nearly empty bottle of champagne and a small, sleeping Jack Russell terrier between them. Nell tugs her hair loose.

***

Henry parks in front at Ainsworth. The house will be quiet for another hour before the staff arrives. They greet Roger, who had been asleep under the sideboard, and climb the staircase side by side, Nell's sandals dangling from her fingers. He follows her down the corridor and opens the door for her.

Nell looks up at him. "You'll stay a minute?"

"Of course."

Henry drapes his jacket over an armchair and unbuttons his collar and cuffs. Nell crosses to the windows and opens the gold silk curtains.

She sits on the bed, close to the padded headboard, then slides over without a word, drawing her skirt aside so there's room for him too. The sandals make a soft thump on the carpet. Henry joins her on top of the matelassé quilt, an inch between them; not quite touching, but close enough to feel her warmth. He rests his hand on the bed, just next to hers. Nell tucks her legs underneath and leans her head on his shoulder, hair brushing against his sleeve.

His arm grows numb from the position, but he doesn't want to move. Instead, he looks around Nell's blush-and-gilt room, notices how her billowing gown spills across his outstretched legs, and listens to the timeless sounds of the house.

Henry closes his eyes and lets the stillness hold them just for a moment as darkness lifts from the dawn. The small space between his hand and hers disappears by the time morning slips into the room, and Henry can't tell who moved first. Light gathers in the windowpanes, turning the glass to gold, and he realizes Nell has been brightening his days in the same way since the moment they met.

18

Oranges and Opportunities

HENRY

THE ORANGERIE AT AINSWORTH stretches along the south side of the house, its tall arched windows running the full length of the room and offering views of the formal gardens. Full-sized orange, lemon, and lime trees grow in glossy emerald green box planters. Henry likes that the air here is always infused with the bittersweet scent of orange blossoms, mingling with the fragrance of waxy green leaves and rich earth.

At the heart of the space, a white marble fountain creates musical sounds with trickling water, the sound bouncing off the high, vaulted ceiling. Plaster walls are painted like a fantastical garden, with a riot of flowering trees arching overhead: orange blossoms, magnolias, and branches trailing wisteria. Bright birds and butterflies perch amid the painted canopy, and beneath, winding trellises cradle meandering jasmine and glimpses of pagodas, urns, and pheasants. Soft green tones in the background lend the entire scene a dreamy, sunlit serenity, blurring the line between the painted world and the living, fragrant jungle inside.

That afternoon, Henry finds Nell there, standing on a three-legged stool, arms deep in a tangle of orange branches, swearing under her breath. She wiggles loose a shriveled orange, launching it to the floor.

"Busy?" Henry asks, eyebrow arching.

"If by busy you mean wearing this orange tree, yes," she says, pushing a tendril of escaped hair back from her face. Roger is lying in the corner, chin on the checkered marble floor, looking from Nell to the fallen orange to Henry and back.

Henry leans against a potting table. "Do you know anything about Biennais? Martin-Guillaume Biennais?"

Nell pauses, balancing on one foot. "Should I?"

"He was Napoleon's go-to man for everything from swords to chamber pots, and, crucially, furniture," Henry says. "His pieces were practically the Fabergé eggs of their day. A single desk could set an auction room vibrating."

"Mrs. Patterson said Philippe Moreau's desk is Biennais. So it's worth quite a lot. Leclair has it priced at forty-thousand pounds. He must know who the maker is." She nudges the shriveled orange toward Roger, who sniffs it and sighs.

"Her inventory lists a curious mark on the desk that you couldn't have seen when you visited the shop, and that Leclair doesn't mention on his website," Henry says.

"Oh?" Nell turns to face him, brushing her hands on her jeans.

"It's a mark that Biennais put on furniture he made for Napoleon himself," Henry says. "Biennais used special marks on almost all of his pieces, sometimes even under the veneer. He must have loved mysteries and puzzles because he was also known for his ingenuity with secret compartments and clever mechanisms in his cabinetry."

"Wouldn't a knowledgeable dealer find a special mark?" Nell says.

"Not necessarily," Henry replies, shifting to a wooden stool under a lemon tree. "These marks were often hidden so well that only the maker and the original owner knew where they were."

"And?" Nell says.

"And," Henry says, "Mrs. Patterson's inventory says this piece has the mark of a bee with an N over it and laurel leaves. Inside the drawer opening, all the way at the back, inside the rail. There's no way anyone would see this unless they knew exactly where to look."

"Let me guess," Nell says. "This is the mark of a piece made for Napoleon."

"Historically," Henry says, leaning back and crossing his arms, "the bee was a principal emblem of Napoleon, chosen for its symbolism of immortality, diligence, and connection to earlier French dynasties. Bees appeared on his robes, official regalia, and personal effects. In furniture, especially pieces made for Napoleon himself, bees appeared in subtle ornamentation like bronze drawer pulls, hidden engravings, or inlaid details."

"You think we had Napoleon's desk here?" Nell says, amazed.

"Nell, I think Philippe's desk might have been a gift to Philippe from Napoleon himself. I think that's why he brought the desk with him all the way from Paris."

"This could be the piece that clears any suspicion about Aleric," Henry says.

Nell gasps. "Henry, it was Philippe who was the spy!"

"Right here under Aleric's nose. It must be Philippe's medal, letter, and button in the garden."

"We need to find that bee," Nell says, "and pronto."

"I'm going tonight," Henry says. "And I have a plan."

***

Eduard Leclair is arranging a trio of snuffboxes in a velvet-lined display case, already glancing at his watch when Henry enters at fifteen minutes before nine.

"Cutting it a bit close, Mr. Templeton?" Leclair's tone is polite, but clipped.

"Sorry to intrude. Her Grace said she was in recently and asked me to stop and find out about restoration work at Ainsworth. I was in the village; I hope you don't mind. Would you tell me about your process?"

Leclair brightens, smoothing a cuff. "It's always bespoke. I start by cleaning every surface. During cleaning, I assess for repairs, old damage, or signs of cover-up. Authenticity is essential."

Henry is surprised to see that Leclair's eyes stray, as if by habit, toward Nell's desk. Leclair would be a terrible poker player, Henry thinks.

"After cleaning," Leclair continues, "I'll strip any failing finish, carefully sand and refinish the wood, and restore missing inlays or brasswork when needed."

"Does that affect the value of a piece?" Henry asks.

Leclair looks smug. "It could. But if done properly, Mr. Templeton, even experts can't see where the original stops and my work starts."

Henry nods slowly. "Is it common to recreate parts that are missing?"

"Very," Leclair replies, brushing dust from his lapel. "Especially for high-value items. I keep molds and exact measurements of every piece I work on. Sometimes I commission joiners for perfect matches. If insurance or clients want a 'safe' version, I can create a facsimile." He pauses, balancing a snuffbox in his hand.

"Is there that much demand for exact replicas?" Henry asks.

"There's always a market for copies. Often, the original is sold, and the replica is kept on display," Leclair says. "May I ask what line of work you're in, Mr. Templeton?"

"I'm the Duchess of Belward's valet and handyman." Henry says.

"Have you always been in service?" Leclair asks.

"No," Henry says, curious about this line of questioning. "Before that, I was in research and analysis."

"Well," Leclair ventures cautiously, "in my line of business, I have a knack for helping owners make historic homes profitable without damaging their character. When a house is full of antiques, there are various creative ways to raise funds."

Henry watches him handle the snuffbox. He reads the implication clearly: sell originals for cash, keep replicas for insurance, massage valuations to move money. Careful, Henry, he tells himself. "The Duchess prioritizes preservation, but your expertise might be useful one day."

Leclair's eyes glint, sensing his interest. "My pleasure, Mr. Templeton. Opportunity favors those who know where to look."

Henry keeps his tone polite. "That's an interesting offer, Mr. Leclair. It's kind of you to think of her."

Leclair smiles, not missing a beat. "Always looking to expand my business."

Henry ventures, "Nell's solicitor mentioned you visited after the funeral. Did anything stand out at Ainsworth that needed work?"

Leclair's eyebrows lift, barely. He turns, busying himself with a silver cupboard. "A few pieces, certainly, but I was just there for a probate valuation. Nothing in particular caught my eye," he says, keys jangling in his palm. "Excuse me, I'll get you some information before I close up."

Using the lull, Henry crosses to the desk. He removes the side drawer, slips his right hand deep inside, and snaps photos with his phone. Drawer back in, he drifts toward an ornate gold-leaf mirror above an antique bureau.

"That mirror is a copy of a Regency mirror I acquired from another dealer," Leclair says, returning. "The original fetches tenfold. Of course, it must be clearly marked as a replica." He passes Henry a brochure. "If you text me photos, I'll take a look, or better yet, come out and give Miss Ainsworth a quote."

Henry notices a lavender sachet tucked inside a half-open drawer of the bureau.

"For moths," Leclair says. "Chemicals are so vulgar."

"I see," Henry nods. "Excellent. Well then, thanks very much. Let's plan on that. Mind if I use your washroom before I head out?"

"Second door on the left," Leclair says, distracted as an attractive woman enters the shop.

As Henry passes the office, he spots Leclair's phone on the desk. Holy cow—it's right there. Let's just take a gamble. He slips a hand into his pocket and closes his fingers around the MI5 device, matte-black and unremarkable. He thumbs the contact pad and, in one smooth motion, presses it to the back of Leclair's phone. A tactile buzz—that's the exploit running, a zero-click handshake on an unpublished protocol vulnerability. He removes the device and sets the phone back on the desk, the tether already engaging.

This is the part he can't rush. He needs ten seconds. Ten perilous seconds.

On his own phone as he walks, Henry taps a onetime authorization code:

Hotspot: BLACKWALL-RELAY | Layer IV encryption.

There is a flash of blue on the MI5 device. *Lock bypass confirmed. Session active.*

Device log: Initializing handshake. Secure pairing—NFC. Fallback: Bluetooth LE. Protocol: Vuln3r-22 exploit successful. UID cloned. Mirror process active.

Done. He breathes, counting the steps to the washroom.

Second door on the left. The connection should hold across the adjoining wall, but if Leclair grabs his phone too soon, the link will fail. Worse, Leclair's phone will warn him about the attempted sync if the protocols trip.

In the washroom, Henry checks his phone again: *Mirror in progress...*

His encrypted hotspot is on, MI5-grade protocols and rolling keys already running, and he watches the transfer: contacts.db, SMS, WhatsApp archive, location cache, any document flagged "Ship" or "Store" pulled across the airwaves and relayed live to the secure drop in London. He takes a slow breath to steady himself and lets the tension bleed off in small, controlled movements. It's the sort of thing MI5 training drills into your bones.

Footsteps sound in the corridor outside the washroom. Time's up.

Mirror transfer 100%. Log scrub complete. No trace left on target.

Henry waits two more seconds, jaw tense, watching for any sign of a transmission blip or network anomaly. Nothing. Clean. He washes his hands, extracts the micro-tether and his phone from his pocket, both cool and inert.

On his way out, Henry glances into the office. The phone on the desk is gone. By the time he steps back onto the shop floor, his expression is all easy composure. Leclair, none the wiser, nods to him, his phone in hand, as he tells Henry he'll follow up with Miss Ainsworth next week.

"Thank you again," Henry says.

He opens the door, and as he glances back, he sees Leclair already speaking softly into his cellphone, voice urgent.

In the car, Henry scrolls through the photos he took of the desk. The first two are blurs, just shadows. But in the third, below the rail, stands a tiny, carved bee topped by a laurelled N: the Napoleonic symbol. Henry's pulse jumps, cold certainty and exhilaration mingling. The provenance, if real, could mean a desk of unimaginable value. "Merry Christmas, Nell."

19

Roses Are Lavender

NELL

THE MOMENT HENRY LEAVES for the village, Nell retreats to the Ballroom to work at her desk. She's contemplating chapter five of her novel, where, as usual, no one speaks plainly and everyone smolders in oak-paneled gloom. She's considering letting her duchess run off with a poet when Mrs. Patterson arrives in the doorway. She's flanked by two footmen in solemn formation, balancing a long, rolled canvas between them like knights bearing a holy relic.

"Ballroom, if you please, gentlemen. Mind the parquet." She leads the formation to the center of the ballroom, then steps aside and straightens her immaculate cuffs as the footmen gently lower the canvas to the floor.

"We were taking down the tapestry in the second-floor hallway, ma'am, for a proper cleaning, which it sorely needed, I might add. We found this nailed up behind it," Mrs. Patterson announces. "I thought it best to bring it straight here, even if it does mean extra work for the already weary and spreads dust from the East Wing across the entirety of the establishment." She glances briefly at Roger, as if seeking his acknowledgment of the excessive dust situation.

"If I may, ma'am," she says.

"Yes, please, Mrs. Patterson."

Mrs. Patterson nods at the footmen, who begin to unroll the canvas under her hawk-eyed supervision. Nell crosses the floor and pushes a brass light switch near the doorway, filling the Ballroom with a glitter storm from the chandeliers. Nell crouches beside the canvas and helps the footmen ease it open. A few old copper nails are still embedded along the edge. Nell coughs at the dust and removes the nails as she sees them. The heavy fabric flattens, and luscious color emerges. The edge of a painted dress, a garden, hints of something extraordinary, and at the lower right edge—*F. Winterhalter*.

Nell sighs. "This is it, Mrs. Patterson. You did it again. This is what we've been searching high and low for."

Mrs. Patterson stands at the edge of the activity—a field marshall surveying a mere inconsequence, hands folded in front of her, forehead raised. Nell grins; this is how pandemonium always begins and ends at Ainsworth: with Mrs. Patterson, unbothered, and her footmen as ceremonial squires.

Nell bends over the painting again as it opens fully. Rose Ainsworth is striking in a white silk dress with a tightly fitted bodice and gathered sleeves. The skirt is full but plain, except for a wide lavender sash cinched at the waist. Its tails lift and flutter in a painted breeze. A gold necklace with an oval locket catches the light at her throat. She stands on a path in front of a graceful stone garden folly. It looks like every other folly at Ainsworth at first glance: a round stone base, a domed copper roof weathered to green, slender pilasters dividing smooth walls and framing tall arched windows, a pane-glass door catching the low sun.

Cascading up trellises on either side of the entrance, clusters of pale lavender roses reach for the dome. Winterhalter has even painted a few delicate petals scattered on the path at Rose's feet. More roses, planted in generous double rows in all shades of lavender, fill the beds along the walkway. Nell can almost smell the soft scent of the flowers merging with the cool evening air, while their color—rare and impossible to ignore—gives the scene an ethereal quality. The symmetry and order of the garden's layout contrast with the wildness of the rose canes, which climb and curve toward the little domed pavilion.

She thanks Mrs. Patterson and the footmen, and tells them the frame is in the East Wing luggage storage.

How ephemeral life is, Nell muses. Everything in this painting is gone now. It's a portrait of ghosts.

Then a thought sharpens. What if this isn't just a portrait? What if this is a piece of a puzzle? Maybe it's a signpost pointing straight at the missing treasure. What if the painting was hidden because it's a map?

Nell's phone rings. She glances at it, expecting Henry, but it's Jenny—the village librarian.

"This is Nell," she says.

"Your Grace," Jenny says. "I wanted to let you know I found some information about your oak tree."

Nell pulls her rolling chair away from the desk and sits, looking at the painting on the floor. "Thank you, Jenny. What is it?"

"On a whim, I searched the local newspaper archives for stories about Ainsworth in the 1800s. Mostly, it was just dry local happenings. Then I found two stories, both from June 1847. Shall I read them?"

"Yes, please do."

"First, in the weather section, it says, *Yesterday evening, a violent storm struck the area, splitting an ancient oak by the Ainsworth rose folly and sending locals rushing out with lanterns.*"

Nell says nothing, only nods. Was the oak tree in the painting struck by lightning the night Rose died?

"Ma'am?" Jenny prompts.

"I'm here. Sorry, Jenny."

"There's more," Jenny says. "The same issue has a small article about the death of Rose Ainsworth. It says, *Miss Rose Ainsworth found dead at the Black Tor cliffs, spirited home by Mr. William Whitby and Mr. Thomas Duval.* The paper describes the two men as *rumored rivals, bearing Rose's body together through the storm.*"

"When did you find this, Jenny?" Nell asks.

"Tonight. I was at home having dinner and had this idea—you know, about searching the old newspapers—and my spine tingled. I just knew there was something, so I came back to the library. I'm here now."

"Please text me a copy of those articles when it's convenient." The articles mark what happened that night and dispel the myth of Thomas fleeing the scene.

"Jenny, you don't have to give me names, but how many people could know about the location of the oak?" Nell asks.

Jenny's voice drops. "Possibly three. Plus you. And me."

Nell hangs up, uneasy. That huge, ancient oak in the painting must be the one the anonymous letter told her to find. Whoever hid this painting must have known it was a key to the treasure—why else nail it out of sight? But if they know the treasure is by an oak near a folly, why haven't they just dug it up? Why bother blackmailing her at all?

Nell's mind whirs through the estate. The roses.

Every garden folly at Ainsworth is ringed with roses. There is a different color rose at each one. There were five follies once; four are still standing now, with beds in red, yellow, white, and pink. There has never been a lavender rose garden at Ainsworth. Not in my lifetime, anyway, she thinks. The only place lavender roses might have stood is where nothing stands any more: the ruined folly on the moor. Nell almost laughs. The answer was right there in the painting all along.

Where on earth is Henry?

Nell stands, heart thudding, and looks again at the lavender roses in the painting. She lets out a breath. What if someone else has finally put the pieces together, just as she has?

The thought snaps through her, bright and sudden. If there is even a chance someone else has worked it out, the tumble-down folly on the moor won't stay quiet for long.

She glances at the clock on her desk. Henry is still in the village. If she waits for him to get back, explain, argue, plan, the light will be gone—and if anyone is already out there, she'll never forgive herself.

"Just a quick look," she mutters. "Reconnaissance."

Nell is already moving. She leaves the painting where it lies on the ballroom floor and strides the length of the Great Hall, heart thudding in her throat as she takes the main stairs down two at a time and pushes through the door to the Boot Room. Her hand goes automatically to her pocket.

Empty.

"Phone," she groans. Right. Still face down on the desk upstairs.

For an instant she hesitates, picturing the trek back up two flights, the wasted minutes, the light slipping away over the moor.

"It's five minutes," she tells herself, grabbing a heavy torch from the shelf by the door. "In and out. Look, don't linger. Who needs a phone for that?"

Roger lies on his plaid bed under the table, watching her as she snaps the torch on to check the batteries.

"See?" she tells him. "Perfectly equipped." She flicks off the light, shoulders into her coat, and steps out into the damp air.

"What could possibly go wrong?"

20

Choices

ROGER

ROGER WATCHES FROM HIS plaid Roger-bed in the shadows under the Boot Room table as Nell pulls on boots, shoulders squared with that stubborn-hero scent that means foolish things are about to happen.

"It'll be nothing, Roger," she says, "just a walk."

He understands enough human words to understand worry. He also understands the way she smells when she's forgotten something important—thin, sharp, like rain on stone. She smells like that now.

"This may be our one chance to get ahead of the blackmailer," Nell says, zipping and snapping her jacket. "Don't give me that look. I have to go now. You don't have to come if you don't want to. You can stay here and be a good boy and watch the house." She opens the Boot Room door, peering under the table at him. "I just want to see what is out there. I won't stay long. I promise. It's just a quick walk," she says again, softer. "If the blackmailer already knows what we know..."

She closes the door behind her.

Roger looks at the Roger-sized flap at the bottom of the big door. He calls it the squeeze-through. It's the gap between his human den and everything that smells like sky. Head low, he noses through the flap, body bending and wriggling. Outside, the air is cold, and the wind ruffles his fur. She's already behind the carriage court, torch cutting a narrow slice through the dark, heading straight for the moor. Roger follows at a distance. Unwilling to go. Unwilling to let her go alone.

Roger's world has boundaries now: hedges, stone, the invisible line where safety ends and wildness begins. The moor yawns far past that line. He failed once before, trusted the wrong person, protected the wrong way. But Nell is walking away from him, her confidence equal parts sweet and reckless. Roger whines low. Stay and be safe, or leave and be hers.

He slinks after her, nose twitching as he ducks close to the shrubbery, wet paws on the sodden grass. The old wisdom snarls at him, turn around! Let the human be foolish in the dark. Each step from the house is a dare, a memory of cold and hunger; of biting for love and being called a monster. Ahead, Nell's lamp bobs, drawing him away from safety through windswept sedges and grasses. Nell pulls up her coat collar against the damp night.

The wind is behind him. This is wrong. The wind should be in his face, not at his back. Every pup learns it. If you're clever, you slip far downwind, circle wide, and come back toward the quarry so the scents fill your nose. But this wind pushes everything away from him. He knows, bone-deep, this is how you miss things. This is how you end up prey instead of hunter.

But Nell walks on. She doesn't pause, doesn't test the air. She can't feel how blind they are. His ears are sleek and cupped for catching the faintest noise, but even sounds fold up and vanish in the gusts. She glances around only once at the shapes in the dark. Oblivious, Roger thinks, but he follows. She can't know what hides. He must know for both of them.

Roger drifts further and further outward through the bristling heather, veering to Nell's right, cutting wide looping arcs that let him challenge the wind for information while keeping her in view. He can't trust the straight walk like Nell does; it keeps his nose dulled, ears muffled. So he moves in long, gentle sweeps, crossing back toward her then away again, each curve searching for scents the wind tries to hide. S pattern, old and true—out, back, out again—trying to circle behind the gusts, snatch at any sign of whatever waits in the dark.

Every loop brings him a hint: a sliver of animal, a bitter tang, the faint scent of Nell herself. It's not enough. Not like it should be, but he keeps working it. His Shepherd's nose is determined. His ears pricked for the softest sound. Safe is a pattern, not a straight line; Roger follows it, hoping to catch what Nell cannot see. She walks on, unaware.

His tail is down. Paws land softly; each tuft of heather touches his belly, wiry and chill. He knows every bump and shadow could rise. If it doesn't move, he is suspicious; if it stirs, he sees it instantly. Above, the sky is too near, heavy with clouds. They travel through boggy places, and dry, craggy places where it is easy to stumble. They walk on until the old garden folly rears from the moor like a shipwreck.

Nell is twenty-five yards away from him now. He stops behind a pile of rocks, watching the darting beam of her torch as she approaches the ruins, stepping over broken limestone. It's a circle of mossy stone walls and toppled statues choked with weeds and thorns.

She picks a tentative path, flashlight wavering, negotiating the jumble of debris, as she sweeps the walls with nervous, muttered commentary. She disappears inside the folly. He creeps closer, crouching beneath a bramble, muscles coiled tight. There is danger here. Tobacco. The scent of the boot print in the garden.

He knows somehow with awful certainty she will not survive the night without him.

"Haunted? Ridiculous. Romantics, all of them... Just stones and—ow," Nell says, bumping her knee on a toppled statue.

He lifts his nose. Every sense howls for retreat, but Nell is an anchor; her voice pulls him back. Back to the strength of his father and the nerve of his mother. Back to the steadfast, lion-hearted pup he was when Fergus chose him from the litter and brought him home.

He presses lower to the ground, nose quivering, ears tuned to every scuff and catch of her breath. She circles the ruin, the torch glancing over mossy benches and twisted ironwork. His nerves vibrate with indecision and dread. It's not too late; he could bolt back to the warm security of the house. Or he can risk everything for the girl who believes in him, even as his heart pounds with something far older than courage. Deep in the thorns, Roger readies himself. Soon, choice will be an illusion, and love will have to be as fierce as survival.

His hackles prickle as Nell's torch slides over a bench at the center of the folly. The bench itself is half-swallowed by brambles and rot; the marble seat cracked with age. She kneels, lips set in a tight line. Underneath, hidden among brittle roots and cobwebs, lay a gold locket crusted dark with age. She holds the locket beneath the light of the torch, a small, incredulous gasp, hands trembling.

Then, from the tangled roses that reach up over the walls, comes the sound: a rustle, deliberate, predatory, too large for a fox or badger. Nell freezes, torch beam stuttering uncertainly in the gloom.

"Who's there?" she whispers.

The darkness offers no answer, just another scrape, another weighted silence. Roger shrinks.

There can be no happy ending now.

A shape bursts from the shadows: masked, furious—a specter twisted by moonlight and malice. The figure runs at Nell with terrifying intent. She screams—then fights back, hands slashing wildly, the locket sent spinning into the weeds.

Roger's limbs are locked with panic and fear.

Nell stumbles, the stranger's grip closing around her arm. She kicks, thrashes, torch skidding across stone. From the undergrowth, it throws monstrous shadows against the crumbling walls.

Shaking, Roger watches as the nightmare unspools—abandonment, injury, the claws of his past digging deep.

But Nell does not stop fighting. Even in shock, she calls him—defiant, reaching for the only lifeline that remains in the ruined, moonlit garden folly:

"Roger!"

Roger's world closes in, shrinking to the bite of thorns at his flanks and the rhythmic, brutal sound of Nell fighting for breath beneath the attacker. Every instinct screams at him to stay hidden. He remembers the hand that once fed him, then struck him. The time he bit, not to harm but to save, and was cursed and cast out to starve. The endless weeks of fear and hunger. Every cell in his body burns with a single command—run now. Run and survive.

Brave dogs bleed. Brave dogs starve. No one saves brave dogs.

But Nell's cry rises again—a desperate plea, rooted in her belief in him, stronger than any fear:

"Roger!"

It shatters the terror clamped around his heart, a summons so raw it leaves no room for the past. Roger's blood roars in his ears. All his fear, his training, the hard, savage lessons of loss collide—and at the center is a single, thin thread of hope. She needs him. He is the last bright piece left in her battered world.

Roger rises on trembling legs. He must choose—now, here, in this moonlit ruin: remain imprisoned by pain or blaze forward, risking everything for this human. But he's already chosen.

"Roger!"

He pushes free of the brambles and races across the open, ears flat to his head, devouring the distance with powerful strides, leaving every ghost and boundary behind. His whole world funnels down to Nell's cry and the hard silhouette of the masked attacker looming over her.

The assailant cannot see Roger, cannot hear him rocketing through the blackness, but Roger sees him clear as day.

For Roger, time slows and his focus narrows to his target—the arm holding the weapon—just as he was trained. He launches, body arcing through the air, the crash of his heartbeat in his chest. Now nothing else matters.

The result is chaos—fur, fists, boots thudding sodden earth. The air shatters with shouting, tumbling bodies, and wild panic. Roger is a snarling whirlwind of fury and loyalty and pent-up courage—a sound torn from deep within, old and new at once. Teeth, muscle, a roar cut loose in the night, and the moor explodes around him, every instinct set free. There is the hot, bitter tang of blood, a gloved hand beating at him, the jarring jolt as his shoulder hits the attacker's leg.

Roger knows he must hold on. He must hold on no matter what. It's a certainty from an ancient past, a drive as old as time. He must hold on and not let go. Roger's claws dig into the mud for purchase. He throws his weight into the assailant and grips deeper on his arm.

He shakes his head and knows, in his brave heart, there is no way out for him now—no backing down. He will win or die.

The attacker curses. Roger holds on, thrashing hard, one back paw spasming with agony as the figure kicks and tries to drag Nell away. A fist swings down, clips Roger's ear, the pain white-hot—but he doesn't let go.

For this instant, suspended between night and morning, Roger is not afraid.

With a final, savage wrench, Roger rips the assailant off Nell, sending them staggering into the stone, knocking Roger off the arm. He snaps for cloth, for any anchor—the world breaking into sharp flashes as he's thrown against the stone wall. The attacker, startled and limping, scrambles over the ruined wall and vanishes into the mist, wheezing in fear.

Roger can't move. His body throbs with pain, and with a new, strange pride. The old terror is gone, replaced by the simple, ragged knowledge that he chose her, even above his greatest fear.

Nell calls his name. Pain sears through his flank and leg; every nerve is on fire. He tries to rise, but his body betrays him, a sharp yelp splitting the quiet. Nell scrambles to his side, tears streaking her muddy face. "Roger, you did it! You saved me, you brave, stupid mutt." But as she reaches to gather him, Roger bares his teeth. It is reflex: a warning, desperate to fend off everything that hurts.

Nell's voice softens, but her resolve is steel. "Roger, I know it hurts. If you're going to bite me, then bite me. Because I'm not leaving you, and we won't survive if we stay out here."

She slides her arms under him, lifting with all the strength she has. Roger growls but doesn't strike. It is the hardest trust of his life.

Nell trips over a clump of grass, falls to her knees, and loses her hold. Roger slumps back to earth, whimpering. But she rises again—breathless, determined—lifting him with wild devotion. He growls again, but she holds steady.

"It's okay, you big dope. I'm not going without you," she whispers, almost fierce, almost broken.

With shaking arms, she hauls him up again. Roger lets his weight press into her. Step by agonizing step, she carries him, lurching, refusing to yield. Roger rests his head on her shoulder at last. Nell stumbles through the moor, clutching him so tightly her arms ache. The wind claws at her jacket, rain stings her cheeks, but she keeps talking to him.

"It's okay... it's okay, just a little farther. You were brave. So, so brave. I'm so proud of you." Her voice trembles, half sob, half plea. "Stay with me, Roger. Please stay with me. I can't—I can't do it without you."

She talks to him nonstop as they weave through the night together. Roger doesn't know what she's saying, but he likes Nell's voice.

"You know, Roger, you are the absolute worst to carry," she huffs, wobbling between tears and laughter. "Why couldn't I have inherited a nice, sensible spaniel? Or, I don't know, a ferret? Ferrets don't weigh a hundred pounds, for the record."

She nearly drops him, but hauls him higher with a grunt. "Next time, could you pick a fight somewhere less soggy? Maybe a nice hotel bar? Oh, sure, go limp, just relax. You did all the hard work back there. We agreed: I handle the talking, you handle the saving. Look at us, sticking to the plan. If any neighbors see me carting you like a sack of potatoes, you're doing the explaining, not me." Her voice fills the emptiness: part pep talk, part scolding, all love. A strand of hair sticks to her forehead; she blows it away, sniffling and snorting in what even she can't tell is more relief or exertion.

"We're almost there, big lad. See? Home. You're my good boy, my best boy," she whispers fiercely, stumbling onward. "Don't you dare leave me now."

She slips again, knees buckling, and Roger tumbles hard into the wet grass with a yelp. Nell collapses beside him, head tipped back, gulping the cold air.

"Oh good lord, you're heavy," she manages, laughing, then crying, then laughing again. "The papers will say, 'Woman Found Clutching Enormous Idiot Dog, Both in Need of Snacks.'"

For one heartbeat, Roger thinks she might give up, might leave him. But no. She presses her face into his wet fur, her words a ragged chant, a prayer and a promise. "We've got this, buddy," she whispers. "We've got this."

Hours drag by before the manor lights glow through the mist, distant and unreal. They nearly fall again. Each time, Nell drags herself up, half-crawling with Roger in her arms, answering every one of his fears with stubborn hope.

Finally, just as her strength seems spent, the Boot Room door is in front of them. Roger whimpers, Nell sobs, and together they breach the line between wilderness and sanctuary. She drops to her knees inside the threshold, cradling him as the world spins. Roger closes his eyes, his body aching, his heart thumping.

He is safe at last. Saved by the girl who refused to let go.

21

Dr. Fairweather

HENRY

NELL AND ROGER SIT sprawled on the flagstones just inside the door, both streaked with mud. Roger leans against Nell's shins, fur matted and blood seeping in lines. Her arm hangs limp, palm bright with scrapes. Both are breathing hard.

Henry drops to his knees, yanks a stack of towels from a drawer: "Let's move him. Here. Nice and slow." He doesn't ask where they were or what happened; he simply meets the emergency as it is, an analyst working the problem at hand.

Nell supports Roger beneath his chest. Henry slides his arms under the dog's hips, and together they ease him onto the towels. Roger settles with a low, rattling huff, one back paw drawn up and stiff.

"Nell, take my phone and call Dr. Fairweather." He unlocks it and brings up the vet's number.

Nell's fingers slip as she taps call. While the phone rings, Henry runs a clean towel gently along Roger's side, scanning for injuries. "Stay with me, big fella," he says, pressing a towel to a bleeding cut. "He's lost a lot of blood. You've got him, Nell? Good. Hold the towel there. Just like that. Keep pressure: five minutes minimum."

"Dr. Fairweather? It's Nell. Roger is hurt. He's bleeding. There's a deep cut on his side, another at his neck. He was limping. He...saved me. Please come. Yes, yes, he's breathing. Please come quickly."

Nell turns to Henry. "Dr. Fairweather wants to know what injuries he has." She taps the speaker and holds the phone out for him, eyes moving from Roger to Henry's calm face.

"Lacerations on his side—at least two, one bleeding heavily. Another cut on his neck, not as deep, but still bleeding. He's holding the back right leg as if it's injured. One ear is torn. Vitals seem stable so far. He's awake; gums are pale. We're pressing towels to stop the bleeding."

Dr. Fairweather's voice crackles through the line, as if she's in an area with spotty cell service. "Keep him warm, but don't let him overheat." She says. "Apply firm, clean pressure to any bleeding. Rinse the muddy wounds gently with clean water if you can. Don't scrub. No ointments. If he's shivering or drifts off, talk to him, keep him calm. If he's struggling to breathe or the bleeding won't slow, call me back straight away. Don't move him unless you have to. I'll be there as soon as I can—thirty, maybe forty-five minutes. Keep him still and comfortable. I'll handle the rest when I arrive."

Working together, Henry and Nell flush the wounds they can find and cover Roger with a towel. Henry stands. washes his hands and looks down at Nell, cross-legged by Roger, talking to him softly and stroking his head. Roger would never have allowed that before. Whatever happened to them out there, it changed their relationship.

"Nell, you're bleeding too." Henry kneels in front of her and gently disinfects a gash at her hairline, his touch soft but unhesitating.

"Tell me what happened."

Nell stares at her hand, lets it fall to her lap. "We walked out to the folly on the moor. There was a man. He hit Roger and shoved me down. I couldn't—Roger got between us." Her words stumble out in bursts.

Henry's voice stays calm. "Mrs. Patterson didn't know where you'd gone. I waited half an hour, then Fergus and I went looking for you. We drove all over the estate. I didn't think you'd walk out to the moor alone."

Nell winces a little as he dabs the cut, but manages a weak, crooked smile. "I wasn't alone. I had Roger."

Henry's eyes meet hers. "Yes," he says quietly. "You did."

"Henry, someone hid the painting of Rose behind a tapestry on the second floor. Someone knew it was a treasure map—that the old oak marking the treasure was near a folly."

"Why didn't they just go get the treasure then?" Henry says.

"Because, just like you, they didn't know which folly. They didn't know about the lavender roses." Nell says. "Whoever attacked me must have figured it out at the same time I did."

"Leclair has your desk," Henry says, showing her the photos on his phone, "and it has Napoleon's bee symbol."

"Oh, wow," Nell says. "That's great...I think? Is it great? Can we get it back?"

Henry glances at her with a wry smile. "We'll try. Leclair knows the desk is valuable but doesn't know it belonged to Napoleon. If it was the blackmailer who attacked you, it's not Leclair—he was with me at his shop."

Mrs. Patterson bustles into the Boot Room, takes one look at Roger, Nell, the mud and blood, the towels in a heap. Her eyebrows arch to the ceiling. "Well, isn't this a fine kettle of frogs trying to herd themselves uphill?" Not waiting for an answer, she pivots out. Two minutes later, she's back—arms loaded with more towels, bandages, and a pale blue hoodie and soft grey sweatpants. She hands them to Henry.

"All right, we're not in the habit of leaving wounded heroes looking like they waded through the Thames. Let's get clean, and then we'll sort out those scrapes, if you please. Can't be bleeding all over the place now, can we? Fergus is on his way to look after Roger."

Fergus barrels in, pajama legs tucked into boots, hands full of bandages—straight to Roger. "There now, old mate. Look at you. What have you gone and done now?" Roger's tail thumps weakly. He lifts his nose to lick Fergus's hand, comforted by the familiar voice.

Henry nods, settles his arm around Nell's shoulders, and guides her into the lounge off the Boot Room.

The newly renovated spaces are strikingly modern for a centuries-old house. In the first room, dark, scraped wood floors support an Oriental rug, deep sofa, comfortable chairs, and a well-stocked bar. Next door is a mirror-lined dressing room, where guests can borrow sports clothes.

The separate bathing area with heated stone floors is cleverly divided: a double washbasin and baskets of plush white towels occupy half, with a row of sumptuous terrycloth robes along one wall. A glass wall separates this space from a spacious walk-in wet room designed for comfort and recovery. Inside, a heated stone bench faces a large jetted tub and an overhead rain-shower. Shampoo, conditioner, and a selection of soaps are arranged on a low teak pedestal. Every detail, from the generous number of empty hooks to the earthy slate tiles, reflects a space perfectly suited to muddy boots and tired riders.

"Let's get you sorted," Henry says, kneeling to slip off Nell's boots and socks, hands gentle over bruises. She rests her hand on his arm for balance, sighing as the stone warms her feet.

"Should I leave you alone, or...do you want help?" He asks.

She manages a shaky, grateful laugh. "Help, please. I'm beyond modesty," and awkwardly peels off shirt and jeans.

Henry lifts the shower wand. Warm mist frames her face. Nell tips her head back under the water and closes her eyes in relief. He shampoos her hair, working in gentle circles with soap from head to toe, never hurrying; always checking her face for pain, waiting for a nod before moving on.

She shifts closer, letting her forehead rest on his shoulder. His shirt and khakis are soaked, but he laughs when she looks up at him and teases, "You're going to need a shower too."

"I'm next," he promises, and tucks a damp lock behind her ear, his thumb lingering for a moment at her jaw. "I was worried about you." He looks into her eyes. She reaches out her hand to touch his face and rests it on his chest instead. Henry shrugs. Suddenly so overcome with emotion, he has to turn away. He takes a deep breath and wraps Nell in a thick robe, composing himself while he ties the belt. Not knowing what else to say.

He offers his arm as she steps into the other room. They say little, but the warmth is genuine. He smiles and dries her hair. "You're alright now," Henry says.

She pulls on the dry clothes, and they trade a look that holds more than words. Side by side, they are more than friends now, Henry thinks. Connected in a partnership unlike anything he's ever known.

Henry tapes a bandage around her wrist. "Did he knock you down, or did you fall? Can you move your fingers?" He runs two fingers along her arm, checking for swelling.

"He was all over us in seconds. Roger was so brave." Nell laughs, voice catching. "I don't know what came over him. He was...fierce..." She closes her eyes.

Henry searches her face, watching for signs of shock. "You still with me?"

Nell opens her eyes and nods. "Yes. I feel better."

"Tell me about the man who did this," Henry says. "How tall? Build?"

She sits on a bench in the lounge, tying one sneaker. She stops and looks up at Henry. "Taller than I am. Not as tall as you. Broad. Moved fast."

Henry kneels to tie the other. "What about his voice? Accent? Anything stand out?"

She shakes her head, trying to summon details. "Said little. Nothing I recognized."

"See his face?" He tilts her chin and puts a bandage on her cheek.

"Mask. Black. Just his eyes, dark, maybe brown. That's all I saw."

Henry nods and stands, then lifts her gently to her feet. "You're safe now. Got more?"

Nell shakes her head, breathes deeply. "No. That's all I've got. I'm sorry. It happened so fast. Roger was a blur. You should have seen him, Henry. He was like a tornado."

Henry squeezes her hand gently, reassurance and admiration threaded together. "You did exactly right."

***

Dr. Sabrina Fairweather is tall and composed in field boots and a Barbour jacket, pockets stuffed with odds and ends, from sheep syringes to emergency chocolate. She brings brisk, capable calm when she sweeps into the Ainsworth Boot Room. She kneels by Roger, placing a hand on Fergus's arm. Fergus, wiping at his eyes but doing his best to comfort Roger, gives her a small nod.

"I raised him from a wee lad," Fergus murmurs, voice quavering.

"It's good to see you, Mr. Macrae," Dr. Fairweather replies, warmth in her voice. "He'll be okay. Mind helping us lift Roger onto the table?"

Henry clears the table while her veterinary assistant brings in supplies. With Fergus's help, Dr. Fairweather eases a soft muzzle over Roger's snout. Then Fergus, the assistant, and Henry each take a corner of the towel Roger is on and lift him carefully onto the big oak table. She checks vitals, gives a sedative, and turns to them.

"Right. Run along, all of you. We'll take it from here." She shoos everyone out. "I'll keep you posted."

Henry walks Nell upstairs to her door. "I'll check on Roger. Just get some sleep. There's nothing you can do right now. Dr. Fairweather may be busy for a couple of hours. I'll file a police report, then head out to the moor—to the folly."

"Wait for me, will you?" Nell says. "I'd rather do this together."

"Absolutely," Henry says. They stand and look at each other.

Nell finally breaks the silence. "I'll understand if you go back to MI5. I'll hate it, but I understand."

"How did you know?" Henry asks.

"I guessed. The text came the evening we dug up the box from the garden, didn't it?"

Henry grimaces and nods.

"You've been thinking so loudly I'm surprised the vicar hasn't dropped by to offer advice," Nell laughs.

He rolls his eyes. "Alright, Holmes. Mind if I ask how you feel about it?"

"Not at all." She beckons him closer.

Henry bends, expecting a conspiratorial whisper. Nell grins, grabs his face, and kisses him.

"That's how," she says, squeezes his hand and slips inside, leaving Henry blinking, surprised and smiling in the hallway.

22

Gold Locket

NELL

NELL PULLS HER FIELD jacket tighter across aching shoulders, muscles tender despite having slept like the dead for a few hours. Every reach, every twist is a sharp reminder of last night—the moonless hike, the slip and slide through mud, the wild moment of Roger's brave defense. She glances at her boots, still flecked with dried blood, mud, and grass. She's chosen her softest old jeans this morning, but even they chafe against scrapes and bruises she can't quite remember collecting. Her hair, damp at the ends, is tucked up under a wool hat, strands already curling loose at her neck.

Henry works in the icy air, khakis tucked into lined wellies. He zips the collar of his field jacket higher, blocking the bite of a typical Cornwall spring, stowing their kit: the flashlight, two shovels, a dented red thermos, and a walking stick for her in the boot with his usual efficiency. The exhaust steams and hangs in the chilly fog.

"Roger will be okay," Henry says, sliding into the driver's seat. His words are gentle, meant for reassurance. "Dr. Fairweather has him settled in the Boot Room. He'll sleep for hours." He chuckles, "Maybe days."

"He deserves it," Nell replies, lifting herself gingerly into the passenger seat, shifting to ease the pull in her wrist.

She glances over. Henry's sandy brown hair is cropped short, a remnant of his MI5 days: practical, easy to manage. It stands in neat contrast to the worn green of his waxed jacket. The early light picks out gold in the close stubble along his jaw. His hands, marked with old scars, grip the wheel strong and sure. He is broad-shouldered in a thick wool jumper and has the capable bearing of someone trained to keep watch and calm chaos. Even tired, he radiates an alertness that reassures her.

His boots, scuffed and sturdy, rest easy on the pedals as the moor rolls past. Nell watches the landscape unspool through the window, frosty heather and gorse sparkling amethyst and topaz. When they reach the ruined folly, she steps out first, shivering, half from cold, half from memory. She retraces her steps, scanning the ground where she was attacked.

Henry walks behind her, patient. "Anything?"

She crouches, fingers sifting through matted grass. "I think it was about here..."

"What was?" Henry asks.

There's a brief glint of gold beneath dead leaves and fresh growth. Nell pinches the locket free, brushing dirt from its surface with her other hand. She holds it for a moment, then walks over to Henry, opening her fingers. On the front, a pair of entwined initials: R.A. & W.W.

"This," Nell says.

Henry takes the locket, weighing it in his palm. "Heavy. Rose Ainsworth is R.A., but who is W.W.? And there's a date."

Nell leans in. "Let me see," April 1846.

"Henry, Jenny told me she found two newspaper articles from the day after Rose died. One said an old oak was struck by lightning, and the other said that Thomas Duval and William Whitby carried her—her body—home together from Black Tor." She pulls on her gloves. "It mentioned that they were rivals. Sarah's diary says Rose and Thomas were in love. It doesn't mention William Whitby at all. But maybe Rose was engaged to William. She's wearing a gold locket in the painting."

Henry glances at her, thoughtful. "Could be. That would make sense." He nods at the locket. "Those initials and the date. Maybe Rose's portrait too."

Nell's heart aches with the sadness of the tragedy. "When I looked at the painting last night, I thought it was just a formal portrait of Rose in a white dress. But maybe..." She trails off, looking at Henry.

Henry finishes her thought. "It was the 1846 version of an engagement photo?"

Nell nods. "Among the gentry, getting engaged meant sitting for a portrait. It often still does."

Henry turns the locket again. "So Rose made promises to both men—one in secret, one in society."

Nell nods again. "It's starting to look that way."

***

Henry takes Nell's hand in his and sets the locket in her palm before heading back to the Range Rover. He retrieves a shovel, its head freshly painted in bright emerald green enamel by Fergus, then hefts the big metal detector. Walking back, he surveys the ruin and wild sweep of land.

"I'll get started," he says, adjusting the detector's strap across his chest and handing Nell the shovel. "If Winterhalter didn't take too much artistic license, the tree in that portrait was about here, just east of the folly's foundation."

Nell tucks the locket safely into her pocket, watching Henry pace the ground. "How deep can that thing pick something up?" she asks.

He shades his eyes to look at her, squinting into the brightening sun. "If it's something substantial, two feet, maybe a bit more." He grins.

She nods, leaning on the shovel for support, sweeping her eyes over the uneven ground for a dip, a marker stone, or the last twisted roots of the old oak. "That letter, the second one we got, says the treasure is *near the old oak.* It doesn't say how near."

Henry swings the detector slowly, working a pattern from the foundation of the folly to the slight slope where he estimates the tree once stood. Twenty minutes later, the detector crackles, then jumps with a distinct whine.

"You've got something?"

Henry nods, kneeling to brush away a swatch of heather and brittle grass. He looks up, face lit with cautious excitement. "It's here." He stands, takes the shovel from Nell, and begins to dig.

Just as his shovel breaks the dirt, a rifle cracks.

Stone splinters less than a yard from Henry's boot. He grabs Nell, and they both leap over the side of a tumbled-down stone wall, dropping flat. A flock of blackbirds erupts from the gorse in a storm of wings and agitated caws. Then nothing.

"Stay down!" Henry shouts, his voice carrying across the moor. He crabs backwards and sideways until he's swung around face to face with her. He covers her hand with his where it presses to the earth, grounding them amidst the confusion, and looks into her eyes. "We've got this," he says with a quick, crooked smile. "Just stay behind this wall, okay? Keep your head down. No matter what."

"Who on earth?" Nell whispers, mind racing as another shot pings off the top of the wall, spilling shards of stone between them. She ducks lower and turns her head to watch Henry crawl to a break in the wall. He's studying the incline of the slick rocks of Black Tor. Probably calculating the shooter's position. Nell notices the firm set of his jaw, how he automatically counts the shots fired under his breath, and the protective way he places his body between her and the danger.

"Stay here, okay? I'll be right back."

Before she can reply, Henry moves to the car, keeping low along the side of the wall. Two more shots strike the ground nearby, one pinging off the blade of the abandoned shovel. He reaches the Range Rover and disappears.

Nell can hear the split tailgate opening, then the sound of him loading the shotgun. He looks over at her and gives a brief, reassuring nod. He almost looks like he's enjoying this, she thinks. He's so calm. Is that normal? And he thinks *she's* reckless.

Another shot rings out, kicking stones across her back and causing her to flatten again. She covers her head with her hands, trusting that Henry knows exactly what to do next.

Suddenly, sirens wail across the moor, blue lights flashing. Nell sees Henry straighten, empty the shotgun and return it to the boot, then hands up and open. Doors slam, shouts rise crisp and urgent, and officers spread out around Black Tor, closing in on the shooter. Moments later, Edgar Whitby steps from behind a rock, arms lifted in surrender, placing his weapon on the ground.

Henry shows his MI5 credentials and has a word with the sergeant in charge. His voice is deep, clipped, and businesslike, and he has that everything-under-control military bearing.

Suddenly exhausted, Nell climbs into the Range Rover, sitting sideways, one shoulder leaning against the seatback. Funny how pain settles in as soon as the adrenaline wears off. She closes her eyes and listens to the radio chatter mingling with Henry's low, authoritative voice.

He finishes with the sergeant in charge and walks over to the car, standing in front of her, hands resting on her knees. He searches her face for a long moment, concern in his eyes.

She looks up at him with a wry smile. "You've turned my life into an action-adventure movie."

He gives a short laugh. "And you've turned mine into a romance novel."

She snorts, shaking her head as she rubs her sore arm. "Which one of us got the better deal?"

He gives her knee a gentle squeeze. "We both walked away, didn't we?"

"We did," Nell says. "You were impressive."

"So were you. I don't think I've ever seen you panic."

"You haven't been around when my jellybean stash runs low."

"Thanks for the heads-up." He grins. "I'll make sure that never happens."

"Edgar Whitby. Can you believe?" Nell says.

"He doesn't fit the profile of a blackmailer. He's working with someone, I'd bet," Henry says.

"Leclair," Nell says, frowning.

At the village police station, Henry and Nell give statements. The process is efficient. They go over what they saw and heard, sticking to the facts. Edgar is booked. Officers thank them and give them permission to leave.

On the way home, the car is silent for a few miles, until finally Nell wonders aloud. "Do you think Edgar will give up Leclair?"

Henry watches the road. "Whitby's not a fool. If Leclair set him up, or paid him off, my guess is he'll keep quiet. For now, anyway."

Nell rubs her bruised knee. "I keep thinking Leclair will get away with all of it."

Henry's phone rings. He glances at the screen and answers, his voice brisk and controlled. "Templeton."

The detective's voice filters through the speakers. "Update for you, Henry. Edgar Whitby isn't giving us anything on Leclair. No mention of the desk, no blackmail, nothing. We can bring Leclair in for questioning, but if he's got an alibi for the night Nell was attacked and bills of sale for the antiques in his shop, there's not much we can hold him on. If you hear anything else, let us know."

Henry hangs up and drums his fingers on the wheel. "Leclair covers his tracks. He'll have paperwork for everything. He's probably been at this for a while."

"I stood three feet away from the desk he stole *from my house,*" she emphasizes, "and he was cool as a cucumber."

Nell stares at the greening countryside outside the window. "But we can't prove he did it. All we have is Mrs. Patterson's inventory. Unless he slips up, he'll get away with it and go on to do it again."

Henry looks over at her briefly and turns into the lane at Ainsworth. "We're not finished, Nell. We have each other. That's more than he's got. Plus, if Leclair is the blackmailer, I have a feeling he won't want to leave without the treasure. We have to get back out to the moor ASAP."

The Range Rover crunches over the gravel of Ainsworth's forecourt and comes to a stop beside Eliza Brooke's car. Nell spots her by the stone steps, and Eliza turns at the sound of the engine. Henry puts the car in park and steps out, Nell close behind.

Eliza wastes no time. "Hi. I must have just missed you at the station. I hoped you'd be heading back here."

Nell shifts, feeling stiffness creep back into her muscles. "What happened, Eliza?"

Eliza shakes her head. "Edgar came home in the middle of the night with bites on his arms and leg. He said something attacked him on the moor. I just knew it was Roger protecting one of you. He left the house this morning with the rifle and said he was going back to 'finish things.' I called the police. I would have called last night, but I was afraid of what he'd do if he were trapped in the house."

She takes a breath. "There's something else. I overheard Leclair tell Edgar he found an old letter that said Napoleon's treasure is buried near an old oak at Ainsworth. It was in a secret compartment of an antique in his shop. He said it also proves Aleric Ainsworth was a traitor."

Nell and Henry exchange a look, both thinking the same thing—the Biennais desk.

Eliza pulls her collar tighter. "Edgar told Leclair he had proof that Thomas Duval killed Rose Ainsworth."

"Sarah's diary?" Nell asks.

"Yes," Eliza says. "I'm so glad I brought that to you. I think Leclair convinced Edgar to search for the treasure and dig it up. He said he had connections to sell it and would split the profits with Edgar. I told the police all of this."

Eliza pulls a folded envelope out of her coat pocket and hands it to Nell. "I found this in Edgar's things. It's a copy. I gave the original to the police. Maybe it will help you solve your mystery."

"Thank you," Nell says, taking the envelope. "So it was you researching the Ainsworth garden plans."

"It was. But I think Edgar and Leclair were looking too. Although I don't think they had much success, because I had all the sources." She gives a small, satisfied smile.

"Someone took garden plans out of one of the buildings at Ainsworth," Henry says, watching Eliza's expression.

"That must have been Leclair or Edgar." Eliza exhales, frustrated. "Mr. Templeton, there are so many tales and rumors about Ainsworth. People from the village have looked for treasure here off and on over the years, but no one ever knew where to look. Ainsworth is a big place." Eliza almost laughs. "And of course, it's private land."

"That it is," Henry says softly. He keeps his hands in his jacket pockets, eyes on Eliza. "Edgar never mentioned blackmail to you?"

Eliza looks truly shocked and takes a step back. "Blackmail? Oh, no! Edgar never planned anything like that. He just wanted the treasure, and Leclair goaded him on and used him. This morning when he left the house, Edgar swore he'd beat Leclair to it. He said if Leclair got it first, Edgar'd never see a penny." She drops her arms to her sides.

"I received a blackmail letter and was instructed to expect a follow-up with further instructions for getting the treasure," Nell says. "But it hasn't come." She knows she's taking a risk telling Eliza this much, but there's something that makes Nell trust her—and hope Eliza has an insight that could help.

Eliza looks thoughtful. "That makes sense," she ventures. "I don't think Leclair knew exactly where the treasure was. I think he planned to push others to find it for him, then let Edgar steal it and take the fall if it came to it."

Nell nods, because that is exactly what happened. "Eliza, why did you bring us Sarah's diary?"

"I wanted it out of the house, just as I said earlier. I thought Edgar hadn't seen it. Now I'm sure he saw it. Maybe even before I did. Edgar was the one who sent me all those threats and warning notes." She shakes her head. "My own husband."

Nell manages a tired smile. "We wouldn't have got this far without you, Eliza. You've been very brave."

Eliza glances at the house. "Edgar always resented the Ainsworths. Hated may be a better word. He thought his family had been cheated out of part of the fortune, though I don't know why." She lifts one shoulder. "I have to go. I'm packing up at Whitby Place. Edgar...he's not a nice person." Her eyes shine. "But Leclair. Leclair is worse. He's devious, ma'am. Be careful."

Nell steps forward and pulls her into a hug. "Will you be okay?" She asks, hands on Eliza's shoulders.

Eliza wipes her eyes. "I will now. I had a good job in London that I gave up for Edgar. I've got an offer, and I'm taking it." She turns, tightens the belt of her trench coat, and heads for her car.

Henry walks with her the rest of the way. He opens the driver's door, waits while she gets in, then closes it gently. When the car pulls away, he turns back to Nell. "Not everyone runs, you know."

Nell watches Eliza drive away. "No. Some of us just move on."

She turns toward the house, taking the letter from the envelope. Henry falls into step beside her, then stops when she does to read the letter over her shoulder.

"French again," Henry says.

Nell reads the letter aloud:

"Dear Papa, I found your medal and treasure by the old oak tree. I shall retrieve it as soon as possible. The woman I had hoped to marry is promised to another. I have one last opportunity tonight to convince her to come away with me. With love, your Thomas."

"Thomas was Philippe's son," Nell breathes. She looks over at Henry.

"If Philippe had to leave the buried treasure on the eve of Waterloo, he must have sent his son back to get it years later. And perhaps his desk and medal too," Henry says. "The letter is dated the day Rose died. Thomas must have hidden it in the desk and forgotten about it when he left so abruptly."

Nell pulls off her gloves and stuffs them into her pocket. "Sarah's diary said Thomas may have run away out of guilt after Rose died. But Jenny's newspaper article says that's not what happened."

***

In the Great Hall, Fergus sits on a stool, studying Roger, who is sporting an oversized plastic cone. Roger's chin rests on the toe of Fergus's boot. He looks groggy and deeply aggrieved. Fergus glances up at Nell. "He's not pleased, miss, but Dr. Fairweather insists." He hands the vet's instructions to Nell.

Nell crouches to scratch Roger's ear just above the rim of the cone, wincing when he does his best to flop onto her lap. "You look the way I feel."

"When he isn't sleeping, he tries to eat the cone," Fergus says. "So we're keeping him mostly asleep. Seems to improve everyone's temper."

"Thank you for looking after him, Fergus," she says, noting Fergus's high sobriety. Perhaps nursing suits him.

"Aye, miss. Roger's m'friend." He touches two fingers to his cap. "Whatever I can do. I'll stay right here as long as it takes."

Henry puts an arm around Nell as stands and brushes away a tear. She takes a deep breath.

From the ballroom, Mrs. Patterson's voice carries into the Hall—imperious, but today a notch softer. Nell pokes her head around the door and sees her, arms crossed, surrounded by a retinue of footmen and garden staff. Two men maneuver an elaborate frame upright. It holds the portrait of Rose Ainsworth. Daniel is at the fireplace calling out measurements.

"Young Daniel is a graduate of St. Martin's," Mrs. Patterson says proudly. "He re-stretched the painting on the original bars from storage, and we've just put it back into the frame. Where do you want her, Your Grace?"

Nell wonders if Mrs. Patterson's uncharacteristic mildness today is because of Nell's injuries or Roger's, or just general bleariness on everyone's part.

"Thank you, Mrs. Patterson. I understand Rose had been above the fireplace when my uncle was alive." Nell glances at the mantel, then nods. "Let's put her back where she belongs. Aleric and his horse can trot back to the library."

Mrs. Patterson nods approvingly at Nell's decision and turns to her assembled troops, lifting her chin. "You heard Her Grace. Let's take His Grace down and put Lady Rose back in her rightful place. Steady hands, gentlemen, and let the chickens fall where they may."

Three men on ladders ease Aleric's portrait off the wall with a great deal of shuffling, balancing, and grunting.

Henry leans close to Nell. "I think we're outnumbered," he says in a low voice. "Ready to trade artwork for buried treasure?"

Nell nods. "Let's go finish what we started." She bends to smooth the fur on Roger's head again and gets a sleepy tail-thump in reply. She looks at Henry and whispers, "He's letting me pet him. Can you believe?"

Henry and a beaming Nell slip out to get sandwiches and coffee, as Rose's portrait finds its way home at last.

23

Buried Treasure

HENRY

HENRY PLANTS HIS BOOTS in the turf, shovel biting into the stubborn earth. The day has warmed, so he peels off his coat and tosses it onto the grass. Nell watches from the Range Rover, feet swinging, probably narrating the moment in her head as if the BBC film crew were already on standby.

He looks back at her and wipes his brow. "Are you sure this is exactly where we left off, Nell?"

She checks the photos on her phone, then swipes to the map pin she dropped. "Yes, sir. You were exactly there, flexing all that public-school muscle to show me how a real dig should look."

He sets the shovel, works the soil methodically. "You can critique my form, Princess Nell, but we need to find this thing soon. The entire village has probably heard about it by now." He leans over, takes a drink from his water bottle, and sets it on his jacket. "We'll have Oxford-educated fortune hunters with drone apps, and fashionistas with TikTok channels out here prospecting by tonight. Private property or not."

Nell hops down. "Philippe could credibly smuggle millions in gems, jewelry, and coins hidden in glazed pottery food jars," Nell says. "If they were sealed with wax, they likely would not have been checked crossing the border. He might have been hired as a tutor before he even left France, so he'd already be considered a member of the Duke's household."

"Let's see what old Philippe left us," Henry says, as his shovel turns up something heavy, flat, and grimy with age. He bends and lifts it free. It's a round sundial plate, antique French, with the gnomon pointer still attached.

"A sundial." He squats and brushes it off with his gloved hand. "I thought it would be Napoleon's lost hoard; instead, we find ancient garden furniture." He looks up at Nell. "Totally on-brand for this family."

Nell leans in, squinting. "What's that on the edge?" She reads aloud, "*Cherchez l'ombre à la neuvième heure*...Seek the shadow at the ninth hour."

Henry says, "There's a ship etched just above the numbers." Then his eyes narrow, appreciative despite himself. "That's not just any ship. Look at the burgee. That's L'Orient, the flagship that carried Napoleon's treasure."

Nell kneels beside him, her mind racing. "Of course. Henry, L'Orient isn't just the name of a ship. In French, it's *the east,* and the root for *to orient.* You know—to find your direction."

Henry is already piecing it together. "So either Philippe had an uproarious sense of humor, or this is a treasure map." He looks at Nell. "Of sorts."

"Yes," Nell says, "the oak tree was the mast of L'Orient, and this sundial is supposed to guide us like a compass. We use the shadow at the ninth hour to orient ourselves."

"But why nine o'clock?" Henry wonders aloud. "Or are we supposed to dig at night with a lantern and cocktails?"

Nell wrinkles her nose, gears turning. "It's not nine p.m.—it's the ninth hour."

"Roman style," Henry says. "Sundials divide the daylight into twelve hours, starting at six a.m., so the ninth hour is about three in the afternoon."

Nell grabs his wrist to check his watch. "Henry, what time is it?"

"Quarter to three. Clever," Henry says. "He hid treasure from a ship named L'Orient, and then buried the directions to it with a sundial."

"A very French solution." Nell smiles, enchanted. "Both practical and poetic." She plants the sundial at the oak's absent roots, lining up the ship with east on Henry's phone compass.

"You have an excellent stabilising influence, Henry," Nell says. "If you hadn't made up your mind about how straightforward this dig would be, I wouldn't have felt so strongly that the universe was boring me on purpose."

"That is not," he says, "how causation usually functions."

"Maybe not for you," Nell says. "For me, it's all perfectly logical."

He takes a breath. "So. Instead of excavating treasure in the most obvious patch of ground on the estate, the place every clue has pointed to, we are going to stand where the old oak was and follow the line of sight of a sundial to the Tor, and then climb down to some perilous ledge and start poking at geology."

"Yes," Nell says brightly. "Now you're getting into the spirit of the thing."

"And at no point might we simply assume the treasure was lost in a landslide and go home," Henry says.

"Certainly not. We've already nearly been shot. We might as well commit to the bit."

"So when Thomas wrote to his father that he found the treasure Philippe buried near the old oak but had not recovered it yet," Henry says slowly, "what he meant was: I have found the spot the sundial points to, but I haven't had an opportunity to the dig portions of the cliff out from underneath the seagulls."

Nell nods.

Henry gives her a long, assessing look. "Very well. We shall proceed with your sundial-as-arrow hypothesis."

They stand and watch as the sun casts a shadow on the dial, pointing like a dark sword straight to Black Tor.

Nell looks thoughtful. "Maybe when L'Orient sank, what Napoleon needed most wasn't gold, but proper direction."

Henry nods. "Napoleon could have been a powerful champion of democracy if he had used his power for good instead of just gaining more power. That's always the problem with wanting to be emperor."

***

The sky is growing dark, and Henry can see the first drops of rain on the windscreen when they park at the base of Black Tor. Not far from the old folly, the rocks rear up dark and indifferent, and the windswept cliff falls away in tiers.

Henry unloads the shovel and the metal detector, then on second thought also grabs a coil of rope, which feels, to his mind, like tempting fate.

"Cheer up," Nell says. "We're simply retrieving misfiled household assets."

"From a cliff," he replies. "In a storm."

"History doesn't keep office hours, Henry."

They reach the same bluff where Rose fell. Far out, the horizon hunkers under clouds, a wide, uneven line that blurs into silver as the sun drops behind it. Gulls skate the updrafts, cutting arcs above the spray. The sweep from the headland takes in all the changes of color: the slate-black rock, the blue-green swells.

The wind is picking up, and Nell eyes the ground with a more practical wariness than usual. She kneels at a shallow hollow in line with the compass azimuth Henry shot from the sundial.

Henry tests the soil a pace back from the crumbling edge. "If one were inclined to bury contraband on this headland, one might choose a spot marginally less suicidal."

"Oh, that's what you would do," Nell says. "You with your sensible shoes and your 'desire to see tomorrow.' But Philippe had flair."

"Philippe is probably smirking about this in the afterlife." Henry says.

They begin to dig in a safer arc, away from the sheer drop. The earth is stubborn and stony, and Nell's romantic notions about treasure hunting evaporate somewhere around the first blister.

"This is much less atmospheric than novels suggest," she pants.

"In novels," Henry says, levering out a rock, "there is usually an under-gardener to do the actual digging."

"Fine. In the next book, I shall acquire one. For now, you're promoted."

"Delighted," he says dryly. "Does the promotion come with hazard pay?"

"It comes with character development."

They strike something hard and hollow.

Henry freezes. "That," he says, "was not a rock."

Between them, they scrape away more earth until a rounded ceramic shoulder emerges: thick, pale stoneware with a crude, dark loop handle. Then another. And another. Four in all, packed close like conspirators.

Nell sits back on her heels, eyes shining. "Oh. Oh, Philippe, you drama queen."

Henry works one jar loose. It's heavy, deathly cold even through his gloves. The wax seal around the lid flakes under his thumb.

"You realise," he says, "that it's at this point in a cautionary tale that something terrible happens."

"Yes, well, I'm editing this one." She nods at the lid. "Go on. Before I expire from curiosity."

He pries it open. "Moment of truth. Marmalade or gold coins?"

"Gold coins. Got to be."

Henry tips the jar, and a cascade of gold sovereigns and Napoleons pours into his hand.

Nell whistles. "That'll buy us some jam and jelly."

The second jar's seal breaks with a pop. Again, gold coins tumble over Henry's palm, some stamped with years, others so polished they gleam.

"I'm seeing a pattern here." Nell says.

He hefts the coins. "I could get used to this."

She pries open the third jar. Inside, cut gems shimmer even in the stormy afternoon, a riot of color: ruby, sapphire, emerald, diamond. She digs out a velvet pouch, tips it, and a flash of blue fire bursts into her palm.

Henry cracks the last jar. Inside, assorted jewelry: chains, rings, a string of large pearls, and a brooch shaped like a fleur-de-lis, tangle together in a nest of faded cloth.

Nell reaches for an emerald brooch, triumph and wonder mixing in her eyes. "This is...Henry, this is real."

Henry just grins, coins running through his fingers, treasure that waited so long to be found. "This is what all the fuss has been about."

"Hello, Regency money laundering." Nell says.

"So Philippe did it," Nell says softly. "Proper Napoleonic treasure. Smuggled, buried. Thomas disinherited by accident. Poor Thomas. Poor Rose."

Henry replaces the lids carefully. "There will be authorities to notify. Legalities. Experts."

"Yes, yes," she says, impatient. "Museums, historians, smug academics. They can all have their share. But the estate will get a reward. A nice, plump one."

She rocks back on her heels, considering the jars with the air of someone mentally filing them under "miscellaneous windfall."

"I," she announces, "am going to buy a horse."

Henry, who had been quietly calculating tax implications, blinks. "A horse...farm?"

"No." She looks offended by the very idea. "Just one. A horse. Singular. And one for you, too."

"For me."

"Of course. I refuse to ride about the countryside alone. It would look tragic. We'll match. What color do you want?"

He opens his mouth, closes it again. "Is there," he ventures, "a color that communicates profound reluctance?"

"We'll start you with something reassuring and brown," she decides. "You can work your way up to dashing and grey once you've accepted your fate."

He eyes the jars. "One assumes we are not paying the farrier in coin out of this directly."

"Oh, we'll be perfectly ethical," she says. "After the paperwork. And the press conference. And the bit where I stand heroically in front of Black Tor looking windswept and clever."

"Very ethical," he agrees.

She falls silent, studying the horizon. The sea is a flat stretch of pewter.

"Also," she says, in the same tone she might use to mention she's low on tea bags, "I've decided I'm not going to let Leclair get away with stealing my desk."

Henry has learned by now that in Nell's universe conversational gear changes do not require a clutch. "Philippe's desk?"

"If he thinks he can gaslight me with bubble wrap and fake invoices. He is mistaken."

Henry considers the list of things he expected to discuss while standing on a perilous cliff over a hoard of Napoleonic contraband. "And the horse will assist in this...desk reclamation?"

"No," she says. "The horse is for fun. The desk is for justice." She turns to him, eyes bright. "I want you to teach me how to do a stakeout."

He just looks at her for a moment, shovel in one hand, his coat dripping rain and sea spray, several million pounds' worth of history at his feet.

"A stakeout," he repeats.

"Yes. You know." She adopts what she clearly believes is a hardened-cop voice. "'We wait. We watch. We drink terrible coffee in a badly parked car and take notes.'"

"Is this because you have been bingeing late-night crime dramas again?"

"Possibly. But that's not the point. The point is, he took my desk. I want it back."

"You wish," Henry says slowly, "to surveil a man over furniture."

"Not just any piece of furniture." She points a dirt-smudged finger at him. "My precious furniture. Philippe's furniture. Napoleon's furniture."

He softens, just a fraction. "And you imagine a stakeout is a...transferable skill from valeting."

"You know logistics," she says. "You know how to be invisible. You own at least three coats that say 'nothing to see here, officer.' Who better to teach me?"

He sighs. "Stakeouts are not inherently compatible with my current job description."

"Neither was treasure hunting," she logically points out. "And yet here we are, accessorized with antique crime."

She leans closer, muddy and determined. "Teach me how to wait in the shadows and watch for an opening. Teach me how not to fall asleep in a car. Teach me how to look boring enough that no one notices me while I'm being wildly interesting."

Henry glances down at the jars, then back at her. "At the very least," he says, "one might instruct you in how not to get arrested."

"Splendid. Lesson one: buy neutral-coloured clothing?"

"Lesson one," he corrects, "is that we remove several kilograms of historically explosive pottery from this cliff without tumbling to our deaths. Stakeout training will begin once you demonstrate basic compliance with the laws of gravity."

She beams at him. "So that's a yes."

"That," he says, lifting one of the jars with a grunt, "is a conditional yes."

"Conditional on what?"

"On you not attempting to conduct your first surveillance operation on horseback."

She considers this, then nods. "Fine. I'll save that for the sequel."

"Of the adventure?" he asks, "or the novel?"

"Both," she says, and bends to help him carry their illicit, perfectly legal future toward home.

24

Three Years Notice

HENRY

AFTER LOADING THE TREASURE into the car, Nell and Henry walk back to mark the excavation site with a map pin. The cliff lifts out of the land abrupt and sheer, shaped by centuries of wind, waves, and rain. At the edge, lichen-covered stone shoulders out over dark water. Below, indigo waves fold in from the Channel, shuddering white against the rocks before sliding back.

Nell turns to Henry. "What do you think happened here that night? Why was the locket on the ground at the folly? Was Rose's fiancé there when she died? Was Thomas?"

Henry looks down at the rocks far below, then out to sea. "If they carried her back together, it seems so," Henry says.

The wind punches across the cliff, blowing Nell's hair into a semaphore of bad decisions while Henry tries, with limited success, to keep her from backing straight into legend.

They're talking about something entirely unromantic—insurance, of all things.

"So if I fall off the cliff," she says, squinting at the drop, "does the policy pay out in a lump sum, or do they dribble it to my heirs in installments like a Victorian serial?"

"I am endeavoring," Henry says, "to ensure that we never find out."

"Yes, yes," Nell waves a hand. "You and your tedious commitment to my continued existence."

The sea roars in the moonlight. Watching the dark water, she says almost absently:

"Henry, will you marry me?"

He goes very still. "Uh...tonight?"

She snorts, "No, silly. In three years."

He blinks, the wind tugging at his coat as he recalibrates both his evening and his life. "May one ask—purely from curiosity—why three?"

"Because," she says, as if explaining something obvious to a particularly handsome but slow child, "I want to get to know you better."

He studies her for a long moment, this woman who treats marriage proposals like footnotes and cliff edges like mildly interesting rugs.

"We have," he notes, "been practically inseparable for weeks."

"Yes, but that's just proximity," she says. "I require data. I need to see how you behave under a range of conditions. Christmas. Flu. My book deadlines. At least one electrical emergency. If after three years of controlled observation I still want to kiss you more than throttle you, then we'll marry. It's very scientific."

"A longitudinal study," he says.

"Exactly." She brightens. "You're terribly clever. This bodes well for the marriage sample."

He exhales something that might be a laugh, might be a prayer. "And...if in the interim I should wish to clarify my own position on this proposed...timetable?"

"You may submit comments in writing," she says. "Or at tea. I'm flexible."

He looks at her, at the cliff, then back at her. "Very well, Your Grace. In that case, consider this my formal notice of intent."

"To survive the next three years?" she teases.

"To give you," he says, "every possible reason to renew the contract."

She rolls her eyes, which does absolutely nothing to disguise the way her hand finds his. "Oh, don't be charming about it. That'll skew the results."

"Perish the thought," he says, and does not let go.

25

Fearless

HENRY

THE RANGE ROVER RATTLES across the moor in the moonlight toward Ainsworth, loaded with its precious cargo.

"I don't know what to do next," Nell says. "Do you?" She's holding up a gold coin and wiping dirt away with her thumb.

"We have treasure, genuine treasure, right here," Henry says. "The next step? We need to declare it."

Nell raises an eyebrow. "How do we declare it?"

"The British government has strict rules," Henry says. "Anything found on private land, especially something this old, has to be reported. We'll need to notify the local coroner. They'll oversee an inquest to determine if it qualifies as treasure."

"That sounds... formal," Nell says.

"It is," Henry nods. "The hoard will be valued, and if it's declared treasure, they can claim it for the Crown. The finder and landowner usually get a reward, but no one gets to keep it outright without permission. We have to follow procedure or risk the whole lot being seized."

"Henry, let's say Philippe was the spy," Nell says. "He took a position in the house of a high-ranking British officer, and buried L'Orient's treasure on the property."

"Okay. I'm with you," Henry says. "If that Légion d'honneur medal was Philippe's, we can assume he was a decorated and trusted officer of Napoleon. Maybe he was heroic at the Battle of the Nile."

"He may be the one who saved the treasure from sinking in L'Orient. That would be a big deal," Nell says. "So Napoleon awards him a medal and gifts him his personal desk in gratitude, and sends him here to use the treasure to pay spies and smugglers on the Cornish coast."

"And Philippe had to leave in a hurry before Waterloo, without taking his desk or the treasure back to France with him," Henry fills in.

"Still, Aleric may have been a part of it, Henry. Philippe had the British battle plans in his possession after all. You said yourself those would not, and should not, ever have left headquarters." Nell looks crestfallen.

"I'm sorry, Nell. That is a possibility," Henry says softly. "If the government believes Aleric was collaborating with a French spy, it could complicate your reward for finding the treasure. With no clear living owner, the government may choose to keep all of it."

Nell nudges a strand of hair behind her ear. "You said the local coroner will come for an inquest?"

"Right," Henry says. "The coroner decides if it's treasure under the law. If yes, the state can claim it, but you'll likely get a substantial reward as finder and landowner, unless Parliament gets ambitious."

She repacks the jewellery she had been inspecting. "Suppose France sends someone to demand it back?"

Henry shakes his head. "They'd have to prove ownership through the courts, and no judge hands back treasure without iron-clad proof."

"For example?"

"An original manifest. A letter from Napoleon." He looks over at her. "A receipt written in blood. That kind of thing."

Nell pokes at the coins. "So... everything depends on the paper-work. That, and proving Aleric wasn't a spy."

"Paperwork and patience," Henry says. "It's a different kind of battle."

She smiles, not quite trusting the fortune but trusting Henry completely.

"Have you ever noticed," Nell says, "that the only people who follow laws are the ones who'd probably act decently anyway? The criminals—for whom the laws are written—couldn't care less."

"You mean criminals, by definition, are people who don't follow laws?" Henry chuckles. "Welcome to my world. Knowing someone's guilty isn't enough. The prosecution has to prove it with evidence. But that's as it should be, Nell. In a civilized country, we'd rather let a few guilty go free than see innocent people jailed."

She looks at him sideways. "What happens now to Edgar? Is he really done for?"

Henry's jaw tightens. "He'll be charged with possession of a firearm with intent to endanger life. Illegal discharge of a firearm. Reckless endangerment. Maybe attempted grievous bodily harm with intent, if the Crown thinks they have evidence. He'll probably get twelve years, out in six or eight if he behaves."

Nell shakes her head. "But Leclair waltzes off and keeps my desk? He set all of this in motion, used Edgar, threatened me with blackmail—and for what?"

Henry sighs, watching the road. "Leclair is clever. We have no confession, no witness tying him directly to the threats, no hard proof of a crime. The letter from Thomas to Philippe is history, not evidence. Unless law enforcement has something concrete on him, they can't hold him. He'll slip through the net."

Nell lets silence fill the car. "So he gets away with everything. All those years, my desk, the threats, the lies, and nothing sticks."

Henry keeps his voice even. "It's maddening, Nell. But the law's the law. Hunches and old papers won't make a case."

She crosses her arms, determination sharpening her tone. "You know I'm not going to let him keep that desk."

Henry glances over. "Just remember, Your Grace, breaking and entering is still illegal."

Nell grins. "So noted."

***

Footsteps have faded, doors are locked for the night, and Roger's snoring drifts into the Ballroom from the Great Hall. The stillness throughout the house tonight is almost unprecedented in a place the size of Ainsworth. The only reason for it this evening is that Nell insisted the staff retire early. It has been a stressful two days for everyone.

She pours a cup of hot chocolate and curls into the corner of the sofa in front of the fireplace, admiring the beautiful young woman in the newly hung portrait. Rose, eyes soft as dusk, is holding court again where she belongs. Henry sets his cup on the nearby side table and settles beside Nell with the newspaper, feeling more at ease than he has in weeks.

Nell traces the shape of Rose's sash with her eyes. "It's odd, isn't it—loving what you shouldn't? I suppose Rose would have made a perfect Whitby. Everyone in her family must have thought so. After all, the marriage would have infused the dynasty with a fresh source of money. But she wanted Thomas, and all it brought her was heartbreak."

"Choices are easy when you know you'll have no regrets. It's the uncertainty that gets you. Love's risky," Henry looks up at the painting. "Do you think Rose made a mistake following her heart?"

Nell tilts her head. "She loved a man her family and society didn't approve of for her. But that doesn't make it a mistake."

"You're a romance author," Henry says. "I read that it's one of the best-selling genres in fiction, and highest-grossing in film. Why do you suppose people love romance as much as they do?"

Nell smiles. "Easy. Because in life, we all wish we could be fearless. Love is as close to fearless as we'll ever get."

"That's why the world loves love stories?" Henry says.

Nell takes a sip of her cocoa. "Not only romantic love. Any love. The love of a dream, of a friend, of a child. Love for an animal, nature, humankind, even love for oneself. We crave stories that show us the heart and soul of love—its true nature: generous, open, forgiving."

"Fearless," Henry says.

Nell nods. "The opposite of love isn't hate; it's fear. Love is accepting that life comes with risks. Love demands we step out of our comfort zone. It pushes us to be bigger and braver than we think we can be."

Henry looks at her and smiles. "Like carrying a hundred-pound dog across the moor."

Nell glances toward the Great Hall, where Roger lies sprawled. "Like what Roger did for me. His love turned out to be bigger than his fear."

Henry leans over and plucks a biscuit from a cut-crystal biscuit barrel on the table, breaking it in two. He passes half to Nell, crumbs catching on the cuff of his shirt.

Nell tucks her feet under, watching Henry stretch his long legs toward the fire. "I don't think he wanted to go out there. I suppose he thought I'd lost my mind and someone had better look after me," she says. "Turns out he was right."

Henry tosses his biscuit half into his mouth, brushing his hands on his trousers. He looks at Nell, warmth settling into the corners of his eyes. "Wherever you are is home now to Roger."

He leans back, arm stretched across the back of the sofa. "I could go back to London and mindlessly solve other people's problems. But you don't leave someone behind after you've learned what home actually feels like."

Nell glances down at her cup, running her finger along the rim, then sets it aside and stretches out her hand, catching Henry's fingers.

"Men have told me I'm a handful, that I'm a pain, that I'm high-maintenance. I've heard I'm difficult. Unpredictable." She laughs, eyebrows lifted. "Let's see...crazy. Beautiful once in a while." She turns to meet his eyes. "But you—you're the only person in my whole life who's ever told me I feel like home."

He lifts her hand and presses his lips to her knuckles. A blonde tendril slips forward, and she brushes it away.

Henry leans in. Their lips meet tentatively at first. She sighs, leaning closer to him. Henry closes his eyes, surprised to find the truth he hadn't known he'd been waiting for.

26

Stakeout 101

NELL

I T IS A TRUTH universally ignored that the best stakeouts involve neither glory nor biscuits.

Nell, notebook in hand and a multi-pack of Oreos, a party-size bag of M&M's, and a half-dozen of Mrs. Patterson's jam biscuits crammed into her coat pockets, sits beside Henry in the chilly gloom of a rainy night in the village. Roger has come along in the back seat in order to be with them, or possibly just to get the cone off his head.

Henry consults the digital clock. "Lesson one: Patience."

Nell grins, her enthusiasm undampened by the cold or the fact that the car is fogging up from the inside. "Is there a theory component, or do I get to leap straight to the part where we chase criminals through moonlit alleys and communicate entirely in acronyms?"

Henry raises a brow. "If possible, avoid chasing anyone. And acronyms should, ideally, relate to some sort of operational purpose."

She flips to a new page in her notebook. "Got it. I've come prepared. If anyone suspicious approaches, I'll initiate LOOPIMO."

He glances over. "LOOPIMO?"

"Yes," she beams. "It's code for Looking at a Possibly Illicit Moving Object."

Henry purses his lips. "Right. And if something genuinely illegal occurs?"

She scribbles furiously. "PICSUIT: Potential Incident Criminal Sighting Under Intense Tension."

He stares. "That's quite a mouthful."

She shrugs. "I figure if actual police can have SITREP and RV point and BLOCS, we can improvise. Plus, it sounds terribly professional."

He reviews her sprawling code list. "And BARKICOMP?"

"That means Roger has started barking and the op is compromised."

Henry sighs, half fond, half resigned. "Very well. And if I need you to stop talking?"

"Simple," Nell flourishes her pen. "You initiate SILENCEN: Subject Instigates Low-Energy Communication Emergency Needed Cease Talking."

"I suspect the government will want to trademark that one," Henry remarks.

She grins, undaunted. "No worries, I'll gift it to MI5 in the acknowledgments."

The stakeout proceeds. Roger briefly interrupts with a squeak toy he finds on the seat, which Nell dubs a SQUEAKINT. Nell insists on whispering updates of every sighting and movement in acronymese, while Henry quietly logs real details and occasionally slips in his own dry commentary.

"Initiate Protocol Yawn," he murmurs once, when absolutely nothing is happening.

At one point, a pizza delivery car turns down the lane. Nell tenses and stage-whispers, "Subject appears. LOOPIMO IRL."

Henry replies, barely audible, "SITREP, no threat detected."

"Henry, you're supposed to say LOOPIMO. Keep up."

"Forgive me, madam," Henry says, "OPERATION CONTIN-UED RESTRAINT IN THE FACE OF NONSENSE. OCRFN."

She snorts, scribbling it in her notebook. "You're secretly enjoying this."

"On the contrary," he replies, "I am considering establishing an acronym solely for enduring this conversation."

She looks at him, eyes bright, and for a moment it's obvious that despite the staged seriousness and the tissue of invented codes, this is exactly where she wants to be. "Henry, Operation Partnership Activated. OPA. We're excellent at this."

He glances at her, then at Roger. "Yes, we rather are."

The world outside their windscreen is dim and slightly drizzly, the kind of English weather that exists purely to make law-abiding people long for a thermos and an alibi.

Nell surveys their "command vehicle," which Henry maintains is perfectly inconspicuous.

She has filled three pages with possible OPs.

Henry, not to be outdone in dry resistance, begins responding solely in acronyms.

OPPA, is Operation Polite Passive Aggression, enacted after the third Oreo lands in his lap, and STATCAT: Catastrophic Crumbs Accumulating Throughout. He coins DOGLINT: Dog Leap Instigating Notable Turbulence, when Roger attempts to leap into the front seat.

Nell, undaunted, adds new scenarios by the minute. When the pizza delivery goes to the wrong house, she whispers, "DIVERPEX: Delivery Intercepted, Van Evidently Re-Routed. Pepperoni eXtravaganza."

Henry says, "DELCOM: Deliverer Encountered Laughably Clueless, Outcome Cold Pizza."

As midnight pushes the boundaries of sanity, they conduct an impromptu AAR, known to professionals as an After Action Review:

What went well? OPERATION BISCUIT TIN kept Roger from eating the stakeout snacks.

What needs work? MISSION SILECEN failed, as Nell could not stop giggling at Henry's deadpan.

Lessons Learned: "Perhaps next time," Henry suggests, "we establish a protocol for JAMMYSPLAT: Jammy Snacks Prone to Landing Against Trousers."

Just as Nell is scrawling this in her notes, a shadow falls across the lot. Both freeze. Now, every invented code snaps into real use.

Nell's whispers, "LOOPIMO is live! VISCON: Visual Contact On Nefariousness."

They hunker lower, and Nell tries not to drop Mrs. Patterson's jam biscuits on the floor. The suspicious figure turns out to be a teen on a midnight snack run. Tension ebbs, replaced by helpless laughter as Nell, still adrenaline-high, insists, "That was excellent! I feel ready for MI5."

Henry softens, watching her glow in the dark.

"OPCON: Optimally Perfect Companion, Ongoing Nonsense," he offers quietly.

She rests her head on his shoulder, smothering a smile, and Operation Stakeout concludes with Roger snoring, Henry quietly content, and Nell sure of two things: she'll never be bored again, and no acronym in the world will ever truly cover how good this feels.

27

Scholarly Intent

HENRY

ENRY WAKES BEFORE DAWN, showers quickly, and dresses on instinct: dark jeans that sit neatly on his hips, a crisp blue-and-white-striped button-down, a navy blazer that skims his shoulders just right, and well-polished penny loafers. He checks his reflection, aiming for casual but scholarly, and decides he looks close enough to both. The routine suits him; three or four runs a week and weights on the alternate days have left his shirts a little tighter across the shoulders than they used to be. Today's workout was cut short only because he is determined to get to London early to see Dr. Penhaligon.

Most days, as a member of staff at Ainsworth, he blends in with everyone else in khakis and a polo or a button-down and blazer. The Ainsworth family gym on the third floor of the West Wing, converted from several bedrooms, is where he usually starts or ends his day. There is also a larger gym by the pool house in the south garden that all staff can use. Daily workouts and an active life around the estate have honed him into something even sharper than he was in his MI5 days, though he prefers to think of it simply as "keeping up."

On the bed, the new Holland & Holland briefcase Nell gave him waits, the leather smooth and stiff at the seams. He opens it and packs maps, files, and his notebook, each disappearing into its place as if the bag had been designed just for his kind of orderliness. When he's finished, he clips the shoulder strap into place and swings it over one shoulder, testing the weight; it settles against his side with an easy, familiar pull that feels just right.

Downstairs, the house is suspended between night and day. The Great Hall is chilly, a shaft of early grey light spilling across the staircase balustrade. As he passes, he's pleased to note that Roger has graduated from spending nights under the Hall sideboard to sleeping contentedly in Nell's room.

The scent of yesterday's ashes drifts from the Ballroom. Mrs. Patterson moves briskly from room to room, throwing open shutters and curtains.

"Good morning, Mrs. Patterson."

"Good morning, sir."

Henry turns right at the bottom of the stairs, passing a junior footman.

"Good morning, sir."

Damn. Is it Michael? Yes, that's it. "Good morning, Michael," Henry says, and moves through the warren of hallways, then down to the kitchen.

Nigel whistles tunelessly at the range.

"Good morning, Chef."

"Morning, sir. Coffee?"

"Yes, please. Thank you. Have a good day."

"You too, sir."

He cuts through servants' passages on the ground floor and grabs a peppermint from a silver bowl in the Boot Room—slightly stale and probably meant for horses; he thinks. Slipping through the Boot

Room door, Henry crosses to the carriage court. Outside, his breath lifts visibly in the violet-edged predawn. The pea gravel shifts under his feet as he unlocks his old car. He glances back at the house, glimpsing staff moving through windows blooming with the first lights.

He is already halfway up the drive, the world liminal and undisturbed, before the sky finishes its slow turn from starless black to a thin, early blue.

At the end of the lane, he thumbs out a text to Nell just in case she's up early:

Heading to London. Found something last night. Think I can clear Aleric's name. Will call you after.

He slips his phone into his blazer, checks his satchel again, his hands nearly trembling with anticipation. He feels less like he's off to see a scholar than running a race with history itself.

Traffic on the M40 is mercifully thin. As streetlights give way to the pale wash of morning, Henry grips the wheel tighter, already rehearsing what he'll say about the error that will overturn a century's worth of suspicion.

***

Penhaligon's office is one of those academic strongholds that time has left behind. The paneled walls bear shelves crammed with leather-bound volumes and heavy military atlases, their gold-embossed spines faded by years of sunlight streaming through narrow, diamond-paned windows. Framed campaign maps wage silent battles in muted colors. The air is tinged with tea, dust, and old paper. On Penhaligon's desk, a large, abused walnut affair, stand a stack of correspondence, a half-eaten scone and various inkwells beside a vase stuffed with regimental ribbons. Henry takes it in, remembering his own time beneath similar ceiling beams, and wonders how rooms at Oxford all manage to achieve this kind of distinctive scholarly disarray.

Experts who study Wellington's headquarters, particularly his intelligence officers, believe that its reputation was built on quicksand. Some dispatches never made it; entire orders went astray. There were rumors even then, whispered but persistent, that certain staff officers concealed more than troop positions. The Dutch-Belgians openly questioned loyalty within the English ranks, especially anyone whose actions seemed too independent. Henry knows from his own research that Penhaligon is not out of line in his suspicion of Aleric Ainsworth.

"Thank you for taking the meeting," Henry says as Penhaligon enters and gestures him to a chair.

"Not at all, Templeton. I live for interruptions from the outside world. What can I do for you?"

Henry places the folder on the desk. "We found these buried in the rose garden at Ainsworth," he says, and lays out the maps and the Legion of Honor, with its bold scarlet sash. "When I first saw them, I thought these plans must have been Wellington's own. To be honest, I had the same concerns you raised about Aleric's allegiance. But since then, we've discovered Philippe Moreau, the family's French tutor, was actually the spy in the house."

Penhaligon steeples his fingers, regarding the vellum skeptically. "If these plans really left Wellington's headquarters in the hands of Aleric Ainsworth, Mr. Templeton, well, it's damning."

Henry unrolls the maps, smoothing the edges. "I don't think they're what you think. When I took time to study them, I noticed the maps are wrong: the order of battle, the troop positions.

Mont-Saint-Jean is off. La Haye Sainte is drawn exposed, not shielded by hedgerows."

Penhaligon stands, fingers moving over the lines. The frown on his brow deepens. "I see...Yes, that's not right. The British center isn't exposed—they're prepared for defense."

Henry traces a road. "Wellington stationed his troops behind the ridge near Mont-Saint-Jean, but these plans show the wrong position of La Haye Sainte. There's a bend in the road that doesn't exist."

Penhaligon leans even closer, glasses slipping down his nose. "Look here. Bijlandt's brigade is marked as attacking the French Grand Battery, but they were behind the ridge until mid-afternoon." He taps a penciled arrow. "This entire position is incorrect."

Henry's eyes sharpen. "You're right. And here, where La Haye Sainte is marked on open ground? The farm is actually shielded by hedgerows and sandpits. If Napoleon's generals thought this map was accurate, they would aim artillery at the wrong spot—just exactly like they did that day."

Penhaligon studies the plan, then shakes his head, almost admiring. "And these troop arrows are incorrect. Wellington's center was reinforced, not pulled back. The maps make it look exposed, when in fact, it was prepared for defense." He looks up, amazement in his voice. "These plans pointed the French straight into mud and confusion. If Aleric leaked these, he helped turn the battle for the British."

Henry feels tension leave his shoulders. "Aleric had to have known that as a member of Wellington's staff, he'd be a prime target for espionage." Henry meets his eyes. "Wellington and Aleric suspected Philippe Moreau was a spy and fed him expertly doctored plans. Everything here is just wrong enough."

Penhaligon sits back, and for the first time, smiles. "The fox outfoxes everyone. Including Napoleon."

"Wellington knew that, of course. That's why Aleric was so lavishly decorated for his service. He helped Wellington win the Battle of Waterloo."

They sit in silence, the full sweep of it settling between them. Finally, Penhaligon shifts tack, the professional reasserting himself. "And your interest in this Templeton? Strictly professional loyalty?"

Henry thinks of Nell, of her shoulders squared against the weight of her ancestor's reputation. "Partly," he says. "And partly because the ninth Duchess of Belward intends to write the third Duke of Belward as a tragic romantic hero. It would be helpful if the official version doesn't brand him a scoundrel while she's busy monetizing his cheekbones."

Penhaligon's mouth twitches in a rare show of amusement. "The novelist, then?"

"The heiress," Henry corrects, with a half-smile. "The novelizing is a symptom."

Henry stands, steady and quietly triumphant. "It's time you set the history straight. Dr. Penhaligon. Waterloo was won, in part, because someone Wellington deeply trusted supplied the enemy with the story he wanted them to believe."

Penhaligon studies Henry, then the plans, respect, possibility, and excitement kindling in his eyes. "Thank you, Mr. Templeton. That is indeed history worth writing. Counterintelligence. British strategy at its best."

Henry nods. "And it worked. Napoleon's decisions at Waterloo—his timing and his choices—all played into Wellington's hands."

Henry almost laughs. "There's more to the story as well. Philippe wasn't simply passing notes. He channeled fabled treasure from the wreck of L'Orient up the Cornish coast, running spies and smugglers under Ainsworth's nose, while also working as a French tutor. The gold he buried paid for an entire network."

Penhaligon exhales sharply, the historian wholly engaged. "And the Duchess plans to write this herself?"

"No," Henry replies, smiling. "We'd rather you did it. Your research, our evidence: maps, ciphered letters, medals. The Ainsworth library is yours to ransack, and Clairview Park's as well if Nell so much as asks."

Penhaligon softens, humbled. "It's the story I always hoped for: the truth, not just the headline. If you trust me, I'll see it through."

"One last thing. Philippe Moreau was a highly decorated soldier. A talented officer, honored by his country. Whatever side he served, he did so with the conviction of a loyal military officer."

Penhaligon nods. "I agree. I'll do him justice in the record as the professional officer he was. I won't turn him into a villain just because the victors write history."

Penhaligon almost smiles. "Tell the Duchess of Belward that being related to a non-spy does not entitle her to conduct her own operations."

Henry pauses at the door. "I assure you, she has no such intention."

He steps out into the afternoon. His confidence, as ever, just a step ahead of the universe's sense of irony.

28

Liberté

NELL

THAT AFTERNOON, NELL HAD scrolled past a cryptic social media post from Leclair announcing "Last Day." Then she noticed that Leclair's best pieces—her Biennais desk included—had been removed from his online inventory.

Nell can feel the universe nudging her to practice her stakeout skills.

"Do you want to come?" she asks Roger. "No is a perfectly acceptable answer."

Roger, after recent events, seems determined never to let her out of his sight again, and fixes her with a look of unwavering canine devotion.

"Stakeout it is, then. Partners in probable cause."

Nell unfolds the new collapsible dog ramp. "Easy does it, big guy. Mind those stitches."

Roger saunters up the ramp into the back seat. She stows the ramp and hands him a treat. "No heroics tonight, mister. We're staying low-profile and high-comfort."

Nell parks two streets away from Leclair's antique shop just before dark. The stakeout playlist for the evening loops true-crime podcasts and the occasional romantic ballad, covering all the emotional bases.

"So," she tells Roger, now curled, sans cone, in the back seat, "lesson one: we observe. Lesson two: we do not get out of the car. Lesson three: we do not commit any crimes without Henry present to do the paperwork."

Ten minutes later, Leclair appears.

He does not look like a villain. He looks like a normal man with a ponytail. An accountant, or someone who charges consulting fees. He directs the operation, clipboard in hand, while two men who do look like villains wrap furniture in blankets and haul boxes out of his shop and into unmarked white vans.

Then she sees it. The desk. Her desk. The French Biennais, all gleaming fruitwood and ormolu. It looks absurd strapped to a dolly, being trundled down the pavement like any old sideboard.

"Oh, absolutely not," she whispers.

Leclair locks the shop, glances down the street, and drives off with the desk in his van like a kidnap victim. His men get into another van and follow. Nell hesitates for exactly one responsible second. Then she starts the car.

"Lesson four: sometimes you have to break lesson three," she tells Roger.

She follows the vans through the village, trying to look inconspicuous, like anyone else who drives slightly too close while wearing binoculars around her neck. Nell tails them through three roundabouts and arrives shortly at a private storage facility on the outskirts of town. It's a plain white block with rows of corrugated metal doors. There is no signage, but plenty of security: surveillance cameras at every corner, and a keypad entry system demanding a code like a digital bouncer. The perimeter is lined with chain-link fencing and topped with aggressive spirals of concertina wire. It's the kind of place where people store things that are almost certainly not all legal.

"Uh-oh," Nell tells Roger. "This could be more Scooby-Doo than Nancy Drew."

Nell circles the facility once, scoping out exits and blind spots. Each time she passes a motion sensor, the floodlights blare on, giving her a warning and a slightly theatrical sense of being on stage. This has low-budget heist movie written all over it.

She snaps a few photos with her phone and watches as Leclair punches in an access code at the gate and rolls through. The gate closes immediately behind him. The trailing van, just seconds behind, is forced to stop and punch in a code of its own before being let in. So much for piggy-backing on someone else's code, Nell thinks. The odds look grim.

"This might be the shortest stakeout in history," she tells Roger.

The white vans park in front of Unit 36C. Leclair, looking impatient, checks his phone, then opens the rear doors of the first van, scanning the lot before wheeling out the contents—including her desk. Nell lifts her binoculars and jots down the license plate numbers. Roger, not needing binoculars, watches the proceedings with typical German Shepherd concern. Nell keeps the engine running and debates texting Henry that Operation BISCUIT: Backup Investigation, Surveillance, and Clandestine Intervention is officially underway.

Leclair and his henchmen unload the second van and lock the unit. His men depart, and Leclair stands outside just long enough to check his phone again and smirk at the door. Clearly, Nell supposes, congratulating himself for outwitting both sentimentality and inheritance law. Then he, too, is gone.

Nell edges up to the keypad. "Time for lateral thinking, partner," she says. "Any guesses?"

Roger stands and noses her ear in solidarity from the backseat.

"The obvious? Good idea." She nods, fingers flying. "*One, two,* then the unit number *thirty-six.*" The machine gives a polite beep. Denied.

"Nice try, buddy." She reaches around the seat and ruffles Roger's fur. "How about classic repetition?" She enters *3636*, repeating the unit. The keypad emits a slightly more peevish beep, warning her.

A tiny screen flashes: *One attempt remaining.*

Nell blows out a breath. "Okay. Let's use crossword logic."

Roger wags.

"Three plus three is six. Six plus six is twelve." She punches in *3612.*

There's a long pause, and she holds her breath.

Then the green light flickers to life. The lock clicks, and the gate shudders open.

Nell lets out a whoop and hands Roger a treat. "Roger, you are a genius. Celebratory snacks for the both of us!"

Nell pulls to a safe distance from 36C and waits. Ten minutes. Fifteen. Long enough to finish her coffee and make six increasingly unhinged notes in her stakeout notebook, including: *Subject displays unhealthy attachment to other people's furniture.* And, *Note: stakeouts are quite boring between moments of thrilling illegality. Next time, bring more snacks.*

When she's reasonably certain no one is coming back, she gets out of the car.

"Right," she says to Roger. "This is the part the workshop warned us about." Breaking and entering, beginner level.

***

The workshop had been called something cheerful, like *Everyday Lock-picking for the Anxious*, which she'd found in a forum thread about women who routinely lock themselves out of their flats. The instructor had been very clear about legality.

"This is for emergencies," he'd said in the video. "You may only use these skills on locks you own or have permission to open."

Nell, watching from the safety of Ainsworth's Wi-Fi, had thought: Future me will definitely find a way to plausibly interpret that.

Future her now stands in front of Unit 36C with a small kit of tension wrenches and picks tucked inside a floral cosmetics case.

"It's basically my lock," she mutters. "My desk is inside. This is like rescuing a hostage."

She glances at the nearest camera and tries to arrange her face into "harmless woman engaged in normal storage behavior" while her hands select the right pick. Her heart is hammering so loudly she can hardly hear the faint clicks, but muscle memory from hours of practice—she is nothing if not a determined student—kicks in.

"Turn, lift, gentle pressure..."

The shackle gives with a sharp, metallic clack that sounds to Nell like a trumpet fanfare.

"Oh my God," she breathes. "I am amazing. And also definitely going to hell."

She shoves the lock into her pocket and rolls up the door.

The unit smells of lavender. What is it with Leclair and lavender? Boxes are stacked against the walls. But in the center sits her desk.

Someone has flung a cheap plastic dust sheet over it, as though to disguise a museum piece as a garden chair.

"Hello, darling," she says.

She whips off the plastic, revealing the full glory of the Biennais: pearwood, bronze lion-head pulls, lines so elegant they make her sigh. It's no surprise he went straight for it at Ainsworth. She wonders if he even gave taking it a moment's thought.

"We are leaving," she informs it. "Right now."

Unfortunately, reality intrudes, as it often does. The desk is significantly heavier than her righteous fury. She manages to edge it onto the dolly; the desk leaning precariously left in the corner, swearing only a little as it threatens to crush her toes.

Roger trots anxiously at her heels, ears swiveling at every sound. In the time it takes to wrestle the desk to the threshold of the unit, Nell is sweating, covered in dust, and giddy with adrenaline.

Then she faces the next challenge: the lip between the concrete floor and the tarmac outside.

"Fine," she pants to Roger. "We drag."

She gets in front of the desk, braces her feet, and hauls. The desk lurches forward, wheels on the cart catching, metal shrieking. It is, she thinks, the single most undignified exit this piece of furniture has ever made, and it once survived a German bombing raid.

A sudden wash of white light floods the interior of the unit.

Roger's ears snap upright. Leclair. I'm about to be caught in flagrante by a man who will happily hand me over to the police for a desk he stole.

Nell dives sideways, dragging Roger and the escaping desk into the narrow strip of shadow by the door. Headlights crawl past, pause at a unit two rows over, then click off. A car door slams; someone coughs; metal rattles. Ordinary storage sounds. She swallows, laughs weakly, and tells both Roger and the desk, "Right, fine, we're on the clock. Hostage rescue continues."

Nell is halfway across the parking lot, leaving a heroic scrape mark behind her, when a man's voice cuts through the air.

Nell freezes. The desk continues its slow, inexorable slide for another four inches.

"Just checking—was furniture moving on your schedule this evening, or is this a spontaneous addition?" Henry approaches, hands in pockets, casually surveying the scene.

"Oh. Hi," Nell says weakly. "You're back early."

"So it would appear," he says. "May one ask what you are doing?"

"Rescuing my desk," she says. "From unlawful imprisonment."

He looks at the storage units, the padlock that has fallen out of her pocket and now rests on the asphalt by her right foot, the priceless French Empire desk that should be in a museum catalogue and is instead acquiring road rash, Roger, and finally the collapsible dog ramp lying neatly beside the car.

"And you elected," he says, "to do so via breaking and entering. Complete with an accessibility plan for your accomplice."

"It's not really breaking," Nell protests. "We opened it very gently."

"Nell."

"I watched an educational video," she says. "It was very clear about tension and listening to the pins. This was homework."

He closes his eyes for a moment, pinching the bridge of his nose. "Lock-picking workshops are not, in the eyes of the law, an exonerating factor."

She straightens, putting dusty hands on the desk like a politician at a podium. "He stole it first. This is repossession."

"You do not," Henry says, "get to unilaterally redefine burglary as 'emotional admin.'"

"But it's mine. And...it's French. And it belongs at Ainsworth, not mouldering in somebody's garage."

His gaze softens for a fraction of a second before the lawyer in his soul reasserts itself. "All of which I am certain can be argued in a civil court. Not, one would hope, from the defendant's table in a criminal one."

"I'm not leaving it," she says. "I've already started dragging. Emotionally, I'm committed."

He walks over and surveys the faint gouge across the tarmac. "So is the car park, apparently."

"I am being heroic," she says. "You're supposed to be impressed."

"Oh, Princess Eleanor," he murmurs, taking hold of the opposite end of the desk, "you have no idea how very impressed I am. That is, regrettably, not the relevant metric."

Together they maneuver the desk the last few feet, Nell panting, Henry maintaining enough dignity for them both. Roger trots behind, a large, hairy security detail.

As they reach the car, Henry says, "Out of scholarly interest, how did you imagine explaining this if the police arrived?"

"I was going to improvise," she says. "Something about chain of title and misappropriated chattels. I took notes when you were on the phone to the solicitor."

He stares. "You took notes."

"Of the good words," she says defensively. "You have excellent outrage vocabulary."

He exhales through his teeth, a sound that might be a laugh if it weren't so frayed. "We are going to have a conversation once this desk is inside, once you are not in handcuffs, about what constitutes an acceptable application of stakeout skills."

She brightens. "So, my stakeout worked, though. I found the lair, followed the target, confirmed the stash."

"And then," he says, "skipped directly to the evidence tampering part of the episode."

"Call it a pilot," she says. "We'll refine the later seasons."

He looks at her, dusty and flushed and grinning over the edge of a piece of furniture that, frankly, belongs in a museum. He thinks of Penhaligon warning him quite explicitly about this exact situation in more dignified terms.

"Get in the car," he says, resigned. "We will load this...absurdly valuable lawsuit magnet, and then we will leave before you give me a heart attack."

"As your future wife," Nell says cheerfully, opening the door for Roger and his ramp, "I consider that feedback actionable. Next time I'll text before I break in."

"There will not," Henry says, heaving the desk with a grunt, "be a next time."

"Of course not," she agrees. "Next time we'll bring you with us from the start."

He shuts the boot a little harder than strictly necessary.

29

Post-heist

HENRY AND NELL

THE DOOR TO NELL'S suite is ajar. Light spills in a golden strip across the hall.

Henry knocks.

"Come in," Nell calls. "Unless you are the police, in which case I have never seen that desk before in my life."

Henry steps inside. The Biennais is in its rightful place near the window, newly polished, its surface already spread with an untidy scatter of pages and notebooks. Nell sits cross-legged on the carpet in front of the fire, laptop open, hair loose, wearing one of his shirts, which she plucked from his wardrobe on the way past without consulting any known protocol.

What appears to be every book Nell owns is stacked in small, tottering towers around the sofa.

He folds his arms. "I see the Ainsworth library has...migrated."

Nell looks up over her reading glasses. "I'm working."

"On what, exactly? Structural testing? See how many hardbacks you can remove before the room collapses?"

She plucks up a nearby volume. "Plot research. Eighteenth-century duelling customs."

He checks the cover. It reads: *What Your Enneagram Type Says About Your Attachment Style.*

"Fascinating," he says. "Very pistols at dawn."

"That one's for dialogue," she says airily, reaching for another. "This is the duel book."

He turns that one over. *The Regency Gentleman's Guide to Dancing and Flirtation.*

Henry raises an eyebrow. "Deadly."

"You're mocking my process," she accuses.

"I'm not mocking," he says. "I'm compiling evidence. There is a serious mismatch between your shelving system and anything recognised by modern cataloguing standards."

She gestures at the piles. "There is a system. Fiction on the left, non-fiction on the right, and anything traumatising goes under the coffee table until I'm ready."

"I wasn't sure you'd be awake," he says.

"I have a book to finish," she replies. "And an accomplice to wait up for."

He tilts his head. "Accomplice?"

"You," she says simply, "sit."

He does, lowering himself beside her. The fire's heat licks his side; the line of her shoulder brushes his. On her laptop screen, he can see the end of a chapter: a line about a woman who jumped to the wrong conclusion and the right man catching her anyway.

"Did Penhaligon cooperate?" she asks.

"Wonderfully well," Henry says. "Aleric is no longer classified as a probable spy. The Ainsworth name is saved, and when his book comes out, you'll be more famous than you already are."

She smiles. "He'd thank you."

"All for you."

They are quiet for a moment, listening to the fire and the wind brushing the old glass.

"Did I ruin your life today?" Nell asks, not quite joking.

"Not entirely," he says. "You did, however, significantly complicate it."

"Good," she says. "You were in danger of becoming comfortable."

Henry turns to look at her. There is soot on her wrist, a healing scratch at her throat from brambles on the moor, ink smudged on the back of her hand from where she annotated as she typed. She is, he thinks, the most beautiful mess he has ever seen.

She catches him staring. "What?"

"Nothing," he says. "Merely cataloguing."

"Cataloguing what?"

"Reasons," he says.

"For what?"

"For why this was inevitable," he says, and leans in.

It is not their first kiss, but the others were provisional, just footnotes. This is...not.

She meets him halfway, hand finding his collar. The kiss is warm, unhurried, thorough. Not a question, not anymore. An answer they have been circling since she lay on the dining room table and declared herself a spiritual antenna.

When they break, she is a little breathless.

"You're very good at that," she says.

"I have had," he replies, "one very intense day of advance notice to prepare."

She laughs, a quick, delighted sound. "You did not spend all of today practising on other people, did you?"

"Certainly not," he says. "There are schedules to consider. And you are, frankly, a full-time occupation."

She eyes him, pleased. "Correct answer."

Her fingers trace the line of his jaw, then drift downward. "Do you know why I said three years?" she asks.

"Because you wanted data," he says. "Holidays, crises, electrical. A longitudinal study."

"Partly." Her hand spreads over his chest, feeling the steady thud beneath. "But also because I need to know if this," she taps lightly, "is going to keep understanding this," she taps her temple, "when everything gets weird."

Henry smiles, slow and startled, the way he does when she lands on something that feels like the centre of things.

"And?" he says.

"And you do," she says simply. "You understand why I break into storage units for furniture and talk to dead girls and write books about people who never existed and then get offended when they don't behave. You... get it. You don't try to tidy me into something less."

"Nell," he says quietly, "of all the things one might wish to tidy in this house, you are the only one that should be left exactly as I found it."

She looks away for a moment, then back.

"One of the first things I noticed about you the day we met," she says, "is that you listen the way I think. Sideways. You pay attention to the throwaway lines. You remember the strange parts. It's like..." She waves a hand, groping for the comparison. "It's like talking to someone who can see the crossword grid behind my sentences."

"That was," he murmurs, "an alarmingly efficient way of describing how very gone I am."

She grins, pleased. "Good."

He kisses her again, and this time her hands slide into his hair, his fingers splay warm at her waist, and the world narrows nicely to the fire's glow and the knowledge that, for once, no one is about to fall off anything.

They shift inelegantly, laughing when she knocks her knee against his. He rolls with it, turning the movement into something smoother, lowering her back onto the carpet with a care that suggests she's the most valuable thing in the room.

"Careful," she whispers, glancing at the Biennais. "That desk has seen enough tonight."

"So have you," he says. "We shall treat you both as irreplaceable." His hand skims her side, unbuttoning the shirt she's stolen from him.

The contact sends a warm jolt through her, pleasure layered over the deeper, steadier thing that has been building under their banter: trust, recognition, the comfort of being witnessed and not edited.

"Nice shirt," Henry says.

"I like yours better than mine."

"So do I," he laughs. "They fit me better, too."

"Do you know," Nell says, voice a little hoarse, "most people either want the writer part of me or the... reasonably functional adult part. Very few sign up for both."

"One hardly sees the point," he says, kissing the hollow just below her ear. "The writer part is the one that breaks into storage units."

She lets out a helpless laugh that turns into a soft sound when his mouth continues its slow, exploratory path. Her hands slide under his shirt now, fingers mapping the real geography of him instead of the neat outline she's been drawing in margins for months.

"Henry," she says.

"Yes?"

"In case this wasn't obvious," she says, "I love you."

He stills for a heartbeat, then lifts his head just enough to look at her properly. Her hair is an angel's halo gone to war; her lavender-blue eyes are clear and utterly un-joking.

"Oh," he says. "Good."

"Good?"

"Because," he says, "I have been entirely in love with you for some time, and it would be deeply inconvenient to discover that was a unilateral condition just now."

She smiles up at him, that fierce, almost private smile she usually reserves for solving impossible plot knots or finding the right last line.

"See?" she says. "Connecting. We're very good at it."

"That," he says, lowering his forehead to hers, "is not the adjective I would have chosen, but far be it from me to argue semantics at this stage."

Outside, the storm breaks, rain drumming its own applause on the slate roof. The fire dips and flares. The house creaks in a way that sounds like a sigh of satisfaction. The conversation dissolves into touches and whispered asides that only they will ever find funny. They move together with the ease of people who have already shared danger, domesticity, and midnight cups of coffee; who know the map of each other's minds well enough that the rest feels like a natural extension.

At one point he murmurs against her skin, a little unsteady, "You do remember this does not constitute an early termination of the three-year clause."

"Obviously," she says. "You're still on probation."

"On...what, precisely?" he asks.

"On working for me until I marry you in three years," she says, perfectly matter-of-fact. "Valet first, husband later. It's a career path."

He laughs. "And tonight's activities fall under...which heading?"

"I'm hoping," she says, "that sleeping with the boss, should I go ahead, will not affect your professional performance. It would be a shame to have to fire you when you're such an excellent worker."

"Nell," he says, "that is not how HR works."

"Fortunately," she replies, tugging him closer, "we don't have HR. We have me."

"Terrifying. And oddly appealing."

He presses closer, and her arms wrap around his neck. When their laughter softens into something quieter, the narrative—theirs and the one on her laptop—decides this is a sensible point to fade out.

Because what comes next is their own, and they have three fascinating years to keep discovering just how well they connect.

30

The Visitor

HENRY

HENRY'S MORNINGS BEGIN WITH Roger loping at his side as the sun pries its way across the lawns. The dog is a miracle on four feet, given what he's come through, and runs ahead along the lane. He's now healed and whole, darting left or right after invisible scents.

Henry runs for rhythm and routine, for the stillness that orders his thoughts. Roger runs for information. Their outings are, Henry imagines, Roger's version of surfing the internet or reading the news: he takes the local gossip from the land and plugs back into his world. The real world.

Henry is supposed to be thinking about the week's loose ends: hiring a butler, the maintenance schedule, a call to MI5. Instead, his mind circles Nell. At first, it was little things, like how she stands at the Ballroom window every night, checks weather reports obsessively, and refuses to drive in the rain. The way she insists on walking him to the car, even for the shortest errand. Then he found the clippings. One was folded beneath manuscript pages on her desk, another filed between photocopies of her driver's license and a list of hospital numbers in a file cabinet.

Both clippings told the same story: a man killed four years ago on a rain-slicked road near Exeter. By the time Henry had put everything back and closed the drawer, it had clicked into place with the precision of a lock turning. Nell's habits aren't quirks; they're grief. She writes romance novels because they give heartbreak scaffolding. To Nell, love is a volatile force that can upend her life and take what it wants.

He crests the rise, slowing to a walk as the house comes into view again. It glows just as it did on that first shocking day he saw it. A silver Rolls-Royce is parked in the forecourt, a uniformed chauffeur inside, nose buried in a book. Henry picks up Roger's water bowl and fills it from the pump near the watering trough, and takes a drink from his own water bottle. Mrs. Patterson meets him just inside the door.

"Mr. Templeton, there is a visitor waiting in the small drawing room. A Madame Duval. Her Grace is there with her now."

The Yellow Drawing Room is just off the Great Hall. It isn't large, but it shares the same high ceiling and dramatic Rubens-esque artwork. A golden flat-weave carpet with an ivory trellis pattern grounds the room. Tall windows look onto a small interior courtyard with a fountain and espaliered pear trees along one wall. Nell and Madame Duval are sitting in gold silk chairs near the French doors when Henry enters.

"Madame Duval," Nell says, "may I present Henry Templeton. Mr. Templeton is my valet and manages Ainsworth."

An elegant woman in her sixties rises and crosses the room toward him, hand extended with unhurried assurance. Her tailored navy suit, mid-heel pumps, jewel-cluster earrings, and silver hair swept into a French twist give the impression of someone perpetually composed, and perfectly aware of it.

"Céleste Duval," she says. "Enchantée." Her voice is soft, cultured, distinctly Parisian.

"How do you do?" Henry replies, returning her smile. "How can we help you?"

"I believe, Mr. Templeton, that I am here to help you. Thomas Duval was my fourth great-grandfather."

Henry senses it instantly, with a certainty that brushes past intuition. "You're the one who sent us the note. You helped us find the treasure."

"Oui." She nods, lips curving. "I have waited many years, never knowing when the right moment would come. But when I learned that the Duchess of Belward had inherited, I hoped..." She gestures toward the Ballroom. "I am glad to see Rose's memory honored here. I hear you found what you were searching for."

"Please, sit down," Henry says, guiding her to the sofa. "If you'll excuse me a moment, I'll ask for tea."

In the Great Hall, he passes a footman, requests tea in the Yellow Drawing Room, then bounds upstairs. He showers quickly and changes into khaki slacks and a fresh dress shirt.

The French windows stand open, and Nell and Madame Duval have settled into comfortable chairs in the courtyard. Spring flowers spill color and fragrance all around, while the trickle of water from the fountain provides a gentle, musical backdrop.

Madame Duval opens the clasp of the leather portfolio in her lap, revealing a packet of faded photographs and ornately scripted documents. She lifts a daguerreotype, her thumbs brushing its edges with the affectionate touch reserved for old memories. "This is Thomas Duval, Philippe's son." The man is older, but unmistakably the same one from the photograph taken earlier in the Ainsworth rose garden.

"Philippe Moreau was a hero, though history hasn't remembered him kindly, as he was, of course, on the wrong side of the war." She says.

"In war, there's no such thing as a winner or loser." Nell says sadly, "The loser is humanity—too many lives destroyed on both sides. We are all on the wrong side of every war."

Henry stands, moving to a table inside the Drawing Room. He returns with a presentation box holding Thomas' letter to Philippe and Philippe's medal. He sits beside Madame Duval and places them on the table in front of her. "These belong to your family."

Madame Duval's eyes glisten as Henry places the Légion d'honneur medal in her hands. She turns it slowly in the sunlight, bright as the day Napoleon pinned it to Philippe's breast. "You would trust me with these?"

"Philippe was your ancestor," Henry says. "These are your family treasures."

Madame Duval nods in agreement. "Philippe fought at Austerlitz, Wagram, and Borodino. Napoleon himself awarded him this Légion d'honneur for saving an entire regiment at Leipzig. But his greatest courage was not on the battlefield. When Napoleon asked him to come to England, Philippe knew it meant exile from everything he loved. Yet he served his Emperor faithfully, even when it cost him his son."

Henry leans forward. "Thomas never returned to France?"

Madame Duval shakes her head, her jeweled earrings brushing her cheeks. "Non. After Rose died, he fled to America to live. He visited Philippe in Paris only a few times. Thomas always believed he had failed in what he felt was his duty."

"The note you sent was perfect timing. But why help us?" Nell says gently.

Madame Duval slips the photograph into a glassine sleeve. "Because Philippe was an honorable man who served his country, and Thomas was a young man destroyed by love. They both deserve remembrance. They should be known as the fine men they were." She looks at both Nell and Henry. "And because I believe we are all ready for this story to have a happy ending. Which is exactly why I'll donate his medal to the Louvre. The French people deserve to know this story."

"We have a desk that belongs to you as well." Nell says.

Madame Duval turns to her, surprised. "The Biennais? Thomas wrote about it in his journals, but I never believed it had survived. I couldn't possibly accept it. It belonged to Napoleon. It is worth...well, more than I can imagine."

Nell shakes her head. "It's yours. If Thomas could have returned it to France, he would have. My uncle told me once that we don't really own anything; we're just the caretakers of this world while we're here. Ainsworth has been the caretaker of this desk for centuries. It's time for it to return to your family."

Madame Duval folds Thomas' letter and slips it into her portfolio. "I have something for you as well." She says.

She draws out a wrapped canvas. It is a portrait in oil of Philippe, young and solemn, the Légion d'honneur bright against his deep blue uniform. She extends it to Nell.

"Every family should have portraits of their heroes," Madame Duval says gently, "even if they fought on different sides. And perhaps to remind us it must never happen again."

As the visit draws to a close, Madame Duval stands, smoothing her skirt, and presses a card into Nell's hand. "If you ever need help in France—research, connections, anything—you must call me. The Duvals pay their debts."

Nell rises to embrace her, feeling history has been redeemed.

In the Great Hall, they pause at the entrance to the Ballroom and look at the portrait of Rose above the fireplace.

"There's just one more thing," Nell says. "Do you know what happened that night? Did Thomas ever say?"

"Rose and Thomas were deeply in love," she replies, "but Rose was promised to someone else."

"William Whitby," Nell supplies.

Madame Duval nods. "Thomas was planning to return the things Philippe had buried in the rose garden. He dug up the box earlier than he'd intended because they were preparing the site for the new sundial."

"He must have been afraid the box would be found, and then Rose discovered him," Nell says, realization dawning.

"Yes," Madame Duval says. "Rose found Thomas with the medal and the war plans and thought it meant her own father was the traitor. She wanted to confront him. Thomas was terribly upset. After the new sundial was installed, he reburied the box and convinced Rose that no one must ever find it. He knew if she learned Philippe was the spy, he would lose her forever." She glances at Nell. "The night Rose died, Thomas met her at the folly on the moor. In his journal, he remembered it as a magical place. They met there often, hidden from the world."

Madame Duval draws a small breath. "That night, Thomas told her the truth—that it was his father who was the spy, not hers. He begged her to run away with him, saying he had a treasure, enough to start a new life, with no need for her family's blessing."

Nell's eyes rest on the portrait. "And William Whitby arrived."

"Oui," Madame Duval says. "There was a storm. William saw Rose with Thomas. He was furious. He snatched the gold locket—the one there, in the painting—and flung it to the ground. Then he challenged Thomas to a duel."

Henry crosses his arms as he listens.

"They took pistols and walked to the cliff's edge, counting their paces. Just before they turned to fire, a bolt of lightning struck the oak, splitting it in two. Thomas' journal said that the lightning ripped the sky open white, turning the tree into a stark black skeleton a heartbeat before it split with a crack that drowned even the sea."

She presses her fingers together as if holding something fragile. "Rose was dazed and ran to them, desperate to stop the duel. Thomas never knew if it was the lightning or the grief. Rose stumbled at the edge of the cliff and fell."

"Perhaps she mistook the strike for gunfire," Nell says.

Madame Duval nods. "Thomas wrote Rose had never meant to run away with him at all. She told him that night that she planned to stay with William. The duel had been pointless; only the damage was real."

They all look up at Rose's portrait. "Thomas and William were both shattered," Madame Duval says. "Together, they carried her home to Ainsworth. Thomas left shortly after."

Henry and Nell walk Madame Duval to the front steps, where her driver waits beside the sleek silver car, the engine quietly idling. The sun warms them all as Madame Duval shakes Henry's hand once more. Then she embraces Nell as if closing a circle.

"If you ever need anything in France, again, you must call me," she says softly. "Thank you for letting me bring some peace to my family."

Henry watches as the car pulls away, the Duval crest catching the light before it disappears down the drive.

"With all the village gossip, I suppose William's father, being the magistrate, must have signed the death certificate quickly. With William involved, no one dared ask too many questions."

Henry nods, turning the story over in his mind. "In reality, it was all just a tragic misunderstanding. An accident. But stories like that get lost easily."

Nell watches the empty curve of gravel. "You know what I keep thinking about?" she says.

Henry shifts beside her. "Apart from whether Mrs. Patterson will ever forgive us for having foreign dignitaries to tea unannounced?"

Nell laughs. "It's all about love. Aleric and his country. Rose and Thomas. Philippe and his emperor. Sarah's journal passed down for centuries. The Ainsworths and this house. Even Madame Duval, crossing the Channel because she couldn't stand to leave the story unfinished."

Henry turns to look at her, listening.

"Love is...messy in real time," Nell says slowly. "People make awful decisions. They run to cliffs in storms and bury medals in rose beds and write letters that aren't sent. It never feels noble when it's happening. It just feels necessary." She folds her arms, gaze still on the drive.

"Rather like a dog risking his life to save a girl, and a girl risking hers to save a dog?" Henry says.

Nell smiles. "Exactly. Love stories are the way we make sense of it afterwards. They give grief a shape so it doesn't just roar around inside you forever. They're how we remember what happened without being destroyed by it. They're how we forgive each other."

"Is that why you write?" Henry asks quietly.

Nell thinks of her folders of emergency contacts, the weather reports, James on the M5 in the rain. "I think it is," she says. "I give love and loss somewhere to go. On the page, it can be tragic and beautiful and survivable, instead of just...an accident that took everything and then stopped."

Henry's hand brushes hers. "And now Rose and Thomas get that, too."

"Yes," Nell says. "Now they're not just a village ghost story. They're a love story. One that finally gets told properly."

Henry looks at her, at their joined hands, at the house beyond. Trust Nell, he thinks, to take a story full of storms and find a way to write it toward a happy ending. With any luck, she might do the same for them.

31

Taking the Reins

HENRY

NELL SITS AT THE breakfast table in the morning room, teacup steaming, Roger sprawled at her feet. She picks up the newspaper folded neatly beside her croissant. She has braced herself for two days, half-expecting to see *Local Heiress and Accomplice in Spectacular Antique Desk Heist!* above the fold.

But the headline in bold type reads:

INTERNATIONAL ANTIQUES SCANDAL: LECLAIR ARRESTED IN MI5 STING

Beneath it, a subhead:

Renowned Dealer Tied to Money Laundering, Art Fraud, and Espionage Ring

"Henry," she says. "You have to see this. I think Leclair just bumped me off the front page."

Henry, still buttoning his shirt cuffs, leans over and kisses the top of her head, eyes widening as he scans the column. Leclair's face stares up at them, all his former smugness replaced by the dull resolve of a caught man.

The article explains Leclair was under MI5 surveillance for three years, suspected of laundering money for several Eastern European and London crime syndicates through high-end art and antiques. He faces a raft of charges: fraud, blackmail, illegal export of national treasures...and, as Henry whistles softly, conspiracy to sell classified materials.

It paints Leclair not merely as a shady opportunist, but as a player in international smuggling and espionage. His gallery, apparently, served as a meeting place for everything from forged paintings to purloined intelligence.

Henry's phone vibrates, and a crisp voice comes through: "Templeton. I'm sure you've seen the papers."

"Yes, sir, just reading about the incident now," Henry says.

"The Bureau would like to thank you formally for your...invaluable role in the Leclair investigation. Quite a coup for the department."

Henry stills, cautious. "Well, you're very welcome. Sir, the Duchess of Belward is understandably concerned about the potential publicity should her name be mentioned."

"Not an issue, Templeton. Leclair has so many criminal counts against him, the Ainsworth desk is not needed in this case."

"Good, sir. I'll pass that on."

"Templeton, I understand you're not seeking full-time employment at present, but our director would be most pleased if you'd consider consulting work. Given your access to certain, ah, strata of society—and your unique skill set. Case by case, of course."

Nell grins shamelessly over her mug. Henry tries and fails to look put-upon. "Thank you very much, sir. I'll certainly consider it," he says as Nell scribbles *007* on a napkin and slides it across the table.

***

Later that morning, the riding arena at Clairview Park is mottled with sun, and there's a fresh breeze carrying the smell of hay and horses. Randolph holds Daisy's reins, watching Deirdre fit a riding helmet onto Henry's head with genuine, if slightly wicked, pleasure.

"I still can't believe your stable manager produced breeches in my size," Henry says, "and boots that fit."

Randolph chuckles. "Seems to suit you. Nell nearly walked into a gate when you came out of the tack room."

Henry adjusts his gloves, aiming for nonchalance and missing. "Yes, she did make a remark about my...legs."

Randolph grins. "Best incentive to learn to ride I've ever found."

"If I survive today," Henry says, "it will be out of sheer vanity." The helmet seems determined to slip over his eyebrows.

Nell hands him a carrot he doesn't remember requesting.

"I'm not hungry, thanks," he says.

Nell and Deirdre laugh.

"Bribes are perfectly legitimate in equestrian affairs," Nell assures him, "even expected."

Henry eyes Daisy. She eyes him back, unimpressed. He offers her a chunk of carrot. "Don't think of this as a bribe. Call it a good-faith gesture."

Deirdre smiles. "I have faith in you—mostly. But I know how you cerebral types love to overthink. Let's not launch yourself into the hedge, all right?"

Deirdre shows him how to stand, holding the reins in his left hand with a bit of mane, and fit his boot in the stirrup, demoing a graceful swing. "Just swing up. It's easy. If you fall, there's a delightful view from the ground. Trust me, most of us have spent plenty of time there."

Henry takes a breath, checks the girth for the fifth time, puts his boot in the stirrup, and swings a leg over, feeling one geometric movement away from disaster. Daisy flicks an ear and sniffs his boot, possibly sizing him up or already missing Deirdre. He sits lightly, conscious of each muscle, empathy for the horse radiating from every line of posture, if a bit too rigid.

Nell walks over and leans on the rail to watch, Roger sprawled at her feet, basking in the sun. "You know, after all the desk excitement, I'm ready for a quiet summer. No more blackmail, no more criminal antiques."

Henry tries the reins, and Daisy ambles a single step sideways. Not forward, not backward, just an experimental sidle. "What happens if the horse is laundering money?" Henry asks.

Nell snorts. "She's more likely laundering carrots."

Randolph, watching Henry settle into the saddle, turns to Nell. "That truly was a remarkable arrest by MI5. All those intermediaries, shell companies, trusts, and piles of cash in private antiques deals make it nearly impossible to see who's really behind anything."

Nell admits, "I had no idea the underworld worked like that."

Randolph nods. "Art forgery, fraud, theft—those are just a few of the ways criminals generate money in the art and antiquities markets. Sounds like Leclair was dabbling in espionage on top of everything else."

"In the end," Nell says, "Henry was right. It all worked out. Leclair's stealing the desk led us to treasure that had been buried for centuries, uncovering the house's history, along with Phillip, Rose and Thomas."

Henry and Daisy make their first circuit of the arena. Randolph applauds, Deirdre cheers, Nell grins and waves a carrot overhead like a trophy.

"See?" Nell calls, almost convincingly. "You're a natural."

"A natural what is yet to be determined," Henry mutters.

Deirdre falls in beside him, gently coaching his posture as they loop the arena at an easy pace. For a moment, Henry truly exhales—ordinary happiness, friends and laughter, carrot bribes, and the first hints of English summer.

32

Owning Her Story

NELL

ELL LASTS EXACTLY SEVEN minutes before declaring reality uncooperative.

By late afternoon, Nell has barricaded herself in the Ballroom with a pot of coffee, a pile of jelly beans, and a sign on the door that reads *Do Not Disturb Unless Something Is On Fire or Bearing Pain Au Chocolat.* The laptop sits open to a document titled *Chapter Fourteen: In Which I Do Not Fall Off a Cliff,* currently containing only the words: *It is a truth universally acknowledged that a girl in possession of one cliff must be in want of a corpse.*

She scowls, deletes *corpse*, types *mystery*, deletes that, then writes: *Nell stood at the edge of Black Tor, brave, windswept, and wearing the sort of coat that implied both emotional depth and a decent tailoring budget.* She pauses, considers her actual coat (bobbling at the cuffs, covered with Roger-fur) and adds, *In reality, she was damp, under-caffeinated, and had seaweed in her shoe.*

"Fine," she mutters, "we'll call it auto-fiction and confuse the critics."

Her fingers pick up speed. *Rose had not been pushed; that was too obvious, too operatic, too third-act twist of a lesser writer. She had slipped in that fatal, ordinary way women always slip—on wet ground, on bad information, on the assumption that two men in love with the same person will behave sensibly on a cliff.*

She likes that line enough to underline it three times in her notebook, then realizes underlining things on a screen is less satisfying than attacking them with ink. Roger thumps his tail under the desk, either in agreement or because she has inadvertently nudged the biscuit tin. Nell stares at the blinking cursor and types: *The valet looked at her with the calm of a man who had already ironed every possible disaster life could throw at him and folded it into thirds.* She hesitates, then gives in and writes his name: *Henry Templeton.*

Henry Templeton was the sort of man one ought to marry, she writes, which is precisely why Nell had given herself three years' grace. A woman needed time to discover whether a man who could look that good in jeans might also... She reads it back, winces, and adds "*metaphorically*" in parentheses.

Now she attempts the proposal scene. *You're going to have to marry me one day,* she types, then stops, fingers hovering. On the page she upgrades herself: *You are obviously in love with me,* Fictional Nell tells Fictional Henry, *and while I understand this is exhausting for you, we may as well make it official after an appropriate vetting period.* Real Nell groans and drops her forehead onto the keys, producing a line of accidental gibberish that looks uncomfortably like Welsh.

"Actual Nell," she reminds herself aloud, "couldn't look him in the eye when she said it and followed up with a remark about dogs. Also, your hair was in your mouth."

She dutifully revises: *She said it badly, as one does at the edge of a cliff when making the sort of statement that rearranges one's future and one's furniture. She said it sideways, looking at the sea instead of the man, and then immediately invoked the dog as a cautionary tale about impulsive choices.* "That's better," she concedes, and underlines it, too.

Her notebook lies open beside the laptop, yesterday's crossword half-finished. Across the middle she has written:

1. Six-letter word for man who brings blankets to a cliff at midnight. She has filled in: *VALET?* then written *HUSBAND?* underneath and circled it aggressively.

2. Seven-letter word for romantic obstruction involving historical corpse. She has: *ROSE???*

She taps the pencil against the margin.

"You know," she tells the empty room, Roger having gone off to find Fergus, "most writers start with a plot and then add trauma. I appear to have started with the trauma and am now workshopping the plot."

The chandelier creaks in an approving way that might be the house settling, or Rose Ainsworth giving notes. She writes, *Chapter 13: In which Henry Interrupts, Professionally.*

There is a soft knock. "Come in unless you're an editor," she calls. "In which case, I'm dead."

Henry appears with a tray. "In that event, madam, it may console you to know that the dead are traditionally not expected to answer emails."

"How many do I have now?" Nell asks.

"68,471. I'm making headway," Henry says.

He sets down tea and something that might be cake under a defensively domed cover. His eyes go to the screen. Nell slams the laptop nearly shut, leaving a cautious two-inch gap like a teenager who definitely isn't watching anything inappropriate.

"Progress?" he inquires.

"Oh, oceans of it," she says. "I've discovered that my heroine is insufferable, the hero is disturbingly competent, and the dog has all the best lines."

"Art imitating life, then," he says mildly.

She narrows her eyes. "Out of curiosity, how would you describe the night I proposed? In one sentence."

Henry considers. "A regrettable breach of health and safety regulations undertaken for the purpose of solving a century-old scandal, concluding with an informal engagement."

She sighs. "You see, that's the problem. In my genre, that's three books."

After he leaves, she reopens the laptop and scrolls to the top. *Chapter Fourteen,* she types, *In Which I Nearly Turn Myself Into Local Folklore and Accidentally Propose.* The words come more easily now: Rose's slip, the coffer, the letters, the awful smallness of the truth compared to the grandeur of the legend. She gives Rose the line she wishes the girl had had time to say: *I only wanted you both to know how important you are to me.* She gives herself no such grace, writing instead, *Nell said something clumsy and enormous and entirely lacking in punctuation, and Henry understood her anyway.*

When she finally closes the document, Roger is back again, snoring at her feet, and the light outside has gone to Cornwall-violet, that melancholy colour that makes everyone's thoughts more dramatic than they actually are. Nell stretches, feeling pleasantly hollowed out the way one does after a good cry or a successful first draft.

"All right, Rose," she says to the portrait. "You get your ending. I'll work mine out in edits."

***

In the garden, Nell and Henry kneel beside the freshly turned earth while Roger leans against Nell's leg. Together, they lower the small chest back into its resting place—empty now but for a single folded note.

Henry reads it aloud, voice steady: "*In memory of Rose Ainsworth and Thomas Duval.*"

They cover the chest and pat the earth smooth, letting the new grass and sun finish the work time began.

Back through the Boot Room, Henry grabs a faded tennis ball from the trophy on the mantel. He gives it an easy bounce, then looks at Nell.

"You know," he says, "once the story goes public, you can't take it back."

"That's exactly the point," Nell answers, joyful and sure. "Love stories are life: how we remember it, survive it, and dare to live it again."

They cross the Great Hall, descend the front steps, and walk to the West Green. The house, grand, weathered, and filled with centuries of love, glows as it always has in the late afternoon sun.

Nell throws the ball for Roger, who bounds after it in a wild arc of happiness.

She pauses and looks back at Ainsworth. People talk about inheritance as if it were only deeds and death duties, but what we truly inherit are love stories: tidy, untidy, half-remembered. For the first time, it feels as though the house belongs to her, and she to it. Not because she owns it; as Uncle Charles said, she is only its caretaker.

It is more that she is part of its legacy now. She will tell Ainsworth Manor's story and write her own within these walls.

Roger drops the ball at her feet, and Henry scoops it up, sending it sailing again. This time, both dog and Nell chase after it, laughter carrying over the lawn. Past and present twist together, bright and light as new hope.

As Nell runs, she hears the wind rustling through the ancient oaks, a sound like a satisfied reader turning a page.

The End

Acknowledgements

Heartfelt thanks to the family and friends who kept believing in this story long before it was bound between covers, and to the professionals and early readers whose insight and care helped The Roses of Ainsworth Manor bloom. To the booksellers, librarians, and bookstagrammers who put these characters into readers' hands, thank you for championing them. And to every reader who turns the pages—especially those returning after The Gilded Talisman—your time is a gift and the reason these worlds exist.

Note from the Author

Thank you for spending time at Ainsworth Manor and following Nell, Henry, and Roger through their adventures. Stories only truly come alive when they find their readers, and it means so much that you chose to spend your reading hours here.

My stories almost always begin with my own travels. This one grew out of a trip to London—wandering the halls of the National Gallery, Tate Britain, and the National Portrait Gallery, and walking through the Wellington Arch and exhibitions on the officers and soldiers who fought on both sides of the Napoleonic Wars. As a former army officer, I was struck by the courage, sacrifice, and even the respect that sometimes existed between opposing commanders.

The moor in this story grew out of visiting wild, windswept places—including the prairies and plains of Texas—and then asking how landscape can become a character in its own right. Roger's chapters, especially his rescue of Nell, come from that same imagination. For some readers, animal-centered danger can be intense, and those scenes are meant to honor how powerful that bond can feel. The moor sequence is where Nell and Roger's relationship becomes more than cute; it becomes a matter of survival. Roger acts on instinct and love, and Nell answers that sacrifice step by painful step on the way home.

As a portrait artist, I am just as fascinated by the lives behind the faces in those paintings. In the galleries, I find myself reading the plaques and imagining the loves, sorrows, dramas, and quiet tragedies of the people on the walls, seeing them as real human beings rather than distant historical figures. The recent John Singer Sargent exhibition at Tate Britain directly inspired the painting in The Gilded Talisman that Alexander grew up with and, in a way, fell in love with. I found myself wondering what it would be like to live with a portrait like that—and then meet someone who seemed to step right out of the frame.

My own portraits are filled with clues about the sitter's life: a certain piece of jewelry, colors, meaningful flowers, or symbols only the family will recognize. One painting holds the birth flowers of every family member; another includes violets as a quiet act of remembrance for someone they lost. Those same instincts—to hide stories in details and to imagine the inner lives of people long gone—shape the worlds, mysteries, and romances you'll find in these pages.

If you enjoyed this book, please consider leaving a quick review or rating on Amazon at https://www.amazon.com/dp/B0G5J76L 9Q or on your favorite book site or retailer. Even a few words help other readers discover the story and make it possible for more visits to Ainsworth Manor in the future.

With gratitude,

Nina Gates

Book Club Questions and Author Notes

Hello, friends!

If you haven't finished the novel yet, you might want to pause here and return when you're ready. What follows includes details from the ending! For everyone else, welcome to the conversation.

Use the questions that appeal to your group, skip the rest, or come up with your own. There are no right or wrong answers. The author notes are from my story log while planning and writing the book.

To continue the adventure, join me on Substack at NinaGates .Substack.com.

You can get in touch with me directly, find book extras, chat with fellow romance fans, and more. I can't wait to see you inside!

Q: What inspired the setting and atmosphere of Ainsworth Manor?

Author's Note:

Ainsworth Manor was inspired by my love of English country houses and the way they hold centuries of secrets through generations. I wanted a setting that felt timeless, layered with both grandeur and the slight melancholy of a vast history that encompasses generations of joy and sorrow, echoing the story's themes of love, loyalty, inheritance, and identity.

Q: Nell is a writer. How does her craft influence the storytelling and her personal journey?

Author's Note:

Nell's career as a writer mirrors her search for truth. Writing gives her the power to shape and reclaim family history, transforming silence into story. Her observations frequently color the narrative and even the ending metaphor—a nod to the writer's role as interpreter and healer. In Chapter 30, Henry also realizes that Nell's writing romance novels may be a way for her to process grief from an earlier romantic relationship.

Q: Henry's background is a blend of espionage and devotion. How did you balance his MI5 skills with romance?

Author's Note:

Henry has one foot in the world of suspense and the other in domestic warmth. His spy skills provide plot momentum, but his loyalty, humor, and empathy ground his relationship with Nell. I enjoyed letting his professionalism clash with—and finally complement—his capacity for love.

Q: What are the most important themes in the novel?

Author's Note:

For me, the core themes are the nature of love and truth. Loyalty, courage, history, and forgiveness intertwine: each secret uncovered is less about scandal and more about personal release. I also explored the idea of a relationship where, though each partner is very different in personality and temperament, they are each valued by the other for their unique abilities and views—not just tolerated, but enjoyed and celebrated.

Q: Did any part of the historical plot (Rose, Thomas, Philippe) come from real events?

Author's Note:

While the narrative is fiction, it's stitched together from real historical details—Napoleonic battles, espionage, antiques, and settings—giving a layered and cinematic scope to the story.

Q: Nell's struggle with grief and her family's history is subtle but significant. How did you approach these elements?

Author's Note:

Grief and trauma shape Nell's decisions—her rituals and hesitations are clues to deeper wounds. I tried to approach grief as both an individual and inherited experience, where healing comes from facing the truth, choosing openness, and choosing connection.

Q: The story balances suspense, humor, and romance. Was it difficult to juggle these tones?

Author's Note:

At times, yes! I wanted the suspense to feel real, but just like real life, there are plenty of moments of lightness. Friendship, banter, and Roger the dog helped keep even the most dramatic scenes from becoming bleak.

Q: How do secrets—family and otherwise—affect the characters' relationships?

Author's Note:

Secrets are both burden and protection. For Nell, Henry, and even secondary characters, the process of uncovering what's hidden deepens intimacy and sometimes strains connection. The process of getting to know each other and allowing hidden aspects to be revealed is part of the character arcs of all of them.

Q: What role does the landscape and weather play in the story?

Author's Note:

It's interesting to me how much weather affects stories—and also the time of day a particular scene is set. In Cornwall, the beautiful but unpredictable English weather mirrors the volatility of the characters' internal lives, especially Nell's. Rain and storms signal both disaster and renewal, linking place with emotion.

Q: How did you choose which historical mysteries to resolve and which to leave open-ended?

Author's Note:

Some mysteries are worth solving; others lose meaning if too tidily answered. I wanted the past at Ainsworth Manor to remain a little enigmatic, echoing how family legends rarely contain the whole truth. And there will be more Nell Ainsworth mysteries coming, so the house and family legends will also reveal themselves throughout other books in the series.

Q: The story ends with the idea of narrative as belonging. Why was this important?

Author's Note:

The somewhat convoluted way that Nell inherits Ainsworth Manor was very intentional. I could have easily made it a very clean process, but I specifically made it a bit muddy. Inheritance isn't just blood or property—it's memory and story. For Nell to claim the house by telling its tales felt truer than making her an heir only by birthright. It also highlights the magic of our lives and how sometimes the craziest, most unexpected things happen. She never, in her wildest dreams, expected to inherit this house or become a duchess in her own right.

Q: Did you empathize more with the women in the story or the men?

Author's Note:

I empathize with all of them; each is fascinating in his or her own way, and I usually wish I could know them better when the book is finished. The women's struggles with silence and societal constraint and the men's battles with honor and duty reflect real tensions—both were necessary for the book's emotional core.

Q: What was your favorite scene to write, and why?

Author's Note:

There were so many. I had a blast writing the scene where Nell is learning how to do a stakeout—I laughed a lot writing this book. I loved the scene where Henry shows up as she is "reclaiming" the desk. My favorite scene is Chapter 20, when Roger and Nell save each other on the moor. Maybe because I have a dog, but I teared up every single time I worked on or edited that chapter. I also love Chapter 2, when Henry sees Nell throwing the ball for Roger and chasing it herself. It was fun to echo that at the end, with Roger chasing it with Nell this time.

Q: Roger the dog plays a subtle but important role. What does he represent?

Author's Note:

Roger is both comic relief and emotional glue—a symbol of resilience and loyalty. His choice to overcome his issues of trust, and the huge choice he makes to save Nell, and subsequent reconnection parallel Nell and Henry's journeys from guardedness to trust.

Q: How do you imagine Nell and Henry's relationship evolving after the novel ends?

Author's Note:

I hope Nell and Henry find laughter and fewer secrets, but their partnership will still thrive on curiosity and occasional capers!

Q: What do you think is the greatest challenge facing the characters?

Author's Note:

Ultimately, the greatest challenge is trusting each other enough to risk telling—and hearing—the truth, and, like all couples, allowing each other to be themselves and having that always be a source of attraction and joy, not annoyance.

Q: Nell's decision to go to the moor alone—without her phone, before Henry returns—feels both brave and reckless. Do you see this choice as a natural extension of her character, or as a turning point where she crosses a new line in risk?

Author's Note:

This scene is meant to sit right on the edge between "this is exactly who she is" and "this is the moment spontaneity nearly costs her everything." The goal is for readers to feel, at the same time, that of course she goes—and that they want to grab her by the sleeve and say, "Wait for backup."

Q: Roger's point of view on the moor emphasizes instincts, boundaries, and his tug-of-war between fear and loyalty, both of which are natural and understandable. How does seeing the danger through his eyes change your sense of the scene, compared to if it were only told from Nell or Henry's perspective?

Author's Note:

Letting Roger "narrate" this stretch is a way to make the familiar landscape feel alien and threatening again. He doesn't think in plot terms—only in wind, scent, distance, and danger—so the same moor that might read as romantic in human POV becomes a place where every tuft of heather could hide something scary.

Q: The rescue and the carry back to the house are physically grueling, but they're also full of humor (the "enormous idiot dog" line, the ferret joke) and tenderness. Did that mix of banter and desperation change how you feel about Nell and Roger's relationship after this chapter?

Author's Note:

It was very hard for me to wait twenty chapters to bring them together, and it was significant when I could finally write it. This sequence functions as a kind of vow between them, told entirely in action rather than declarations. The humor is there partly to keep the scene from becoming unbearably heavy, but also to show that even when Nell is exhausted, frightened, and in pain, her first instinct is still to comfort him.

Q: Why include an international element (France, Napoleonic history) in this English setting?

Author's Note:

To show how family histories spill over borders and centuries. The international intrigue adds stakes but also underscores the universality of love and regret. I am also interested in how much of what we think is so significant today, over time and over the course of history, blends together or is lost entirely.

Q: How do the secondary characters—Randolph, Deirdre, Mrs. Patterson—shape the atmosphere and main characters' choices?

Author's Note:

Secondary characters add so much to a story. They serve as sounding boards, confidantes, and sometimes gentle critics. Their humor, kindness, and perspective anchor Nell and Henry when the plot gets stormy. They also help shape the architecture of the story.

Q: If you could write a sequel, whose story would you tell?

Author's Note:

I'd love to write about Deirdre and Randolph—surely they, and Clairview Park, have secrets of their own! But we'll see Nell and Henry again in The Vanishing Violinist, so stay tuned!

Q: The attack on the moor and Roger's rescue of Nell are among the most intense scenes in the book. How did you feel reading this sequence—more frightened, more moved, or both?

Author's Note:

This scene was written to feel physically and emotionally costly for both Nell and Roger. It's meant to show that the "stakes" in the story are not just clues and reputations, but people, animals, and bonds.

Q: Roger's choice to intervene—knowing, in his way, that he might not survive—pushes the story into a darker, more dangerous space. Do you see this as a necessary risk for the plot, or did it feel almost too far for you as a reader?

Author's Note:

It's important to acknowledge that, for some readers (including me), animal peril is harder to read than human peril. I'm one of those "I will not watch the movie if the dog dies" people. The scene is intended as a true crucible for their relationship, not as gratuitous harm. I found it incredibly moving and teared up literally every time I re-wrote or edited that chapter.

Further Discussion

• In what ways does Ainsworth Manor function as both a setting and a character throughout the novel?

• How do various characters' relationships with secrets shape their destinies?

• How does the uncovering of history impact the characters' choices and sense of self?

• What role do symbols play in the story's unfolding and in the characters' healing?

• Did your perception of any character change by the end of the book? If so, what triggered that shift?

• How does humor function in the novel—especially in scenes balancing suspense or sadness?

• In what ways does the novel explore the idea of inheritance in various forms?

- Which scene or subplot resonated with you most emotionally, and why?
- How does the book use weather (rain, storms, sunlight) as a metaphor, and to what effect?
- If you could ask the author one question about the story or her creative process, what would it be?

About the Author

Nina Gates is an American author known for mystery, romance, and literary fiction with depth and heart, and for witty contemporary heroines who blend glamour and sharp comedic timing with elegantly profound insights. An acclaimed artist and former army officer, she holds a bachelor's degree in political science. She lives in Texas and is currently at work on her next novel.

Connect with her on Instagram @NinaGatesAuthor or on her Amazon Author page for book news and extras.

Also by Nina Gates

The Gilded Talisman

The Gilded Talisman sweeps readers into an opulent world of history, intrigue, and romance as gifted art restorer Maren Bennett's unconventional life is upended by tragedy and a single cryptic message: "Come to Venice as soon as possible—trust no one." Drawn into the city's shadows, and the secrets surrounding a mysterious ring, Maren is tasked by the enigmatic Marquise de Saint-Clair to recover Roxelana, a legendary sixteenth-century Ottoman talisman lost to history. Her pursuit becomes a globe-spanning race between those who would protect the talisman's legacy and rivals willing to kill for its power, carrying her from the legendary Orient Express—where luxury masks danger—to Parisian designer salons and glittering Istanbul ballrooms. Complicating her mission is Alexander: devastatingly handsome, impossibly wealthy, and bound to the talisman's dark past in ways he refuses to admit. Blending old-world glamour with the heart of romantic suspense, The Gilded Talisman is a novel of bravery, obsession, and the transforming power of self-discovery.

www.ingramcontent.com/pod-product-compliance
Lightning Source LLC
Chambersburg PA
CBHW031610240626
47153CB00002B/706